BLACKFLIES

ARE

MURDER

BLACKFLIES
ARE
MURDER

A Belle Palmer Mystery

by **Lou Allin**

RENDEZVOUS
PRESS

Cover art: Christopher Chuckry

Le Conseil des Arts | The Canada Council
DU CANADA | FOR THE ARTS
DEPUIS 1957 | SINCE 1957

We gratefully acknowledge the support of the Canada Council for the Arts for our publishing program.

Napoleon Publishing/RendezVous Press
Toronto, Ontario, Canada
www.rendezvouspress.com

Printed in Canada

05 04 03 02   5 4 3 2 1

National Library of Canada Cataloguing in Publication Data

Allin, Lou, date-
    Blackflies are murder

A Belle Palmer Mystery
ISBN 0-929141-92-X

I. Title. II. Series: Lou Allin, date- . Belle Palmer mystery.

PS8551.L5564B53 2002   C813'.6   C2002-900210-9
PR9199.3.A3963B53 2002

Dedicated to Freya (1984-1997), waiting at Rainbow Bridge
with Mr. Chile in her mouth.

Acknowledgments
Merci mille fois to my insightful readers, Sheila, Tim
and Nan. To my editor/publisher Sylvia, who faced any
foreign language challenge and never balked at a *hostie*.
To Lillian, the best Mac's manager in Canada.
And always to Jan, for whom second best
is out of the question.

PROLOGUE

The small room was quiet, a glass prism in the window shooting rainbows onto the simple pine floor. On the wall, a picture of a smiling, round-faced man beamed approval. Below him a cot with a rough grey blanket, a young boy hunched beside it. He was worrying a hole in the arm of his sweater, passing his fingers in and out, unravelling the wool. "Don't do that," the voice said, well-modulated, comforting at other times, in other places. "Stand straight. What do I teach you?"

A sniffle, nose swiped with a sleeve. "Never mind. Come closer." Outside, far away, a bell tolled. "Had we but world enough…"

A small sob. Then a shudder, quickly mastered. A straightening of limbs and clothing, and a sigh. Out of a pocket came a flash of silver. "Do you know what this is?"

"A whistle?"

"Clever lad. But a special toy for our new game. When I blow it twice before supper, you are to come here. Immediately." Steel arrows nailed the boy's eyes as he backed away. "Do you understand?"

In the palpable silence, the hole grew larger, more ragged, like a scream for help.

ONE

Who cares if they pollinate the blueberries?" Belle Palmer mumbled to herself as she raked at the bloody crusts behind her ears. You could eat only so much pie. Damn blackflies. Would some genius ever invent repellent that wasn't an oily, sticky solvent for plastic? Cheer up, they'll be gone in a month, ushering in mosquitos, cluster flies, horse flies, moose flies, deer flies and pernicious no-seeums, which require a tent screen finer than silk. Welcome to Northern Ontario, where bugs are an equal opportunity employer: O positive is as full-bodied as A or B.

Belle usually avoided the woods until the hotter weather switched off the worst biters, but her German shepherd Freya was eager for a trek. The dog brought up the rear, browsing every ten feet for an educated sniff at her p-mail. Was it like reading a book? Tracing Braille? Red squirrels, the stunted northern variety, chittered teasingly from the cedars; foxes had scheduled night manoeuvers, littering the path with grouse feathers; and under the bracken, a rabbit hopped to safety, newly metamorphosed from white to brown in seasonal camouflage. Under the arms of a massive yellow birch, Belle spied a tiny, freeze-dried wintergreen fruit, popped it into her mouth and enjoyed a teaberry gum moment. She realized that she had stopped singing, a strategic mistake in bruin territory, especially when they were foraging frantically for tender grass, grubs, and roots before the berries arrived.

Suddenly her third-class human nose wrinkled. What a stink! Yet not cloyingly sweet like carrion. Rancid, sharp, even burnt. The dog had picked it up and veered off past hills of white trilliums and delicate ferns, leading her deep into the bush to a scene from an absurdist movie. Tied into the brushy alders were a dozen doughnuts—grape jelly, under examination —and stale. A lemon pie, ravaged by joyous ants, rested on top of a table rock. Miss Havisham's wedding feast? Moving toward a glittery hanging object, Belle skidded to her knees, breaking her fall against a rotten log shining in the sun. Soaked with used fry oil, a generous gallon. The glitter came from a cheap plastic timer set with fishing line, Salvador Dali's surrealistic contribution. No salt lick this, no appleyard for moose or deer, but an ursine smorgasbord. In its big-city wisdom, the Ontario government had cancelled the spring bear hunt. Someone was poaching.

Belle narrowed her eyes in disgust and rubbed her hands on the grass with dubious success at removing the tacky mess. The hunt itself posed no problem. Ontario had 75,000 of the critters, and rising. If a bowhunter or stalker offered fair odds, let them fill a freezer. Bear meat could be delicious in stews and savory sausages. It was the baiting that bothered her, ticket to the fifth circle of hell if she'd been devising poetic punishments for the afterlife. Rich Americans from Michigan, New York and Ohio tooled Lincoln Town Cars up to the distant lodges north of Sudbury and waved ever-inflating dollars. The scenario was simple. Set out tempting pastries, garbage or even rotten meat, then climb into a tree perch, rough boards or fancy metal frames out of the Cabela outfitter's catalogue. Despite the morning frost, a pleasant wait with a few sandwiches, munchies, renowned Canuck beer or a mickey of rye, and presto, Bruno with insouciant pie face became an instant rug.

There was another motive more sinister than trophies—the burgeoning demand for ancient Chinese medicines based on animal parts, especially in Vancouver, where Hong Kong barons were enlarging their power base. Squeaky clean Canada's shameful cousin to the rhino horn or ivory trade. And now that the loonie dollar coin had a new bimetal big brother (the twoonie, toonie, tunie?) featuring a polar bear, all the more ironic.

"Let's get out of this reek. I don't want to become a statistic." Bear attacks were very unusual, but recently a female jogger in Quebec had suffered a fatal bite on the neck. Freya was, in sad fact, an insurance policy.

As Belle returned to the trail, she saw a familiar figure approaching, yelping beagle and loopy golden retriever heralding the procession. It was Anni Jacobs, who had cut and tramped these webs of peaty paths. A slight but vigorous widow nearly seventy, she forged out daily to impress herself softly upon the forests. Her unruly dogs earned no respect from Belle, but Anni's late husband had prized these two for bird hunting, so she was coddling them into ripe old age. The women shared a reverence for the woods, yet respected each other's privacy, passing a few words on the road at intervals. Childless, Anni devoted her spare time to volunteering at the Canadian Blood Services. Belle thought that she had better relate her discovery, for though the area was Crown land, Anni's name was on it, so personal and firm were her footsteps.

Dressed in L.L. Bean's prime chinos, a light anorak and a green net that covered her face, she greeted Belle as the Beagle barked mindlessly. "Didn't recognize you at first. Life through a bug hat darkly. Haven't trampled any of my early

4

mushrooms, have you?" she said in a mock scold, raising the face net and bending to pull at the yellow roots of a clover-leafed plant with a white star flower. "I see our goldthread's back. Pharmacopoeia of the woods. Aboriginals used the roots for cankers, sore gums and teething."

"We have a problem worse than a toothache," Belle said. "I found a baiting spot not far from that grandfather yellow birch with the lightning scar."

"Should have suspected that. I heard gunfire Saturday morning, and more than one strange truck's passed. It's ruining the hiking. If I'm not ducking at a shot, I'm looking over my shoulder for bears straying from their territory, attracted to the free lunch." A black look crossed the healthy old face. "Last week a mother and two cubs were foraging near the swamp. Bears don't scare me, mind you, but I do want to know where they are. Likely they feel the same. Still singing George M. Cohen songs?"

"On the same two notes, just like Cagney in *Yankee Doodle Dandy*." Belle ran a hand through her short reddish hair, discovering a delta-winged deer fly looking for a home in the greying strands.

"I thought the spring would be safe now." Anni bristled like a venerable porcupine at bay, a slight sag to one eye lending an arch expression. "Cubs are learning to feed with their mothers. Fresh from their dens and hungry. God knows enough of them get shot in the fall."

"Where the quota is limited to boars, but who checks? Shouldn't we call the Ministry of Natural Resources?"

"Overworked and underpaid, the MNR. Don't-call-us department, if you can get through that phone maze. Press this, press that. And last week in town they tranquillized a mother sixty feet up a tree. Died in the fall and orphaned two cubs." With her stout oak walking stick she prodded the Beagle's rump to prevent him from poking his nose into an anthill. "Tell me where you found this hellish site."

Frowning at the description, turning over possibilities like coins in her hand, Anni said, "This calls for extreme measures. I don't suffer fools gladly. Enough is enough."

"What are you going to do?"

With a conspiratorial grin, she ticked off steps on her wrinkled fingers. "One, search and destroy. Rip everything down and bury it. And I'll give a good, solid burn to that oily log, safe enough before the dry season. Two, any strange vehicle up to mischief gets tires flattened or a spark plug tossed into the brush. They'll get the message."

"Uh," Belle said, shifting her feet uncomfortably in consideration of the Russell belt knife at Anni's side, "that could be dangerous. Especially if they figure out who did it."

A wry smile teased one corner of the puckered mouth, as innocent as Lillian Gish's in *The Whales of August.* "But, my dear, how can they? There are so many cottages. And I have a perfect disguise. The old are as invisible as children. You have to do what is right. And in the end, we're all bear bait, and nobody gets out of the forest alive. Not even the bears."

No arguments there, Belle thought with mingled admiration and uneasiness at the picture of a senior citizen guerrilla. "Please be careful. And keep me posted." She watched the slender form stride down the trail, a five-foot challenge to osteoarthritis, one tough person, living alone twenty-five kilometres from town. What else to expect from a daughter of Manitoba, a rugged place where men are men and moose take precautions?

Back down Edgewater Road Belle walked, heeling the dog, alert to the sounds of approaching vehicles muffled by the hills, noticing, as she passed smoking barbecues and laughing children, that life on Lake Wapiti had shifted seasons. The varying sounds of motorboats had returned, a different tenor from the guttural roar of snowmobiles. On April 20th, the last ice floes had drifted out, and until Labour Day, the boats would hold dominion.

She turned at the Parliament of Owls sign that marked her driveway. Serving as personal totems were Horny, a foot-high brown owl with yellow marble eyes and threatening eyebrows, and Corny, his innocent snowy brother. Ever hopeful, Freya dug up a pebble and dropped it at her feet like a precious gem. Shepherds were notorious stone-swallowers. Probably the bouncing rock resembled some chaseable creature in a Jungian doggie symbol mindset. "Chip your fangs, but remember that you can't get falsies. This isn't Toronto," Belle said, skipping the prize across the gravel and climbing to the deck where ruby-throated hummingbirds back from Gulf Coast condos duelled for a sugar fix from the bright red plastic flowers of the feeder.

Inside the two-storey cedar house, "Fireworks Polka" by Strauss was playing on the CD player, a lively treat with explosions of gunfire. Belle took a bath, talced up, and chose a T-shirt with a picture of Clayoquot Sound: "Pardon me, thou bleeding piece of earth." After pouring a glass of tankcar red wine, she opened *The Toronto Star*. Referendum, wheneverendum, neverendum. Would the Quebec dilemma plague Canada until the rest of the provinces joined the US along with the multi-cultural city of Montreal? Protection of Francophone heritage or just plain blackmail? Humiliated spouse or whining wife? Nervous ethnic and Anglo votes had tipped the last "Leave Canada" results to a narrow 50.6% NO victory, though the shenanigans with balloting resembled the Florida mess. None of this uncertainty was helping the confidence of the nation, interest rates, the stock market and Palmer Realty—her own *gagne-pain*—bread and butter.

Mealtime in a rush meant sensible Kraft dinner. Why were people so snobbish about the legendary blue box? Hard to beat the price, the convenience, the taste, or the plenitude, and the stuff was undeniably nourishing. Leftovers fried up into crusty magic. A salad of California red lettuce, artichoke hearts and green peppers rounded out the meal with a vinaigrette of balsamic vinegar and extra-virgin olive oil. Now there was a paradox. The satellite dish on the dock creaked to the American Movie Classic channel and brought Garbo's growl in *Anna Christie*: "Gif me a viskey. Ginger ale on the side. And don' be stingy, baby." Between noisy bites, Belle mouthed the words along with the young prostitute and smiled on cue at the scene where Marie Dressler (a fellow Canadian from Cobourg), the archetypal barfly, maneuvered her bulldog face and bag-of-toys body, weaving a hand through a hole in her tattered sweater with drunken bemusement. "Know what? You're me thirty years from now." Had they really had an affair? The spate of kiss-and-tell books after Garbo's death at eighty-five had been a gothic horror parade. Handstands after intercourse as a birth control method? Blasphemy. At fifteen, Belle had seen her first glimpse of the enigmatical ice goddess. Now, at forty-five and ten pounds over fighting weight, she was beginning to identify with Marie.

TWO

Driving by Anni's house a few days later, Belle craned her neck to spot the woman's rusty little Geo, but it was gone. Anni was a woman of her word, no-nonsense, expedient. If she said she was going to demolish the site, she would. Might be a good idea to give her a call soon.

Belle's four-by-four van, a compromise between comfort, space and the practical needs of a Northerner, passed along the Airport Road, the puffs of the 1250 foot Superstack in the distance, emblem of the International Nickel Company, aka INCO, the once-dominant employer. Supposedly the friendly giant cleansed the exhaust of 90% of pollutants and was monitored like a preemie, though intermittently it gave a dyspeptic burp that hit the papers. A molten bombshell from space nearly two billion years ago had crowned Sudbury with a thirty-mile ring of ore deposits, a blessing and a curse. The region was finally recovering from the systematic rape of resources that had left a war zone around the Nickel Capital. First, its timbers had been shipped to Chicago after the Great Fire of 1871. Then open pit smelting had destroyed secondary vegetation and leached soil from the hills. No wonder astronauts had come to the blackened moonscape to train. Fortunately the last decades had seen a massive liming and seeding campaign. Acid-tolerant pines and rye grass were covering the scars, and trout, pickerel and pike were biting again as the lakes recovered.

En route to her office downtown, Belle stopped at the latest addition to their food chain, a bagel shop. She scanned the counter, barely mastering the canine urge to drool. Fifteen kinds, including sourdough, cheese and bacon, and a dubious chocolate chip. A cooler offered cream cheese in tempting flavours: dill, olive, peach and smoked salmon. For less than five dollars, she snatched an assortment.

Palmer Realty occupied a large mock-Victorian house on a quiet street with mammoth cottonwoods, a fast-growing and resilient tree. Twenty years ago in Toronto, Belle had left a punishing career as an English teacher before a love of literature became an apology, and with only a suitcase and her *Compleat Shakespeare*, had boarded a bus to join her Uncle Harold in his business. With 160,000 people in the newly amalgamated region, not to mention cottage buyers from the south, all hungering for a spot on one of the ninety lakes, he had established a lucrative and satisfied clientele. Until his death at eighty, he had strolled through the door every morning, unfiltered Camel cigarette in his mouth, red bow tie bobbling over his Adam's apple. Every now and then she expected him to reappear, quizzing her on every pond, puddle and pool. Anyone with the confidence to wear a bow tie might come back from the dead.

"Can lattes be far behind?" she asked Miriam MacDonald, rustling the bag. Her mistress of all trades, former itinerant bookkeeper, brushed back a lock of frizzy iron gray hair, surveyed one, smelled it, poked it and finally gave a tentative nibble. "A real bagel like on TV? No more gnawing like a beaver on those frozen hockey pucks from Toronto?" She rummaged through the bag. "And peach cream cheese? Today I work for nothing." A sigh broke from her lips. "Hell, I do that anyway, and I need a holiday."

"Victoria Day's around the corner. Anything new and exciting?" Belle made a face as she refilled Miriam's cup and poured herself a coffee. "Don't you hate that phrase?"

The fax machine ironed out a message. Miriam yanked it off, eyes widening in comic disbelief. "What's this? Do we have any waterfront under fifty thousand? Must have lake large enough for a jet boat, year-round road access, modern cottage with septic, boathouse, sauna, dock, all within an hour of town." She mimed a dealer tossing out cards. "This guy'd get better odds playing the slots at Sudbury Downs."

Belle flashed her an encouraging smile. "Everything sells at the right price. What about the Darwin property? Has the old coot come down as we suggested?" The crafty owner had given an imitation pine facelift to the leaning shack, but she suspected lurking problems, a buried heating oil tank for the "septic," dry rot in the boathouse. Unless the buyer wanted to use the outhouse (Class 5 sanitation system), he'd need a field bed at a cost of perhaps ten thousand. A realtor wore two hats, one for the buyer and one for the seller. It was her job to be optimistic yet realistic, since legal troubles came from hiding information.

"Hanging tough," Miriam said, scanning the bulletin board, snatching off a note and tapping her favourite repository of Frenglish slang. "*Tabernac* on toast!. This call came yesterday as I left. A Mr. Sullivan seemed very interested in that property near you. He noticed the ad in *The Sudbury Star*. I made you a date. Three sharp."

Miriam licked a pencil point and drew dollar signs on the prospectus, passing it over. "Do you think he has the money? He'll be paying for the acreage more than the small house."

Belle didn't have to open the folder. She had walked to all four corners checking survey stakes. Smack at the end of her road past the schoolbus turnaround. Five glorious acres backing onto Crown land. A boathouse, drive-in shed and 800 square-foot cottage. Oil furnace. Decent siding and insulation. Plow truck and small tractor. Its salient point was privacy, nestled into birch, poplar and maple forest. The property had belonged to Jason Brown. A year ago, the old man had suffered a stroke and been taken to Rainbow Country Nursing Home, where Belle's father lived. Unable or unwilling to speak, Jason was as communicative as a rutabaga. He had taken good care of his home, but last time she had visited, a piece of siding was blowing off, and the boathouse needed fresh paint.

At three o'clock precisely, the door opened. Silvery hair brushed to a sheen, a Burberry topcoat over his arm, the man wore a light beige three-piece suit, maroon puff in the pocket, matching striped tie. Very Toronto Bay Street broker, if it hadn't been for the carefully trimmed white beard. "I'm Charles Sullivan. I've come about the Edgewater Road property."

Belle introduced herself and presented the file, which he scanned with interest. His hands were immaculately manicured, and a light scent of bay rum reminded her of Uncle Harold.

"I've retired," he added, "and always dreamed of living on a quiet lake. If there are a few problems to fix, all the better. I'm pretty handy with a hammer and saw, and I like to keep busy."

Belle found his courtly manner refreshingly old-fashioned. He listened with an intelligence signalling a profession. Doctor? Lawyer? Clergyman? It seemed presumptuous to ask. Not a patrician eyebrow rose at the price, and when she suggested a visit, he followed her from town in his white Ford Taurus, fresh from a car wash.

Half an hour later, at the junction of Edgewater Road, Belle signalled for a stop at the assembly of Canada Post mailboxes.

After getting out of the van, she called over her shoulder as she opened her pigeonnier. "Believe it or not, we lobbied long and hard for this small privilege. The alternative was to collect our mail in Garson, the little suburb we passed through." As she sifted the letters, she discovered one for Anni, 1703 instead of her 1903, and placed it on the dashboard.

With Creedence Clearwater Revival banging out "Down on the Corner," Belle drove past the swamp where moose crossed the road for a dawn slurp and three deer, a rarer sight, had danced a midnight ballet one moonlit night. Dreaming of her flaming youth over the words "Look at all the happy creatures dancing on the lawn," she swerved to avoid an oncoming green Escort gobbling more than its share of gravel. Patsy Sommers, one neighbour short on manners. Behind her, Sullivan stayed well to the right. She hoped that the incident wouldn't discourage him. Nothing like a fender-bender introduction to rural living.

A mile beyond her house, they passed the school bus turnaround and stopped by a farm-style gate. The property had the bonus of chain-link fencing along its road boundary to foil snowmobilers or people pulling boat trailers looking for lake access, she explained, opening the padlock. "Pretty safe out here," she said. "Occasionally the snowbirds lose portable temptations like chain saws, shotguns or stereo equipment."

They parked in the large lot at the end of the lane, where red osiers sported their umbilical flowers. She pointed out raspberry bushes, the new canes green promise. "These make great jam. Wild ones always taste better than commercial berries. People say Mr. Brown was famous for his wine, too," she said.

"Is that so? I used to be a dab hand with that art myself." He looked up as a small dark red-barked tree with a host of white blossoms showered them like bride and groom. "Pale pink like lemonade, but proofing out at over 20%, especially if aged in old rum barrels."

Belle laughed and warmed to his enthusiasm, not to mention her rising hopes for the sale. "Might call it 'firewater.' Medicinal purposes only, eh?"

"Nature knows best."

The little house needed a good airing. It was musty, the heavy curtains pulled tight to discourage nosy intruders. Originally a one-room post-and-beam camp, when a foundation had been added, the upstairs had been divided into a living area, bedroom, kitchen and bathroom with shower. Belle opened a window to let in fresh air. A collection of castoffs, the furniture mixed decades like an eclectic museum. Massive Forties overstuffed chairs merged with the drab Fifties nubbly couch in a vomitous colour and the Sixties black and white television. "Silverware and dishes in your choice of patterns," she said with a laugh as they passed through the kitchen. In the bedroom, they paused to consider a swaybacked mattress on a metal frame. Belle shook her head. "Multiple lumps or a sag that you fight all night seems part of cottage life." Downstairs, the oil furnace gave the cinder block basement a definite wang, but Sullivan didn't comment, nodding as she showed him the new jet pump. "The house is well-insulated," she added. "Pink batts in the crawl space and blown-in fibre in the walls."

Was the man interested? He hadn't spoken more than a "um-hum" since they had come inside. When they returned to the yard, she asked, "Have you lived in the country?"

He hesitated, then looked at her pleasantly. "Not for years. Ottawa's been my home."

"If you're used to city life, what I'm getting at is this.

Everything looks so benign in the summer. But we get plenty of snow. Eleven feet this year. Not much thawing, either, like the chinooks out west. The road is plowed, better be with the taxes we grouse about, but you'll have to clear your drive with Brown's old truck or arrange for a contract. Ed DesRosiers's very reliable. I use him myself, and often I'm away by seven."

He waved his hand in polite dismissal. "The Capital City gets a lion's share, and I think I'd like plowing. Make technology do the dirty work. It seems productive and relaxing. Enjoy tinkering with cantankerous motors, too."

That sounded better. Belle took a deep breath. After expenses, namely Miriam, the six-percent commission would pay for a new refrigerator, maybe a down payment on a van. And it really was a splendid place, much larger and far more private than hers.

He retrieved a small leather notebook from his coat pocket and jotted notes with a gold Cross pen. "Septic OK? And how about the drinking water? Is there a well?"

"Whoa! You're no amateur." Belle pointed to a grassy knoll. "Field bed's back there. Natural drainage slope, so you don't have the worry of a lift chamber. Most of us have our tanks pumped every two years to be on the safe side. A grant's available, too. And as for the water…" Spread out like a melted Prussian blue crayon was Lake Wapiti, an eight-by-eight mile meteor crater, deeper than the Underworld itself and as frigid as the other place was sizzling. "There's the best well in the world. Brown has a heated waterline like mine. A bit of colour in spring run-off, but you can get filters at Canadian Tire if you're squeamish about algae or sediment. Even a reverse-osmosis system is available now. Big bucks, though."

What they found next in the large shed made Sullivan clap his hands. "He left all his tools? They're worth a fortune." He studied the table saw, chop saw, lathe, router, shop vacuum, grinder and rows of assorted jars of nails and screws neatly affixed to the wall. A pegboard with hooks held graduated series of screwdrivers and wrenches.

"He's in a nursing home. The relatives down south took only the bass boat. Cottages are usually sold all-inclusive," she said as if bestowing a personal gift. "Never know what you'll find. Maybe five sets of rusty bedsprings. Maybe buried treasure. His nephew told me that Brown had hinted at some secret hideyhole. Family joke, I guess."

The central part of the property was cleared, which allowed the breezes to blow off the bugs, with a few well-placed large oaks and maples saved for shade. At one side, flanked by dwarf plum and apple trees, a weedy garden sprouted asparagus feathers and the broad rhubarb leaves of the ubiquitous Canadian staple. "Hurts to see a garden gone to seed," Belle said. "Before he started going downhill, this used to be the best on the road, especially the tomatoes. Once he even grew a prize-winning pumpkin. Milk-fed, but don't ask me how."

Sullivan knelt stiffly and sifted the soil with his hands. "Fine stuff. Just the right mix of organic material, clay and sand. Must have taken him many years, hauling in the soil."

Belle broke off a thumb-thick asparagus spear to munch on. "Don't tell me you garden, too?"

Pulling out a plantain weed, he tossed it aside. "Oh, I'm hoping to have time for many hobbies now."

Belle led him to the dock, bolstered by a formidable rock wall for ice and wave protection. Far across the water, flanking the North River, the hills leapfrogged each other in layers of teal and black under shadows of scudding clouds. A loon called to its mate, ululating and then diving, only to surface a hundred feet away. "Marvellous swimmers," he said.

"Can't ever guess where they're going to rise. One thing's sure, it proves that there are plenty of fish in Wapiti. Are you an angler, Mr. Sullivan?"

He beamed like an uncle. "Call me Charles. I'm a catch-and-release man, in it for the fight. Will confess something, though. I do eat the perch."

Belle bent down and peered into the clear depths. "Perch? Are they worth the trouble? They're so small and bony."

"That's true. Most folks don't bother. Consider them trashy, to use their word. Five or six make a pretty good feed, and I don't mind the cleaning." He stepped forward and tossed a twig into the water, following its drift with a trained eye. "My Lord, just look at the little devils down there. Wish I had my tackle," he said, grinning broadly. "Tell you what. I'll catch a pailful and invite you for dinner."

Belle's heart rang like the drawer of an old-fashioned cash register, and she wondered if dollar signs had snapped into her saucery eyes. "Do you mean that…"

"That's right, my dear lady. I like it. I'll take it. Not even going to insult you and our Mr. Brown by dickering. Not my style."

Wondering if he had forgotten the steep price, she tried to cement the bargain. "I know it seems high, but you do have 650 feet frontage. You could split off a lot, sacrifice a little privacy, and realize sixty or seventy thousand at the right time."

He closed his eyes, folded hands behind his back and took a deep breath. Belle could smell the clean tang of the water as the wind ruffled their hair. "Why spoil paradise?" he asked.

It was after six by the time she left Charles surveying his kingdom. "Yesssssss!" Belle said, clenching her fist. Satisfied buyer, satisfied seller. Whether or not Brown ever connected with reality, she had obtained a fair price which might buy him some comforts. As the van rounded a corner, the letter to Anni dropped from the dash onto her lap. Better take it on down. Besides, she wanted an update on the mind games with the hunters. Women, take back the woods!

The rusty Geo sat in Anni's driveway like a wounded veteran, a faded Support the Right to Arm Bears sticker on its rear windshield and its muffler dangling an inch from the ground. How the woman kept the beast chugging was a miracle, but money was short for a widow. She lived frugally, her greatest asset the property itself. Parking on the neatly swept gravel, Belle marvelled at the perennial garden surrounding the modest frame house. A pastel rainbow of graduated tulips and hosts of sunny daffodils lent Wordsworthian splendour to the tidy beds. She raised an eyebrow to notice that Anni's Oriental lilies were already a foot tall. Her own bulbs had become a late spring snack for some discriminating vermin. Around the corner dashed the dogs, yapping and jumping. Belle gave a surreptitious knee to the unruly golden trying to romance her leg. The door opened, and Anni appeared in jeans and a patched corduroy shirt, holding a book and probably wondering about the unusual social call.

"I have a letter for you. Wrong box again." Belle passed her the envelope with a Government of Canada return address.

Anni swept her arm graciously. "Well, then you deserve a reward. Come in and talk over a crone's tipple. I usually eat later in the summer."

The few times Belle had been inside, some new puzzle decorated the wall, this time an eye-crossing Jackson Pollock full of paint blots and streaks. Anni had explained that the concept of "dissected maps" had developed in late eighteenth-century England as a teaching tool. Her husband Cece had started her on the hobby, bringing back specimens from his world travels as a metallurgical engineer. One Japanese wooden puzzle hung vertically without glue, sold with tweezers and magnifying glass to assemble twenty-five pieces per square inch. To add to the museum flavour, purple velvet plants trailed their vines, winding among Boston ferns and an assortment of prickly cacti including an Old Man variety sporting a gray wig. In a brass container in the corner stood Anni's walking stick and an umbrella. The polished wood floors shone like honey. No traces of dog claws, though, with the mutts likely relegated to the basement at night.

Belle stopped to inspect a curious landscape peopled by small figures making their way from the Barren Land of Ignorance to the Hill of Science, detoured by the Mansion of Appetite, the Wood of Error and the Fields of Fiction. "Anni, is this new? Give me a room in the Mansion of Appetite."

Her friend set her reading glasses aside, pleased at the observation. "A Pilgrim's Progress variation, circa 1800. Probably no one bothers with that in school anymore, but it's always been a comfort to me. Couldn't resist buying the little treasure."

"Wouldn't it be great if life were that simple? Good, evil, black, white. Mind your manners and advance to the next square."

Sitting on the chintz sofa, her hands folded as she stared at the envelope, Anni turned pensive. "We never know where some paths may lead us. At any rate, I did the deed," she said with a grave tone. "All of that abomination is gone."

"Did anyone see you?" Belle asked, choosing a rocker.

"I don't think so."

"So nothing has happened? No phone calls or other dirty work?"

"For precautions, I left town that night to stay with an old friend in Muskoka for several days. Since I've been back, I haven't heard any shots, or seen anyone who didn't belong on the road." Sighing, she rose and went to the credenza, reaching for a cut glass decanter and pouring small glasses of sherry with a shaky hand. Several drops spilled, but Anni didn't seem to notice.

"So what's wrong? They learned their lesson," Belle said, accepting the drink.

Anni gestured at a picture of a grinning young man on her mantel. It was her nephew, whom she mentioned occasionally, always with a curious mixture of love and exasperation. "Another wild scheme of Zack's."

"Again? Not another budgie sitting service or balloon delivery from Batman. Or is he opening a chip stand across from McDonald's? Too bad he missed the pet rock craze. Can you imagine the raw material around here?"

The Gatling gun humour had misfired. Anni blinked her cinnamon brown eyes, shadowed with concern. "He has an idea for a used book store, compact discs, too. Maybe computer games. It's true that he's my only relative and welcome to his legacy. God knows he's given me a hand with the spring and fall chores and made sure I got good care when I broke my arm last year, but I'm not made of money. Why can't he find a rich wife or rob a bank?" She managed a weak smile.

Belle sipped at the sherry, a tiny dose of Bristol Cream, but "cherce" as Spencer Tracy would say of his Kate. "Small businesses are risky," she said. "Half of the new ones go belly-up every year."

"I know. Lack of planning, faulty demographics, too much staff or overhead, heavy competition. And some, like men's clothing, are extremely perilous." She realigned a ruby glass paperweight on the coffee table and took a deep breath.

"Listen to me lecturing like Zack. Says he's read enough books and made all the right mistakes to succeed. The infallible logic of the young, bless them. They'll learn as we did." Her eyes grew moist as she looked away.

Belle wondered if he had considered the obvious. "Tell you what's big in this aging town. Home care. Assistive devices, help with daily chores. Special clothing, too, now there's a gold mine. Silvert's comes up from Toronto several times a year to make the rounds of the nursing homes. Surely he could beat their prices. I paid sixty dollars for my father's ordinary sweatsuit with Velcro fastenings."

Finally, Anni laughed. "That's the last venture Zack would try. Except for me, and he tells me I'm really twenty-five, he can't handle old people."

"What do you mean?"

"Well, face the concept, I guess. When his mother, my sister Nell, had to be put into a nursing home because of Alzheimer's, he became so depressed that he had to take tranquillizers every visit. Says he'll kill himself before he reaches that stage. Early dementia runs in families." Her voice trailed off.

"I can understand. First time through the door at Rainbow Country, my legs turned to rubber. You and I can't imagine living in helplessness." Belle shrugged and made a palms-up gesture. "But for some, a word or a wave brightens their day. Not that I'm bucking for sainthood, but I can't just skulk in and out with his lunch. These people I see every week. They deserve acknowledgement."

Anni's slender fingers curled around each other as if to husband strength against a growing vulnerability. Her eyes flickered toward the kitchen. "I've...been forgetting things lately. The odd bill, the time I left the dogs out all night, and

I'm forever losing my keys. I made the mistake of telling Zack, and you should have seen his face."

Belle gave a light laugh of reassurance, took off her glasses and twisted the titanium frames, which sprang back obligingly. "I'm always losing these, or sitting on them. Happens to everyone. You're safe as long as you remember that you wear them."

"I hope you're right. Anyway, enough family problems. Thanks for listening and for bringing the cheque. I've been a bit short this month." Anni tossed back the last of her glass gamely, but the droop of her shoulders told a different story. "I'm not sure how long I can keep the Geo going. Rollins Automotive said that it needed a valve job and a new 'tranny,' I think the word was."

Swallowing, Belle tried to keep a neutral face. Big time expensive, but why worry the woman more? As they walked outside, her eye was attracted to a contorted woody shrub. "What is that bizarre plant?" she asked.

Her friend hummed a tune. "A clue? You're the film buff."

"The puzzle lady. It's familiar, but so far away. Another era. 'You are my dearie...da da da. Sweet as sugar candy' and something, something brandy." She snapped her fingers. "Greer Garson in *Random Harvest*. She did a little dance. Cute kilt. So what's the connection?"

"You know your movies, but not your music halls. The Scottish entertainer she was imitating. Harry Lauder's Walking Stick, it's called. Common name: hazel."

"Will it grow here?"

"Zone Five."

"Risky. I lost my lavender last year in that -35° stretch."

"We'll see. It's in a sunny spot, and the bay is sheltered. In a few years I'll whittle a stick for you."

Belle drove home with a nagging concern for her friend. Dementia, what a cruel spectre for someone with a healthy body. Belle's father had been so vigorous, at eighty-one keeping pace with her all over Epcot Centre. Then, a few months later, he had needed full-time care.

THREE

S everal weeks later, a giant wicker basket on her porch snapped Belle out of the doldrums of a Friday afternoon. Wrapped in bright red cellophane was an assortment of fresh fruit, California zinfandel, cabernet and chardonnay, no shoddy brands either, and expensive cheeses sampled only on holidays: triple-crème French Brie, Emmanthaler and a butterscotch square of Gjetost. A pound of cashews and a jar of macadamias completed the feast, along with palm hearts and marinated olives. What gourmet angel had been monitoring her wish list? The card was inscribed with a copperplate style that recalled her mother's careful hand: "From a grateful client. If you're free tonight around six, I have some perch who wish to make your acquaintance." Belle grinned. Mr. Sullivan, Charles, had settled in.

She popped a macadamia into her mouth, moaning at the milky crunch, and took Freya scampering up a path behind her house. Checking the time carefully, she doubled back at Skunk Brook after the animal enjoyed a brief, peaty slurp and was home in time for a bath. As she prepared to leave, ladling out Mature Purina, extra oil and Metamucil, which the vet had recommended for the older dog, she rubbed the velvet ears. "We'll find out if he likes pups, and maybe next time you can go."

She strolled to the end of the road, encountering Charles

beaming at the gate. He had a proprietorial touch in the way he escorted her down the lane. Wearing crisply pressed khaki shorts, a zippered safari jacket and dark green knee sox, he might be serving with the Raj in rural India, except for the spotless apron around his waist. "You didn't have to bring anything," he said as he studied the bottle she presented. "But the chardonnay should complement our friends." He escorted her to a picnic table by the house, appointed with an Irish linen tablecloth along with an assortment of covered dishes. With a flourish, he filled two crystal goblets, and they relaxed in lawn chairs under a shady grandfather oak next to the house. Old-fashioned citronella candles warded off the bugs with less distraction than the popular electrical lanterns which crackled ruthlessly but dispatched only innocent moths.

"You're all moved. I wish you had given me a call to lend a hand," she said.

"No difficulty there, my dear. I'm a simple man and a frugal one. Hired transport can be expensive, so I packed only the bare necessities, as they say, my library and phonograph records notwithstanding." He coughed and rubbed his back. "You were right about the wretched beds. My Lord, what white nights I spent until the new furniture arrived. Aspirins every hour. My ears are still ringing the 'Anvil Chorus'."

She laughed out of hard-gained wisdom. "My cottage had three varieties of chiropractic mine fields."

He appeared surprised. "But your house is new. When did you build?"

"A couple of years ago. My uncle left me enough in his will for the basic package, and I added the rest a bit at a time. Did the painting and clean-up myself." She didn't confess how she had nearly blown the central vacuum by sucking up drywall dust.

Sullivan cocked an eyebrow. "Very wise. So many people

overextend. Try to have everything at once. Not the way my family operated, nor yours, I'll wager."

"True enough. My parents waited until their forties for our first bungalow. They constructed a basement, covered it with plywood and tarpaper, and we lived there like blind moles until they could afford to finish. Suburban Toronto was loaded with blocks of flat structures with a doorway sticking up. Kids thought it was the way everybody lived."

A few glasses of wine later, Belle went inside to use the washroom and was amazed at the transformation of the camp. Neutral curtains and paint, a tasteful brown corduroy sofa and a glass coffee table. One wall was covered with books, mostly music and philosophy at a glance. A stereo system played Brahms symphony which floated outside like a blessing. On other shelves sat a few keepsakes, a Toby jug of Falstaff bearing a droll resemblance to its owner, onyx boxes and a folded wooden shape which attracted her. She opened it tentatively to find a delicate carved triptych.

A throat cleared behind her. "Ready for our repast?"

She felt like a kid caught with its hand in a candy jar. "I'm being nosy, but I couldn't help marvelling at this. What is it, Charles?"

His face seemed more disappointed than stern, though he softened at her appreciative tone. "You have an eye for antiquities. That's fourteenth-century beechwood. Wiser to preserve it in a safe deposit box, but I enjoy the medieval presence, a link to a lost world of craftsmanship and faith." Belle replaced the treasure with careful reverence.

The diminutive perch deserved its reputation, cornmeal-crusty chunks sweet and tender within. Steaming baked potatoes arrived with sour cream, chives and grated Monterey Jack, then a deliciously bitter salad of baby greens with tarragon vinaigrette, and for dessert, a mud pie. "Good old James Beard. Louisiana cuisine travels anywhere," he said.

"Chocolate may unite the world." Belle wiped her mouth in slight embarrassment after wolfing the pie. When he brought seconds without asking, she decided that he would make a toothsome addition to the lake.

Later that month, with the hot weather coaxing the loaded fields to sweet fruition, strawberry season began. Joining the hordes who had driven on a Sunday morning to the Valley, a rich glacial till deposit where farms thrived, she was entertained by the babble between rows as she knelt to scoot her canister along. "Old man's no problem," a woman in a tattered straw hat said to her nodding friend, their sweating faces as plump and scarlet as the berries. "Park him under a tree with a couple of beers, and he's happy as a clam for hours." At the cash, Belle found herself overloaded with quarts. Criminal to waste them. Anni might like some. Their paths hadn't crossed in weeks.

As she turned later into her neighbour's driveway, Belle thought that someone was visiting. By the house sat a gigantic General Motors van loaded like a dowager empress. Her nose pressed against the tinted windows. Leather seats. Keyless entry. Power everything. Yet where was the Geo? A firm knock on the back door brought no answer, and she was inhaling the redolent attar from a wild rose bush when she heard a scuffling. The dogs were peering timidly from behind the shed instead of clamouring for attention. Perhaps Anni had given them a two-by-four lesson. They weren't even decent protectors, not a mean bone in their silly bodies. Anyone could cart off the last stick of furniture by wiggling a slice of bologna. Wouldn't work with a shepherd, bred for healthy suspicion and territoriality.

She rapped again, then tried the door and found it open. "Hello? It's Belle." Not a sound. On a hunch, she paced the grounds in case the woman was puttering somewhere. On a boat ride? Anni's small outboard often trolled down the lake on a windless morning, but the dogs always sat in the bow. Back at the door again, canine panting loud in the silence, Belle tried to shake off a growing uneasiness.

Best to leave the perishable gift safely inside on the counter. She tiptoed into the kitchen, resorting to the silly phrase, "Are you decent? I have something for you." At each step she stopped and listened, hearing only the ticking of a clock and the hum of the refrigerator. Placing the berries by the sink, she glanced toward the living room. In the doorway was a foot. A foot in a beaded moccasin, then another, followed by legs, torso, arms and head, the conventional arrangement. On the glowing pine floor, her friend lay on her stomach. Dressed in cotton pants and a man's striped shirt, she might have been sleeping if not for the dark, matted hair.

Enough, Belle thought as her head spun and she calculated the miles to the couch. Her knees weakening, she sat down heavily on the floor, trying to deny the ugly reality. Perhaps Anni was alive, could be saved, healed, restored to that brave posture. Without really believing the possibility, she averted her eyes and groped down the thin arm for a pulse. So still, and the skin quite cool. Had Anni fallen on the slippery pine boards? Rising shakily to her feet and grasping a chair for support, Belle scanned the room with an economy of movement to minimize dizziness. Several feet away, the oaken walking stick protruded from under an end table. Why wasn't it in its usual place?

Sweat breaking out on her forehead, stricken as if by a sudden flu, Belle collected the familiar sherry decanter from the credenza and took a large slug, another and another until she fell back onto the couch, mastering with difficulty the urge to retch, hoping that the liquor would work its tranquillizing miracle. After a few minutes of deep breathing, she got up to search for the phone, lifted the receiver with two fingers and dialled the police, reminding herself to shut the door lest the animals seek out what their body language signalled they already knew.

"Is Steve Davis there? Please find him. It's important," she said in strangled tones to the switchboard operator.

"What's up?" Steve asked, several eternities later. "Another restaurant we can case out?"

"A friend of mine is dead. Anni Jacobs. I found the body. Her house is down from mine. 1703."

His even tone felt like a cool hand on her brow. Steve never wasted words. "I'm on my way. Half an hour tops."

Steve had been Uncle Harold's good friend before Belle had arrived in the mining town. With reluctance, he'd left his roots behind on a remote reserve, joined the navy and had risen through the ranks of Sudbury's finest. A few years younger and overly protective, he often tried to give her unwelcome advice, which she shot back in kind, especially concerning his rocky marriage. Recently he and Janet had bandaged their wounds and adopted a three-year-old girl with serious emotional trauma. The fight to gain her confidence had been difficult.

The Bristol Cream had clouded reality by the time Steve arrived with several officers and a plump blond man in wire-rimmed glasses whom he introduced as Dr. Mitch Graveline. Apparently it was necessary to certify the body one hundred percent unlikely to rise again like Lazarus. Later, one of the town's part-time coroners would conduct a post-mortem

Helen Keller could have deciphered, given the head wound and the nearby stick.

Steve toured the room, pushing back a shock of thick black hair from his face, its coppery complexion highlighting a proud Ojibwa heritage. He glanced back over his shoulder. "We usually send the nearest patrol car to secure the scene. I pulled rank to take the call. Did you touch anything?"

"Did I what? Haven't you told me a hundred times about people corrupting a crime scene?" She marshalled consonants in the rolling wake of the liquor. All able-bodied vowels could fend for themselves.

His six-six frame leaned toward her, and he narrowed his dark eyes as he gave an educated sniff. "Are you drunk?"

She waved off the accusation in cavalier fashion. "So I borrowed some of the sherry. And it was the sommelier's choice for an impromptu wake. Check my prints and file them for future reference. Better scrape up some DNA, too, or however they collect the stuff."

Zeroing in on the empty bottle at her side, he frowned like a principal preparing to issue a detention, then spoke firmly. "I won't tell you to calm down, because if you get any calmer, you'll pass out."

"I came, I saw, I took her pulse and headed for happy hour." Scattered thoughts outraced her manners. Following routine, Steve made her repeat the narrative. How many times would she have to tell this ugly story?

"Her pulse, right," he said. Meanwhile Dr. Graveline, the invisible man, pulled on plastic gloves for the examination. She had been unaware he had remained in the room, so quiet and efficient were his movements.

"She might have fainted. I didn't notice her stick at first," Belle said, feeling foolish as she pointed to the end table.

"Hers, eh? Bag that when the doctor's finished," he said, with a motion to an officer hovering with an evidence kit. "What's the wound like, Mitch? Could it have been a fall?"

"Trauma to the back of the head." Gingerly the physician examined the stick, its knob darkened. "Let's see now."

One corner of Steve's mouth rose. "The traditional blunt instrument?"

Graveline retrieved a giant magnifying glass and rotated the stick under a table lamp, examining the grain. "I'd say so. Oak's a tough wood. Won't split like pine. There's minimal damage to the skull and little bleeding. We'll know more later, but one solid crack in the right place would have done the job."

"Only one?" Belle asked with blurry astonishment. "I know she was old, but wouldn't the blow have to be pretty lucky? Or rather, unlucky?"

The doctor scribbled into his notebook and gazed up with the innocent liquid eyes of a Jersey calf. "Tell you a story made the rounds in Medical School. Seems that a band was playing 'When the Saints Go Marching In' when a trombone player got so carried away with Dixieland spirit that he rammed his slide into a trumpet player's head. Smack into the most vulnerable spot behind the ear. One more saint joined the chorus."

"Murder by ragtime," Belle said with a thin smile.

Steve cleared his throat pointedly. "How long ago?"

Sheltered partially by a wing chair, Graveline removed a thermometer he had placed unseen. Then he tested the flex of the joints. "Rigor is a temperaturmental creature, pardon the pun. So many variables. On average, it's well underway after twelve hours. Offhand I'd say sometime last night, if no elves fiddled with the furnace or turned on an air conditioner. And with the consistent lividity, I think we can conclude that the body wasn't moved."

The atmosphere turned from laboratory to kindergarten when a stocky young woman clumped in, chewing like a mad cow. "No broken glass, forced locks. Nothing out of place outside. Doesn't look like no robbery." She blew an enormous bubble. "Those mutts are stupid. Could care less who runs around."

Steve flashed her a punishing look. "That's all, Officer. Check the grounds and make your report. First thing in the morning on my desk."

Hoping that the bubble would splatter all over her ungrammatical and vacuous lips, Belle glared at her without effect. A woman was dead, for God's sake. Then a bark sounded from the yard. She stood with the hint of a totter, the perennial animal lover. "The dogs are probably hungry. Missed a couple of meals. May I give them some food, Steve? I doubt if their prints will be a factor."

At his nod, she left to rummage in the kitchen's obvious places, locating a large bag of kibble, but when she took their bowls to the porch, they turned their heads away, same as Freya would react under serious stress.

Steve tapped his watch and flipped through notes as she returned to the couch. "All right. Dinner's over. And mine's getting colder somewhere between here and town. So much for a quiet Sunday afternoon shift. Let's start at the beginning."

Belle began with the bear-baiting, the campaign to foil the hunters, her innocuous day, ending with the sherry overdose turning her mouth into a sugary cesspool.

"Get serious. Are you saying that she caught someone in the act? And if so, why come back here? More logical that with all the attention they would simply have packed up and found a more remote spot." Suddenly Steve rose from the couch and moved around Graveline to look at Anni's shoes.

"Moccasins. But household ones. No sign of outside wear.

So we're clear there. She wasn't marched back at gunpoint." He raised a coal-black, expressive eyebrow. "What exactly did the woman do? Did she damage any vehicles like she threatened?"

"She said that she had torn the place down. I don't know about any other sabotage. It's been a while since we talked." A picture of Anni on a mission impossible flashed through her mind. "She'd have told me. We had a kind of compact, a stew…ardship." Sobering fast, she thought, flexing her vocabulary.

"A dangerous one. Playing Rambo. Could have made big trouble."

Belle bristled, her eyes beginning to refocus. "So she was furious. You would be, too, if you were worried about pot shots at you or your family." Yet "furious" was the wrong word, she thought. Anni was far too methodical and organized. For her, revenge would be a dish best eaten cold.

"OK, I get the point. But what else do we have? Nothing seems to have been taken. Break-ins are common, except that in cottage country, robbers don't arrive when people are home. Most places are isolated enough for them to wait until the owners are away." He paused. "Change the channel. Who might want her dead? This house on the lake is expensive property. And whose van is that, anyway? Don't tell me she drove that monster?"

"Hold on. My head is hurting. One question at a time. The new van doesn't fit, Steve, because all I've seen is a tubercular Geo that could hardly make the big hill. Small pensions. As a realtor, I'd estimate that this place is probably her best asset. Just a guess, though. She didn't flash bank statements. Anni was a private lady."

He gestured like an irritated director speeding the pace. "What about relatives?"

"She's a widow, no children, but there is a nephew. Zack Meredith, a local man."

"And what's our nephew like?"

She pointed at the picture on the mantel. College graduation maybe. Short dark hair with a glint of fashionable styling gel. An open face. Boyish more than handsome. "That's the fellow. I've never met him, but she described him as a wannabe entrepreneur. Hare-brained plans that he's always urging her to bankroll. She was worried about that last time we talked."

Steve's scribbling speed increased with this disclosure, making her uncomfortable. "It's not as bad as that. He gave her a lot of help with chores, and I know she loved him. Still, if nothing turns up, he's your number one suspect. *Cui bono?*"

"Stop showing off. We'll see who's Mr. Bono when we find out if she left a will, which, at a conservative guess, she probably did. If we don't find it here, we'll contact the local law firms. She's not new to the area, is she?"

Given Graveline's smooth movements and her own bleary concentration, Belle had almost forgotten that a body lay nearby. Suddenly the back door opened and slammed, and figures moved into the room, rolling a gurney. Even though the attendants performed with surprising grace and dignity, Belle hit nine out of ten on the screaming mimi scale as a still, sheeted form was placed on a stretcher. I'm on the nerge of a vervous breakdown, she told herself.

Then they were alone again, after what seemed like a hideous dream. She swallowed hard and forced her gaze back to Steve. "I think she and her husband had lived here twenty, twenty-five years. Built the place themselves." She looked around sadly, then closed her eyes, felt the breeze through the screens and heard a gentle lap of waves from the shore. "And she was so independent, Steve. This is no place for bingo lovers, mall hoppers, or people who expect fresh cream for their coffee the morning after two feet of snow."

"She must have been a tough character. Know anything about her friends?"

Belle considered her words carefully, her mouth dry and sour. "I guess you'd call me her friend. In connection with our love for the woods. She didn't seem to socialize out here. Did a lot of volunteer work at the Canadian Blood Services, though." Her fidgeting hands seemed to have a mind of their own. They looked older, more wrinkled. She pressed them together as if in prayer, blinking the sting from her eyes. "I'll miss her."

Steve stood up. "This one's going to be trouble if the nephew has an alibi. No sign of forced entry or any violence other than stick meeting head." He paused as she gave him a disgusted look. "Sorry about that. Missed lunch and you know me. Anyway, we'll be checking her records, financial statements, whatever might provide a lead. For one thing, I'd like to know who owns that van, if she doesn't. And where's her car?"

Outside, the smell of the roses had become cloying, funereal. Belle fought the urge to drive home at top speed and jump into a bath of purifying water, sloughing off every horrid detail, growing a new skin. Wordlessly, she passed Steve the strawberries she had retrieved. It would be a long time before she enjoyed them again. Their sun-drenched redolence would remind her of the sight of blood. Steve popped a handful into his mouth, tucked the rest into the white patrol car, then pointed down the road to a hollow where a small path began. "Before you leave, tell me something. Is that the trail that leads to the baiting site?"

"Yes, about half an hour in. But everything's gone. Torn down and buried, remember?"

"These hunters sound like a wild card, but I might as well

take a look now as later." He thumped her back. "Sober enough to travel?"

Belle paused at the water tap at the side of the house and took a long drink. Then she filled her lungs with forest air, its piney coolness clearing her head. "I'll be five hundred yards ahead of those black cop shoes, Mr. Spitshine." She took off at a trot, glad to run off the sherry.

At the quick march, the half-hour dropped to twenty minutes. The sun had fallen below the hills, casting eerie shadows across the trail. Belle stepped lightly on the peaty turf, spongy and kind to the feet except for an occasional rock or root. Something fragrant was in the air, Labrador tea, perhaps.

But the wind shifted ominously, bringing a large order of carrion. As they passed the familiar carpet of trilliums now tinged with brown, Belle had a sinking feeling that Anni's plan hadn't worked after all. Nothing could have erased that aromatic picnic from the bruins' primal memory bank. Bait was bait, the smellier the better. At the base of a striped maple lay a large black mound next to a small hump of fur. Steve covered his face with a handkerchief and waved Belle away. She sat glumly on a cedar stump, contemplating a parade of ants and gulping against returning nausea. "Let's go," he said a minute later, wiping his hands with distaste. "I've seen enough. That was a mother and this year's cub. Half Freya's size."

"Mutilated?"

"Animals have been at them, maybe even other bears, but they've been cut open…and the paws are gone." With a groan, he pocketed the handkerchief. "Hunting was part of life for my family on the Reserve. No fancy grocery stores in the back of beyond. Not even a town. We depended on wild game. But it was a partnership, a pact of respect. Leaving meat to rot would have been a crime."

Belle coughed into her sleeve, breathing through her mouth. "It's profit, Steve. Bear gallbladders are valuable. Why don't you talk to the MNR about any similar reports. A car or truck might have been seen in another area."

"This could fit the time if she caught them in the act, but we've been over that. Remember that she went home of her own accord," he said as they walked, warm with sweat. "We still don't know if she damaged a car or truck. Maybe they saw her near their vehicle or knew she walked the paths. Put two and two together and followed her."

Belle shrugged. "A pitiful motive for murder. And why her stick? Wouldn't they have had weapons? A shotgun or rifle?"

"Maybe they tried to scare her, and it got out of hand." He brushed his ears and neck against the mosquitos swarming in the dusk. "Anyway, I'll get the boys to hunt for tire tracks, although it's probably useless with the dust and traffic. One other thing, Belle."

Frustrated and ready for the soft womb of her waterbed, she couldn't keep irritation from her answer. It was more like a whine. "I hate that. It's so classic Columbo."

"Where were you last night?" He touched her shoulder like a concerned brother. "Don't take offense. I have to ask."

She rubbed her eyes, then raised her hands in submission. "No alibi unless the dog will talk. I was home for dinner at six. Read a couple of magazines. In bed by ten. Am I going to hang?"

"Canada hasn't hanged anyone since 1962. The end of capital punishment in fact, if not in law. And don't worry. Only the guilty have air-tight alibis."

"That's a comfort."

"Oh, and I need your prints for elimination." He stepped back at her exasperated look. "No need to come downtown. I keep a kit in the car. Handiwipes, too."

To save the dogs from the upset of a kennel, Belle persuaded Steve to let her take them until Zack was contacted. Later, cleaned and minimally fed, she sat on her deck in the darkness. A barred owl called from its perch to remind her that some predators earned an honest living.

FOUR

Captain and Sam weren't the ideal boarders. The golden had shredded Belle's red plush bedroom slippers and made Freya so nervous that she had scuttled to the basement laundry room. The hyperactive beagle yapped at the shudder of the ancient refrigerator, the electronic blips of the computer as Belle logged onto "Canoenews" and the occasional drone of a plane circling the airport for approach. They hadn't stinted themselves at breakfast, though, declining the Purina and inhaling three cans of expensive beef stew saved for a rainy day. By 7:30 a.m., Belle was approaching meltdown and worrying the clock for Zack's call.

Her mug splashed at the first ring, a muttered prayer for delivery proving that there was a God. "It's Zack Meredith, Anni's nephew. I hear you have the dogs at your place," a subdued voice said.

"Yes, they're fine. I'm so sorry about your aunt." She swallowed and groped for a comforting phrase, but none arrived.

There was a long pause, what sounded like an embarrassed sniffle, then a throat clearing. "I can't believe it. Out there where she felt so safe. Why didn't she follow my advice and move into that seniors' condo downtown after Uncle Cece died?"

Apologizing for the delay, he agreed to come that evening. "I rent a small house in the Valley, and of course Captain and

Sam are welcome. They won't get the same attention or freedom, but Aunt Anni would have wanted me to take them. We're great pals."

On the way to town later, Belle thought for a moment about the brief conversation. He'd sounded sincere enough, and certainly protective about his aunt. How protective, though? Enough to want to send her to Cece to spare her the humiliations of old age, leaving him with a tidy inheritance? Now that was a cynical thesis. She opened up the office, surprised not to hear the tick-tick of a keyboard. Usually Miriam arrived first, living in a nearby townhouse. After giving the coffee maker a token swipe, Belle brewed a pot and banished preoccupations with the murder to a mental broom closet. By the time her friend came in, she had sifted through paperwork like Schliemann uncovering the ruins of Troy.

"Watching too many late movies?" Belle asked. Often she passed Miriam tapes of her favourite classics. They agreed that Bette Davis had been well behind the door when Beauty called, climbing to the top on sheer acting ability and a dose of grit.

The older woman looked harried, her eyes puffy and bleary. "This awful film, well, I mean it was powerful, that was the problem. I couldn't keep my mind on my quilting. Had to rip out a whole section. Then I stayed awake in a rage for hours."

Miriam could sew in her sleep, any pattern, any size. She'd won first prize at the Quilts on the Rocks competition last year. "What was it?"

"*The Boys of St. Vincent's*, that child abuse exposé at a so-called training school. What frosts me is that these men were trusted. They had such absolute power. Either the kids clammed up out of fear or no one believed their stories." She snorted in disgust.

"Power corrupts, and there's nothing more absolute than organized religion. Public schools aren't immune. That teacher in the Sault who got away with abusing girls for over twenty years." Belle drummed a pencil on the table. "Still, they say that most molesting is done by relatives."

"And those excuses. 'Willing participants.' The right to have sex with children. 'Intergenerational' love. Now they're prowling the Internet, popping Disney names into their sites to attract youngsters." Miriam's face paled under her Brillo pad hair, and she turned away for a moment. Then she grabbed a paper and scribbled a few notes. When the lead broke, she stuffed the pencil into a sharpener and began grinding with a passion. "*Hostie.* Neuter every one of the bastards."

More Frenglish curses were a grim way to start the morning, and her own sad news hadn't been delivered. "Say, I didn't have the calmest night myself."

Miriam slipped off her shoes, engaged the wooden foot roller under her desk, and passed Belle the "Are We Having Fun Yet?" mug, wiggling it in sign language. "What could happen in the quiet life of a realtor? No sugar. I'm hyped enough."

"Try a murder. My neighbour, a retired lady on that nice little picturesque lakefront road where everyone wants to live." She followed up with the details as she poured her friend a coffee.

Ears pricked like a terrier's, Miriam was herself again, quizzing in expert fashion. She was devoted to murder mysteries, wished she had been born into genteel poverty in England like Miss Silver and had been combing antique shops for a bog oak brooch for years. Once Belle had found her zooming in on an Agatha Christie tribute page on the Internet. "The dogs. Why didn't the dogs bark? Wasn't that one of Holmes' arguments?"

"They're wimps. Even if they had barked, no one lives close enough to take much note. Sometimes you can't hear anything but wind and waves. She was killed inside the house. Everything nice and neat. Guess she let the murderer in."

"Sounds funny to me. You said she was a sharp old woman. Suspicious as hell. Why ever would she open her door to a stranger? Anyway, don't you have any good news?"

Belle clapped her on the back and blew her a quick kiss. "After that Sullivan sale, now that the bills are paid, I'm declaring a bonus for you. Sun yourself in Cuba next December. Take your daughter."

"She's in North Bay taking summer courses for her teaching certificate. That apartment is costing me plenty." Miriam turned to the night's faxes, then chuckled like a parrot with a hunk of papaya. "This sounds promising. A Toronto couple transferred here to the Taxation Centre wants a house on the water."

"Plump government salaries. The very sound tickles my ears. What are they looking for?"

Miriam's head tipped up to adjust the bifocals. "I hate these glasses, can't wait until you're tortured with them, too. Something fairly new. Three or four bedrooms. Two baths. Maintenance free. Garage. Half-hour drive from town. Jostle any brain cells?"

Belle rubbed the bridge of her nose in concentration. "What about the distress sale on Kalmo Lake? That's a bargain. 40K below value."

"I wondered about that. Somebody die?"

"What a grisly attitude. It was a case, in my cautious new neighbour's words, of overextension. The Marches bought a large wooded property. Too large. The access road broke them. All that backfilling over boulders sucked up pit-run gravel like quicksand. In a week they blew twenty thousand. Then his salary was frozen at the hospital. To top it off, the wife got pregnant."

"Perfect for Mr. and Mrs. T-O. Silver lining to every cloud, isn't there?"

Even where murder was concerned, Belle wondered? What was Zack's alibi?

As she passed the airport on the way home, she glanced at the kettle lakes, one of many geological curiosities which brought international scientists to Sudbury. Over a sandy delta deposited in Pleistocene times, a glacial re-advance had scoured the area and left blocks of grounded ice to melt, forming conical potholes later filled by cool springs favoured by brook trout. The largest she had named "Philosopher's Pond," where she had spent afternoons floating on a makeshift raft and dangling an optimistic hook over hundreds of pairs of globular eyes. Well-fed by minnows, the fish had been a wary challenge for anglers since the turn of the century, if an art deco brown medicine bottle she had found were any proof. Charles didn't have a boat yet. Would he like to try his luck here?

Later that evening, after turning up their noses again at dry chow, Captain and Sam barked at a noise outside. "Quiet!" Belle scolded with a maddening lack of effect. A yellow Firefly pulled into the yard as she opened the door. "Come on up, Zack. Your babies are waiting."

He took the steps two at a time like a prom date, bearing a bunch of carnations instead of a corsage. "A simple offering," he said, "but I'm grateful you looked after the guys." As the beasts probed his groin, wagging their tails, he thumped them in hearty masculine fashion. "If you have time to talk, maybe you can tell me more about my aunt. The police asked about my trip to Detroit, but they didn't say much about how she…how she…" The words seemed to come hard for him.

Belle brought out coffees, and they sat on the deck as the lake fanned out its majesty. On cue, a white triangle of sail cut the waves. "What a view," he said, a longing in his eyes common to visitors. "It's like a fairy tale. Aunt Anni's place is so sheltered in the bay."

Belle laughed at the urban perspective. "Yes, but being on a point puts me at the mercy of the wind. At ice-out it's touch and go for the boathouse and satellite dish, even with the rock wall. Watching the floes shelf up, I pray like hell for a combination of hot sun and windless days. When he got back from Florida this year, my neighbour's waterslide sat on his lawn, and his dock was a pile of pick-up sticks."

Dressed in a University of Toronto sweatshirt and jeans, his dark brown hair fresh from a summer buzz, Zack sipped in silence for a moment, his mug gripped in both hands. He set it down shakily. Feeling sisterly or more likely motherly, Belle took the initiative. "You wanted to talk about Anni?"

He braced his shoulders and exhaled slowly in a effort to marshall his resources. "I'm glad I wasn't the one to find her."

"She didn't suffer. It was sudden and…final." Not going well, she thought. Stale words. Trite. Abrupt. Hardly comforting.

His voice grew bitter and self-accusing. "Yes, so final. No more chances. The last time I saw her, what was I doing? Telling her how much I loved her? I don't ever remember saying those words."

"Depends on how you're raised. Some families aren't very vocal or demonstrative with hugs and kisses. It's actions that count. And you tried—"

He pounded a fist on his knee as if passing sentence on his failures. "Tried to borrow more money, you mean. But

44

'borrow' is a joke. When could I ever hope to pay her back?"

"No, I meant that you tried to help. With the house. With the yard. She loved you, Zack. She was going to leave you everything." Belle blurted out the fact, nearly slapping her mouth.

If she had expected naked greed at this bombshell, she was mistaken. For a tremulous minute he looked as if he were going to cry. Then he massaged his temples, leaving white marks on the tanned skin. Belle switched gears. Grief counselling was not her forte. "I remember when we first met. I was shambling along the road like a whipped puppy. My uncle had been diagnosed with lung cancer, and he was handling it better than I was." He nodded in sympathy as she continued. "Then a magical voice emerged from a birch grove. 'I know where the wild clematis grows,' it whispered as if confiding a precious secret."

He sniffed and then pulled out a handkerchief, twisting it instead of blowing his nose. "Aunt Anni was a great one for wildflowers. I was going to give her a new Peterson's guide for Christmas, hers got so ragged. It was her Bible."

Her eyes closed, her heart remembering the drone of the forest that day. "This woman dressed in denim strolled out, holding a fragile pink flower like the holy grail. Took me back for tea and got my mind off myself by talking about her trails and their wonders. Later I found out that she'd lost Cece the year before, so she knew what I was feeling." The roar of duelling jet-skis woke her from the reverie, and to her surprise, Zack had folded his hands in resignation, calm once again as he took comfort in the vitality of Anni's life.

"She had that knack. When Mother died, she came to my apartment and packed my suitcase. Insisted I stay here for a few days. Know what we did together by the fire that night? Read

Hans Christian Andersen. Just like when I was a kid. Aunt Anni was Danish, you know. Her maiden name was Blixen."

Finally Belle told him about the baiting. "We'll have to wait until the investigation moves along. My friend Steve is touching bases with the MNR. There's a bizarre possibility that someone took offense to her actions, and it escalated."

"Are you sure? She didn't mention anything, even when I called her from Detroit." He paused as an idea crossed his face. "We always played a game. I tried to disguise my voice. Like phone sales, something to throw her off. She was so sharp, though. Never missed a trick. Said her ears were better than her eyes."

"Aunts don't brief nephews about commando raids. Exactly when did you talk to her, anyway? It will help fix the time of death."

"I left here at dawn to beat the traffic. Got there around two, so that's when I called. Took all my spare change. Brutal trip in my tin can car. Wish I had borrowed the van."

That sounded selfish to Belle, but he was like a kid to Anni, and kids did take advantage. How sound was his alibi? He had given no more specifics. "We've been wondering about the van."

He whistled, and a faint smile played on his lips as he swatted at a mosquito. "The Queen Mary, you mean. Rides like a living room sofa. We went to Science North the weekend she got it. Saw a bear movie at the IMAX, then over to the Farmer's Market for fresh bread, smoked trout from Manitoulin. That vehicle must cost a mint. Air, CD, cruise control. She was so careful with money. Maybe she had a nest egg." He stopped short at her expression. "I mean, why not? She deserved to go first class."

Belle's momentary good will was flagging. Was he genuinely

moved by the death or merely acting? The comments about money seemed ungracious. Still, it was no time for recriminations. She waved her hand casually. "The police will make enquiries. She must have seen one of the local dealers."

"They've got to find out who killed her. Is there something I can do? That's the only repayment I can make."

The sun was setting on their collection of bug bites when Belle and Zack said goodnight. Coaxing Freya from the basement, she went up to the master suite and poured a purifying soak, dripping liberal portions of kiwi bubble bath for aromatherapy. "Serenity," the bottle read as if it might be consumed. Or maybe the AA prayer. The things we can and cannot change and the wisdom to know the difference. Nothing could return Anni to life, but nothing could stop Belle from finding out how, then why, then who. A tedious but logical order. Mahler's "Kindertotenlieder" drifted upstairs. "Songs for Dead Children" sounded so mellifluous in German.

FIVE

A few days later the phone rang at dawn as Belle was mounding hot salsa onto a cheddar omelette. Crammed with sourdough toast, she answered with oral gymnastics. "Hurrogh."

"It's Steve. Thought you might like to know what we've found so far, early bird. Say, are you chewing something?"

"I was. Don't keep me in suspenders."

"That old joke ages you twenty years."

Belle cringed, vowing to bury Uncle Harold's favourite chestnut. "OK. Three questions. How could she afford that van? Zack told me it was hers. How did she die? And *cui bono*, our tie-breaker?"

"Least to most interesting. As for the death, Graveline had it down straight. The oak stick had traces of her blood, minute particles of wood in the wound, but for prints, only hers were retrievable. Some smudging could have been made by gloves or a quick wipe. The blow caused a massive haematoma. To get technical, the upper occipital region, on the lambdoidal suture. She never regained consciousness and died where she fell. Sometime after dinner, going by the stomach contents."

Belle coughed, reaching for the grapefruit juice. Suddenly her mouth felt dry. "Now I'm sorry I asked. A blurry memory of that scene suits me better. And the van?"

"No mystery there. Her name was on the registration in the

glove box. Purchased it a couple of weeks ago at Crosstown. Turned in her vehicle for next to nothing. Price was thirty-five thousand and change. But guess what?"

"GM is desperate? One per cent financing and no payments for a year?" In a town known for a boom-bust economy and labour disputes, local stores often advertised generous plans to drum up business. "No payments until after the strike" was a familiar come-on.

"Our lady bountiful paid in cash."

Belle released her breath slowly, her eyes bugging like a Peke's. "Curiouser and curiouser. The third envelope, puh-lease."

"Except for the mysterious source of money, and that's a big except, we're looking at the nephew first. Claims he was in Detroit for the weekend looking for used CDs."

"So he told me. Makes sense. She mentioned his plans." Belle's fingers drummed a paradiddle as she thought about Zack's immediate and long term needs. "Did you find the will?"

"Tucked in the desk neat as pie along with a property deed, bankbooks, income tax statements and utility bills. And you were right. Small pensions were her only income. Let's see." He paused and the sound of shuffling papers echoed over the line. "She banked at the Toronto Dominion in Garson. Few hundred in a chequing account. Three thousand in term deposits. RRSPs of around eighty thousand. Pin money, really. No action on any withdrawals. Her own life insurance ended with the husband's death. *C'est tout*. People have been murdered for less, though."

"But how did she pay? Could there be records someplace else? Maybe n bank in Manitoba or somewhere she used to live?"

"Not under the married name. And we checked Blixen,

too. Computers make it easy to hunt cross-country. Wasn't some old hoard mouldering under the mattress, either. The bills were nice crisp purple thousands, according to the salesman, some polyester sleaze. A neat stack barely half an inch. How often does someone count out cash like that?"

"Think she robbed a bank?"

"Not around here, and besides, she'd make an unlikely candidate with her age, not to mention her sex." For a moment Belle conjured up the image of Ruth Gordon brandishing a yam in her babushka to shake down the tellers. "So our FOURTH question is, why the cash?" he asked before he rang off.

Exactly, Belle thought, finishing the eggs and washing up. Why not a safe, conventional cheque? Anni was not the high-rolling type. And a van? That was no old lady vehicle, more the choice of a young parent or someone running errands. For the Canadian Blood Services perhaps? Would someone there have any answers? One of these days she should donate.

Meanwhile, she had to take her father his lunch at the nursing home. It was "Tuesday, Tuesday," the cadences of the sing-song game he had invented when she and Mama Cass had been babies. He was eighty-four years old. Not long ago he had been living in his own house in Florida, adjusting to her mother's death, finding a stylishly-coiffured, much younger Italian girlfriend named Mary at a Life Goes On meeting. Then came cumulative TIA's, tiny punches to the brain, lurking Alzheimer's, plain old senility. Who cared about the official diagnosis? He grew too tottery and confused to stay by himself. With his zaftig girlfriend waving a tearful good-bye, Belle rushed him back to Canada before his diminishing abilities flashed a red light to Immigration, which frowned on incoming drains to the health care system.

For a fraction of the U.S. costs, he had a private room at Rainbow Country, a small competitor of the anonymous pretty-faced high rises where the upper middle class preferred to warehouse their parents. The facility was a bit tattered around the edges, but clean as a new penny, and with matchless personal care. The nurses and attendants chronicled every sneeze and sniffle, each bite of food, pill and missing sock.

After a blow-by at the office, she pulled into Granny's Kitchen, the friendly family restaurant where they had enjoyed a weekly meal when he could still walk. "Hi, Maria. The usual. Shrimp, french fries and cole slaw. Hold the seafood sauce. And pie and ice cream. Cherry if possible. Cheeseburger and milk for me." Belle passed a few words with one of the regulars, a man about thirty-five whose shambling manner made him appear drunk. The sad truth was that Fred had lingered in a coma for a year after a devastating industrial accident. Intensive physical therapy and a large injection of courage had restored enough coordination to get him on his feet and enrolled in a few marketing courses.

"Did you register for the summer sessions at Nickel City College, Fred?" Belle enjoyed hearing about his progress.

"A big runaround. Workman's Comp won't authorize the program. They say I'd have to drive to work in marketing up here, be mobile, you know? And I'm driving, for sure. But it's like they don't believe I have any right to." His laboured speech was difficult to understand, so she watched his lips carefully. He looked as if he needed a shave, or perhaps he was giving up. With a fumbly bow, he presented her with his *Sudbury Star* as he left. "The old dog just might have another trick left."

Belle opened the paper. It was hard to understand why he wasn't bitter. Maybe he was merely glad to enjoy what pleasures remained, a good meal, restoring his Camaro. On the front page were details about another residential school lawsuit, this time in Fort Albany, an isolated Cree community on Hudson Bay. Leaving an ugly trail back to the Fifties, the priests, nuns and lay workers had been charged with fondling, rapes and illegal abortions. How had the community remained silent? Easy. Parents who complained were told that their government cheques wouldn't be cashed, nor would the company store provide credit. Thank God the last of these "schools" had closed in the early Eighties.

"No charge today," Maria said, appearing like a benevolent dervish and setting the bags on the table. "This is my final shift, so I want to thank my best customer."

Belle looked up in mild confusion. "Going on vacation?"

"I have needed one for some years. An eighty-hour week, you know, running this place. My son Tony helps in the kitchen, but he wants to study to be a chef in Montreal, and I am not so young anymore." She shook her wattles like a weary ox, as wide as she was tall. "So I have sold the restaurant."

Belle took her tiny, talented hand and offered good wishes. For her father's sake, she hoped that the new owner would keep the same menu. Routines were important to old folks.

At Rainbow Country, she passed a few lawn chairs on the small porch, saluting the coughing brigade who had abandoned the free tar and nicotine of the dreary smoking room. Under nursing home rules, smokers were allowed one cigarette an hour, receiving lights from the staff. Abby, a grizzled veteran nearly blind behind mirrored sunglasses, recognized Belle's voice. "Got to grab some fresh air with our smokes," she said with a wheeze and rummaged in the bag attached to her walker.

Belle opened the pack and lit one for her, then went inside to collect a bib, towel and silverware from the supply cabinets.

Along the hall, she noted the subtle, depressing changes, the pixie with two canes now a blanketed shape in bed, the empty blue chair where the cadaverous man who chuckled over Janet Evanovich's *Deep Six* once rocked. Father's television was blasting out an exercise program, a Jane Fonda clone in spandex hip-hopping to unearthly perfection.

She shrank a bit as always to see him in his "gerry" chair, designed to guard against a fall, but a cruel jailer. Broken hips were a nightmare ending with blank spaces on the name board by the nurses' station. She remembered the day she had bought it. He'd been found on the floor twice, too proud to call for help. In the Model Sick Room at a local pharmacy, she'd sat down to test the comfort, and the officious clerk had leaped forward to lock the lap table into place. The sudden confinement in a padded cell on wheels had nearly forced a scream from Belle's tightened lips. Holding her breath, she 'd unlocked the clasp with paralytic fingers and scrawled a check for nearly a thousand dollars while tears dried on her face.

"Hi, handsome. It's Tuesday, Tuesday, and I've brought your shrimp." She unpacked the boxes and arranged his bib.

"I thought you weren't coming." He recited the same line with a calculated pout, even after her scrupulous visits through blizzards and ice storms. The rare times she left town for more than a few days, she arranged for an aide to deliver the lunch.

His thick white hair was fresh cut and brushed, baby blue eyes large and clear, glasses long abandoned in a drawer. For some reason he no longer used them, even to read, or perhaps he had forgotten that he wore glasses. A Maple Leafs' shirt and machine washable work pants completed the easy-care outfit. Despite the extra effort, the staff was religious in making sure everyone was up and dressed by nine so that they didn't sit around in nightclothes.

Filling a glass with water from his tiny bathroom, she bumped an elbow against a cumbersome Hoyer lift straddling the toilet like an enormous mantis. Then she set up his lunch, sat back and let him enjoy the food without conversation. Not only was his speech unintelligible with his mouth full, but he needed concentration to coordinate chews and swallows. A minced or puréed diet might soon be required, the dietician had noted. Belle had tried to keep his bridges battened down, but getting him to the dentist was a navigational minefield, and it didn't take much to wrench a back, helping him in and out of the van. Saner to operate without teeth at all. Bridges and dentures often went missing anyway with the cob-webbed female wanderers who collected small items on their "clean-up" rounds.

The cheeseburger, milk and his *Maclean's* magazine kept her attention, though she cocked an eyebrow at the fanatical exercise woman flogging a Nordic Track. How senseless to buy costly steppers and treadmills to compensate for sedentary lives instead of choosing a relaxing walk. Belle's quiet paths were the best reason for living in the wilderness instead of in a city where five-year-olds took classes in street smarts. Then she thought glumly of Anni and put away the rest of the cheeseburger. To be banished from the world outside to a little room like this would not have been her choice, but to leave so soon, upon the whisper of a breath?

Her father wiped his mouth with a tiny burp after the last french fry had vanished. "What's up? You're pretty quiet."

She had no qualms about telling him about the murder. He loved excitement. When he had worked as a booker for Odeon Theatres in Toronto, a gas explosion had levelled a building across from his office. The disaster had been his number one story for fifty years. "Hold your horses. First the coffee." She cleared away the debris and opened the pie box, fetching from the kitchen a mug bearing a picture of him with his arm around his lovely girlfriend. "My neighbour was murdered."

A gleam lit his eyes, and his voice strengthened. "Murdered? In Canada? I don't believe it."

"Neither do I, but trust me." She paused for the dramatic effect he enjoyed. "I found the body."

His pitch jumped an octave as he ate up the details as fast as his dessert. "No kidding? Tell me everything." And so she did.

"Her name was Jacobs? Was she a Hebe, then? Pretty rare birds in this neck of the woods."

Belle frowned. "Father, really. That's not politically correct these days, a word like that."

"What does politics have to do with it? The whole fillum business was Jewish when I worked there. That's what they called each other, Hebes."

She sighed, wondering how to span the decades, explain the evolution of manners into diction. "It's one thing for an ethnic group to use those names, but for an outsider, it's quite rude."

"So I'm a Scot. Like Arnold Palmer. Is that rude? The Pope's a Pole. Is that rude?"

"Well, I only…"

He stared her down, stubborn in his innocence. "And besides, I nearly married Eva Rosenblum. Except her parents lined her up with a rich doctor, a fancy one, a gyro…gyro…"

"Gynaecologist. Lucky Eva, or maybe not. Anyway, Jacobs was the married name. Anni was Danish."

He beamed. "A Dane. See?"

Old dogs and new tricks. Maybe he had a point. As she left, he stabbed an index finger on his lap table. "Appearances can be deceiving, girl. Look underneath. Use your peepers." He drifted off for a moment. "Remember what you said to that clown at the Christmas parade who asked where you got those eyes so blue?"

"Right, Father. 'Out of the sky as I came through.' Except that my eyes aren't that blue anymore. And speaking of precocious brats…" She kissed him and returned to the van. Such observations might be the ravings of an old man seduced by films, but sometimes, like Mr. Dick in *David Copperfield,* he grasped an idea that sliced the fog. Would she have to play Edna May Oliver and chase the donkeys from the yard? "Peepers." What was there to look at? Were any of the puzzles valuable? Had Anni been having work done at the house where calculating eyes might have tucked away information? Word got around in the casual labour market.

SIX

After asking Hélène and Ed DesRosiers for dinner that night, a feast starring her no-fail chicken casserole, Belle set out for her favourite real estate activity: reconnaissance, checking out a property. She chose twill pants and a turtleneck along with Reeboks designed for a hike in the bush. On a sunny morning, the drive fifty miles north to Onaping Lake was a pleasant diversion, despite the blackflies organizing a Jonestown massacre on the windshield. She passed time working on her country song, imagining Nashville fame through an instant hit. "Come on up to Mama's table," the refrain went, and as she flinched at the endless timber trucks roaring back from remote towns, the next verse wrote itself:

I've been on the road since Christmas
Driving trucks across the land.
I've raced across the Pecos
And crossed the Rio Grande.

I've spent some long and lonely nights
Looking at a motel wall,
But down that endless highway
I could hear my mama call.

At a small marina she rented a five-horse motorboat,

ripping the cord to goose the old Evinrude into action. The lake was a good size with a reputation for excellent bass fishing. Luckily the wind was down, the silken surface reflecting pillowy clouds. She plastered on industrial strength bug dope loaded with Deet. The expensive aerosol used by tourists lasted about as long as a non-filter cigarette and had the same transitory effect on the pests.

The seller's crude map guided her to the site, where she pulled up onto a long sandy beach, an attractive feature. The rest was rocky but level. With several acres backing into the hills of maple and poplar, a small woodlot might be maintained. Lots of privacy, too, only five or six other cottages in view. Using a fist-sized boulder and a couple of nails, she pounded a realty sign onto a prominent birch, then tramped the property to determine if a field bed could be located the requisite fifty feet from the lake. Building would cost more, but the land was a bargain for someone who prized seclusion and didn't mind the limitations of water access.

She sat awhile on the shore, checking her watch with a reluctance to restart the roar of the motor. A clump of tiger lilies caught her attention, naturally prolific and tenacious, Dylan Thomas's "force that through the green fuse". Anni loved lilies. Now she was pushing them up. Belle felt frustration at the slow investigation. Perhaps Steve had searched the house thoroughly, but what about visiting the Canadian Blood Services? And that Geo. If only cars could talk. Yet perhaps it could whisper a few ideas…if it weren't a recycled blob of metal by now.

An hour later, she drove by Crosstown Motors. Would Anni's old vehicle still be in the yard? The wretched little soul had more likely been passed to one of the lower-end used car lots which sold affordable transportation to folk on minimum wage. A salesman oozed out the door and eyed her aging but serviceable vehicle, perfect for a trade. "Interested in another van?" he asked, lighting a stogie. "We have a great selection of new Ventures and Trans Sports set to wipe up the competition."

"Just looking," she said indifferently, measuring him from the corner of her eye to Steve's description of Mr. Polyester. The scant hairs feathering his pink scalp were woven for maximum coverage, but the effect was more pathetic than artful.

"Most powerful standard engine, 3.4 litre V-6," he said, stroking the driver's seat of a handsome cobalt blue model the colour of Lake Wapiti before a thunderstorm. "Twenty-six storage compartments, hidden front wipers, three choices of seat styles. And priced to sell. You can cruise home, tax and all charges, for less than you'd dream, especially if our manager Mel is in a good mood. Free air this month, too."

"CD player, of course."

He waved his hand in an expansive gesture. "Whatever you want, Madame. Plus dual stereo systems. One up front and one in back for the kiddies. Relax with Sinatra while they blast their ears with head-banger music."

Bristling about being pushed into his decade, Belle eased into the cushy quad chair and leafed through a brochure on the dash, the new car smell calling her like a lover. "Up to ten cup holders?"

She climbed out, accepting the card he presented with a hopeful smile. "A friend of mine bought one of these sweethearts recently. Traded in her old Geo. Poor thing was on its last legs," she said.

Her girlish snicker didn't earn a blink. He puffed and pondered, thumbing a monster ash from his cigar which narrowly missed her foot. "Gotcha, the rust bucket. I remember now. Muffler fell off in the lot. Gone for scrap to

Rock City over on the Kingsway. Funny old gal, though."

"What do you mean?"

"Well, just as she left, I told her again what a plum she had chosen, selection reinforcement, you know. She muttered something under her breath, sounded like an ill wind bringing good." He winked knowingly and fixed red oyster eyes on Belle. "Bible maybe. She looked a strict one. Preacher's wife. Librarian."

A cryptic observation for Anni, Belle thought. What could she have meant? She headed for Rock City, hoping that the car had been saved from the crusher.

As children, she and her friends had loved to sneak around junkyards, searching for fresh wrecks, broken glass a gory delight. "Blood! Ten points!" they screamed at any dark stain, the fate of the unlucky riders beyond the comprehension of chocolate-bar minds. The gawky attendant at the metallurgical cemetery turned a page in a Spiderman comic and sent her to the rear of the yard in search of a right front seat to match the one her bad little child had peed on.

Next to a pyramid of tires, the old Geo sat like an abandoned pet. Belle started with the trunk, then moved to the glove box and seats. Nothing, not a gum wrapper, parking ticket stub, or roll-up-the-rim-and-win coffee cup. Even the jack was cleaned and oiled. Anni had been too fastidious to have laid a trail to her murderer. Then folded up in the visor, the edge of an envelope caught her eye. No inscription, nothing inside, just a fine cream paper alien to a society which had traded ink and stationery for prosaic e-mail. Into her pocket it went as she headed for the gate, calling over her shoulder, "Wrong colour."

Following the paper trail, she dropped into the nearby Staples, a megalith threatening to eliminate the smaller office supply stores. Such disloyalty it was to deal there, but the prices and selection were unbeatable. Every time she entered with the firm intention of buying a small box of computer disks, she exited with exotic coloured pens, plastic file organizers, and once, an ergonomic chair cancelling a week's profits.

A slow learner, she cruised the aisles like a magnet out of control, attracting a battery-operated pencil sharpener for Miriam, then depositing it with chagrin in a paper clip bin. "May I help you?" an older woman asked, permed raven hair unnaturally black but a motherly smile lightening her face.

Belle produced the envelope. "Do you sell anything like this?"

The woman smoothed it with admiring fingers and shook her head. "This is quality rag paper I used to see on special orders years ago in my old days at Muirhead's Supply. 'Vellum,' they call it, though of course it isn't. An unusually large size, too. We had a sample book for fine stationery. Ladies liked their personalized writing paper and envelopes." She sighed as if recalling her wedding night. "A lost art now."

This affectation seemed wrong for sensible Anni, but who knew where the envelope might have come from? A gift, perhaps. Might have been sitting in a drawer since Trudeau left office. With no address, it hadn't been sent through the mail.

On the way home, Belle pulled into Tim Hortons, the premier chain of doughnut shops, even if it did ignore the apostrophe. Typically Canadian: immaculate and safe, but with an American gluttony of choices, the best of both worlds. Now in addition to at least twenty-five doughnut varieties as well as tea biscuits, pies and cakes, Tim's offered soup, sandwiches, and even chili.

As she ordered a coffee, a butterscotch pie caught her attention, a rich and frothy concoction that she'd never bother to make. Hélène might suspect, but she'd be too polite to comment. Delighted to find a discarded *Sudbury Star* on the table, she was turning to the real estate supplement to check her ads, make sure that "doll house" didn't turn out "dull house" or that "three batrooms" didn't appear, when suddenly she locked onto the bottom of the front page. "Teen Held on Lakeside Murder." An unnamed young offender in Skead had confessed to the brutal killing of Anni Jacobs on Lake Wapiti. There were few details to this late-breaking nugget, just the note that he had a history of petty theft, including a robbery at the Skead Seniors' Centre, and had spent time recently at Cecil Facer, a youth detention facility. Her face flamed as she crumpled up the paper and tossed it into a waste can. Why hadn't Steve told her? What was she, chopped moose meat? Quick police work, though. Maybe he was at his desk dunking doughnuts and licking powdered sugar from his fingers.

The DesRosiers were sitting on her front steps when she arrived home, Ed drawing designs in the gravel with his cane while Rusty, their chocolatey-red mutt, slurped water on the beach. "I told him you said six, but he didn't believe me. Thinks the world eats on the dot of five like we do. Anyway, here's some of my jerky. Cajun flavour." Hélène said, placing a plump plastic bag in Belle's hands.

"Sorry, guys. I guess I cut it short. Why didn't you go right in? You know where the liquor is. But everything's made. Call me a miracle of time management." She sniffed the present with delight while Rusty skidded up, exposing a pink belly with a pattern of bug bites. "I'll have to fight Freya for this."

Scotch was poured around, and Belle shoved the combination of chicken, mushroom soup, artichoke hearts, mushrooms, onions and red peppers mixed with rotini into the oven for a complementary gratin in the final browning.

Placing the last of Charles' cheese assortment onto the coffee table with a box of crackers, she flopped onto the couch and looked warmly at her best friends. Ed, a retired plumber, had just hit sixty-five. Chained lovingly to an excellent cook, Ed battled an extra forty pounds which pushed his stomach over his belt. His svelte wife, younger by a few years, was immune to the results of her delicious efforts.

"I seen in the paper where Anni's killer confessed," he said, shifting his sore hip and biffing crackers to the dogs. "Always knew it'd be some dope-crazed kid."

"Didn't say he was on drugs, Ed," Hélène broke in. "Plain old robbery attempt, most like."

Belle scowled into her glass, letting the smoky Highland ether braise her throat. She was glad to have splurged on J&B. "I read about it. And Steve's going to have to answer. Left me in the dark after all I'd been through. I can still see her body. So small, like a broken toy."

Hélène gave her a look which could signal "womanly support" from across a hockey rink. "I wish I had known her better, but Anni kept to herself." She glanced pointedly at her husband. "Wish some others would. I can't tell you how many men, married men, make my kitchen a doughnut shop. And you encourage them, Ed." She poked his ample paunch.

"I'm still confused about that splashy van," Belle added, finishing her drink. "How in the world could she have afforded it?"

"Some change," Ed said with an affable snort. "She either scored on the trifecta at Sudbury Downs, or…" He paused as their eyes grew sceptical. "She was growing wacky tobaccy in that garden, or…she was blackmailing someone." Tension-breaking laughs followed over the Peyton Place nature of the road where everyone knew everything and nothing. The pie fulfilled its mandate, and, to Belle's mixed feelings, the casserole vanished without the benison of leftovers for the chef.

"Forgot to tell you. We're getting a pontoon boat next week. Ed woke up long enough to put in a new bathroom and kitchen over at St. Bernadine's," Hélène said as Ed nodded proudly. "You'll have to come for a ride."

"One of those…" Belle caught the pleased look on Hélène's face and changed "monsters" to "party barges." The image of a Cleopatran majesty with all its riotous implications seemed far from her friends' needs. And yet, perhaps not. With grown sons and grandchildren expected hourly, they weren't out for a fast time, just a leisurely one.

When the DesRosiers left promptly at nine, Belle pounded Steve's number with a vengeance. She could hardly keep froth from her lips. With no answer, she slunk to bed, shrinking her anger into a tiny black walnut by surrendering to routine. Into her Adolphe Menjou filigreed holder from the MGM Studios gift shop went one of five nightly cigarettes. On their last trip to the Florida theme parks after her mother died, her father had snapped his Visa card like a roué to buy a bit of nostalgia.

Freya scrabbled after chipmunks in her sleep. Lucky animal didn't need tranquillizers, but she didn't have bills, deadlines and a murdered neighbour. Belle poured a Scotch and hunted for a book. Usually she bucked the seasons, James Lee Burke's steamy New Orleans jambalaya in January and cold fare in July. The night was unusually warm for northern Canadian summers where a light duvet was often necessary. She gazed at the framed silhouette of her mother, caught in time at what must have been Belle's present age. Now the daughter grew older than the image she addressed each night. "The old man's about the same. You should have talked me into becoming a nurse...I mean a doctor." She sighed. "But high school chemistry axed that idea. Give me moles over mols." Turning to her book, she dipped her feet into the frigid Arctic waters of Dana Stabenow's Alaska adventure.

SEVEN

Still no answer at Steve's house the next morning. Why didn't he invest in a machine like the rest of the uncivilized world? Belle would read him the riot act soon enough. Meanwhile, a picnic at Surprise Lake sounded like a peaceful plan for a hot Saturday. With the aquarium, she had hiked there to trap minnows for her live eaters. But the pampered beasts had grown too fast, so she had donated the big boys to Science North, where they would enjoy a giant tank, and given the rest to Popeye's Pet Store. The delicate little discus had been the last to go. How she missed their luminous blue stripes and dainty acrobatics at feeding time.

At the schoolbus turnaround where the path began, she noticed Nick Delvecchio's old Ford truck. Half an hour later, Surprise Lake spread out like a painting from Tom Thomson and the Group of Seven gang, whose daring interpretations had galvanized Canadian art. Shimmering aquamarine water and spiky black spruce were framed by light green poplars and birch. At the far end, a huge beaver dam held water from the bubbly creek and allowed enough depth for a lodge. Her fast clip had outpaced the bugs; now the blackflies dived for the tender space behind her ears while a mosquito inserted a tiny syringe into her sweaty arm. "Whose blood, I wonder? And no side order of the West Nile virus, please," she said as she mashed the insect. A plastic bag held a hooded bug shirt saturated with dope. After the first few heady moments when the chemicals hit her nose, the loose mesh shirt allowed freedom from the discomfort of heavy clothes. Noticing that Freya was shaking her head and nipping her flanks, she rubbed a few drops of repellent into the exposed flesh on her ears and pink groin, prime insect real estate.

Out of the backpack came lunch, an eight-foot sausage lasso, banana and soda water. The meat label alarmed her. Best before 2006? What comprised this petrified stuff from Chicago, hog butcher of the world? Pork, beef, salt, sugar, cayenne pepper. So far so good, but then sodium ascorbate, sodium bicarbonate, followed by more sodium, this time in tandem with nitrite and nitrate. Cheaper than day rates but worrisome. "A little knowledge…" she corrected herself, "a little learning is a dangerous thing." Still, she champed down half and gave the attendant dog the rest.

While Freya splashed after frogs and chased chippies up trees, Belle parked under a sheltering white pine, relishing the sudden breeze which dispersed the mosquitos. The air was redolent with the spicy fragrance of Labrador tea leaves. At hand was a patch of delicate pink lady slippers, their tumescent bulbs streaked with crimson. A few unfurled fiddleheads poked up, delicious fried in butter, but dangerous to confuse with the feathery bracken which invited digestive problems. Along the edge of the swamp swooped a great blue heron, wings a graceful metronome. Perhaps it nested high in the Jack pines where she spied a dark mass. Though usually this largest of birds shied away from people, in the mists of an early morning, one had posed on her rock wall like an exiled prince. Throughout the woods, the distinctive calls of white-throated sparrows played a lively symphony, males beckoning females or staking out their territory.

Is Anni missing this, she wondered? Or forging new paths in the undiscovered land from which no traveller returns? For a moment she wished that she had brought her friend here, repaid a fraction of the wisdom and reverence for nature passed on by the mage who knew where the wild clematis grew. Belle felt at home in the bush, far safer than glancing over her shoulder on the midnight streets of Toronto, but the recent violence pressed upon her Eden like a nameless evil. Why was she so nervous? The killer had been caught. She jumped as a noisy whiskey-jack claimed its territory. Too many lurking horror movies. Soon she'd be seeing the Creature from the Black Lagoon waving scaly hands among the lily pads, ooze seeping from its gaping mouth.

Belle shuffled lunch debris into the backpack and whistled for the dog, sorry at the result. Freya had paddled into slime and needed a bath in clean water. Before heading back, she followed old blazes marking an overgrown trail to the lake, fringed with purple stalks of pickerelweed. Kneeling, she leaned cautiously and drew a plant forward to plumb its secrets. Another week to blossom. She ran gentle fingers over a hummingbird's nest in the crook of an alder, the clever weavings of twigs, birch bark and soft feathers sheltering a clutch of pea-sized eggs.

Gazing down the shore following the skimming takeoff of a merganser duck, she noticed something alien disturbing the natural splendour with the abruptness of a fast food billboard. Leaning against a tall pine tree was a crude homemade wooden ladder leading to a platform ten feet above, just enough space for one person to play lord of the lake. Looped at the top was a birch bark cone any Northerner would recognize as a homemade moose caller. Belle pounded the scaly trunk with her fist, absorbing the painful abrasions as a sickening feeling crawled over her. Now the hunters had invaded her home. Maybe they were from the bear-baiting site, stocking more game for their freezers.

"I hear you, Anni," she said in a low voice full of contempt. "Tomorrow this place is coming down."

With the blistering pace back, Freya lagged behind with wayward sniffs. At a juncture, Belle nearly crashed into a hiker. "Sorry," she said without looking, irked at another intruder. It was Nick Delvecchio. His great-uncle Sal had run traplines on the far end of Surprise Lake. Every April when the trail cleared, Nick's battered truck with a British Columbia plate parked at the turnaround. He stayed in the old camp until the first flurries of late October, ruling out the possibility that he was a student, though his fresh face placed him under twenty-five. Shy and reclusive, he rarely spoke to anyone, but meeting Belle in the ambience of the woods seemed to relax his guard. Usually he carried an expensive backpack, sported two-hundred-dollar hiking boots, and wore a Rolex, she had noted with envy. Once settled in, he made few trips to town. Sharp eyes on the lake had led to speculation about his isolation. "On the lam from authorities," Ed had decided one beery night, wiggling his bushy eyebrows to reinforce his theory.

"Come on. The last place to hide would be the house of a relative," Belle said. "Do you know the Delvecchios?"

He shook his head. "Not very well. Old Sal used to trap beaver and fox around World War Two, when my Uncle Louis was logging out that way. Never saw much of him. Camp had been boarded up for years until young Nick showed up."

Catching her breath, she pointed to his shotgun. "Hello, Nick," she said with a hint of anger. "You're not the one put up that moose perch at the other end of the lake, are you?"

"That's been there for about a week. Heard someone

hammering. I'm no big gamer, though. Can't store meat without a fridge." He mocked a sight into a tree toward a small cooing. "Partridge pie. Makes a break from pasta."

"Got to lead the bird, though. Otherwise you're picking shot out of your teeth." She gave him a wave and continued down the path. What was Nick's source of income? Seasonal job? A remittance man? Some went so far as to suspect him of the occasional thefts along the road, but she doubted it. A few fish, some dead-and-down wood for cold fall nights, he took only what he needed from the bush. Maybe she'd hike in a loaf of fresh bread and wangle an invitation. What did the mystery man do on those long evenings with no electricityand scant room in the pack for books or magazines? Perhaps he was a writer, the old-fashioned kind.

When she had soaped Freya to decency at home, tossing a tennis ball into the lake for her rinsing and hoping that no neighbours would spot the detergent scum, Belle turned to the garden she had planted June 5th, still risky at that late date. The lettuce and spinach, early risers, were greening nicely. Another two weeks to a salad crisper than any supermarket cello-pack. Carrots, beets, peas, beans, broccoli, zucchini and tomatoes would provision her through Labour Day, and she might even summon energy to can the rest. The asparagus patch had been slowed by the short growing season. "Three years and nothing larger than a piece of spaghetti," she said with a growl. Perhaps she should have baptized it with a chamber pot like an old hippie friend from university who swore by natural nitrogen. Though she shovelled bags of pasteurized moo poo onto her gardens with religious fervour, Belle resisted chemical weed and feed stuff, fearful that residue would leach into the drinking water.

As she walked under the deck to the basement patio doors,

a swooping form made her duck. On one of the high joists sat a nest with barely enough room for a fat red-breasted robin with accusing black eyes. Five other beams held nests in graduated stages of construction. Apparently this dimwit couldn't determine the original site, so had covered her bets. "Some of us aren't cut out for motherhood," Belle said, heading for a beer. Five pages into *Canadian Gardening*, she heard a crunch on the gravel.

A dapper figure in a Panama hat strolled down the driveway. It was Charles Sullivan, bearing a box of peat pots. "Cherry tomatoes," he said, depositing his gifts in the shade. "Had a couple extra. Wanted to wish you a happy Canada Day, too."

It was July 1st, the national holiday which stole a march on the Yanks' 4th. She grinned, imagining their luscious globes exploding in her mouth like liquid starshine. "Never too many of those sweethearts. Trade you for a beer?"

Drinking together, enjoying the quiet afternoon until a speedboat flew by trailing an inner tube with shrieking kids, they caught up on the road news. "I guess you heard about Anni Jacobs," Belle said.

"Yes, poor lady." He shook his head. "Very shocking. I thought that I left violence behind in the city. It seems to have been a break-in. Glad they have the fellow in hand. What's happened to young people these days?"

After Belle told him about discovering Anni, he spoke in quiet recollection. "We met once at the mailboxes, cleaning up some flyers littering the ground. Had she any family?"

"Only a nephew. Seemed decent. Likes dogs, anyway." That was her character barometer, a tip-off in *Undercurrent,* where the angelic Robert Taylor had proved the villain instead of cleft-jawed bad boy Robert Mitchum.

"Never trust anyone who doesn't," he agreed, picking up a Mr. Chile toy and inspecting its fiery tongue and bloodshot eyes before he gave it a squeak and sent Freya scrabbling across the deck.

"Anni'd been bothered by hunters recently. Have you heard any gunfire? One trail heads off back of your property."

He frowned. "I wasn't sure. Sound carries some nights and not others. Sunday at dawn I thought I heard a shot or two."

"That ties in with the new moose perch I discovered today. Don't go hiking in there unless you're wearing red."

"Walking the road's my limit. Fewer surprises from man or beast. Say, I came to ask you for supper. Pork baby back ribs. I found the best little meat store. Tarini's, it's called."

Belle slapped the table in mock exasperation. "Not again. I haven't repaid you for the last feast." But her wilful stomach had a greedy mind of its own.

As the western sky layered a Neapolitan ice cream parfait of pinks and blues across billowing vanilla whipped cream clouds, shortly after six, she eased the Grummon canoe into the water and clamped the mighty 1.2 horsepower to the side bracket. Sounded like a blender grinding coffee beans, but it cruised across the lake on a cup of gas.

Passing a dozen properties, she waved at people in their yards or on docks, some hoisting a beer in friendly response and motioning her in. Flags were flying, including the occasional Québecois fleur-de-lys, a New Brunswick provincial banner, and even the stars and stripes. Charles rushed to help her tie up, and soon she was sitting in her usual lawn chair, listening to Mahler's tones issue from the cottage windows, licking sticky sauce from her fingers in contentment and feeling as if they had been friends for years. "Dirty rice, too, Monsieur Prudhomme. I wouldn't eat chicken livers any other way.

What other talents do you have?"

The comical expression on his face pinked by sun lent a Puckish look. "Oh, a talent to amuse, I hope."

She glanced around in wonderment. "I doubt Noel Coward did landscaping and carpentry. You have this place pretty spruce. New siding on the boathouse, the garden starting to burgeon. And is that a sauna you're building?" With unselfconscious flair, she pointed a rib bone toward a framed structure behind the house.

He gestured like a prospective father. "A four-seater. You'll get to inaugurate it next week if the stove arrives. Special order from Toronto."

"Count on me for the birch switches," she added, which brought a clearing of throat which she interpreted as embarrassment. Perhaps she had gone too far. Suggestive banter was second nature to her neighbours, but Charles would have been more at home in Jane Austen's Pump Room. To change the subject, she proposed an *après-souper* canoe ride to a special place.

"It's only half an hour with the motor. You'll sit in front, so you won't go deaf from my little monster. And I always carry two life jackets."

"I had been hoping you'd ask. Lead on."

He went to the house, returning with a large paper bag and field glasses. Belle was glad that he seemed to have good balance entering the canoe. It wouldn't have been the first time someone had capsized beside a dock. Due to his greater weight, however, the nose was riding low, so to correct the trim she lugged a large stone from the shore, tucking it under her seat. A power boat with an engine the size of a Chevy truck's blasted by, eroding the beach with huge wakes. Why didn't they haul those three-bedroom hogs to Lake Huron?

God knows what they did secretly with the effluent from the head. As the waves calmed and Charles pushed off, she pulled the starter cord. He covered his ears in mock protest.

"I know it's noisy, but twelve pounds is all I can muscle. Besides, if you want to see scenery, really see it, you have to go slowly."

No cottages dotted this quarter of the lake. Rough terrain and lack of access roads kept it as wild and breathtaking as when Champlain had canoed down the nearby French and Pickerel Rivers to Georgian Bay and lost his astrolabe. With the noise of the motor, conversation was impossible, but Charles sat alert, scanning with the binoculars while his smile widened in pleasure. She circled a few rocky islands stopping at a shoal less than a foot above water. One gnarled Jack pine leaned with the prevailing wind direction like a faithful sentinel.

"Flowergull Island. My biological microcosm. I come here from time to time to see what's landed and taken root. Smaller than my deck, but you can see daisies, blue flag irises and one pale corydalis. Oh, and a Saskatoon berry bush. The nesting gulls help fertilize." Charles followed her directions with interest, as if he welcomed any knowledge about his new world.

She headed toward the shore again, aiming for one of the long, narrow inlets. Soon they were cozying in beneath rugged cliffs shooting up a hundred feet, tapered into the forest where huge chunks of granite had fallen. Often she climbed among these giant's building blocks, always aware that a fall might break her leg. Why did most memorable experiences contain a frisson of danger? "Raven Cliff, I call it," she said. "You can barely see a nest below that twisted cedar. The fledglings are gone."

He trained his glasses to the right with a curve on his lips. "We might have another. Look on that shelf under the pine."

A shadow with long, pointed wings and a narrow tail swept

past. "We'chew," was its call, followed by a series of "cack-cacks" and a wailing note. Belle whistled softly. "Peregrine falcons, aka duck hawks, a less dramatic name. Always noisy near the eyrie. They're documented on the northeast side of the lake, but this is a first. I'll have to tell my birder friends from Shield University to bring their summer classes here."

Tying up at a spar of weathered cedar, they wiggled their fingers at curious bass which peered up through the clear water. Charles sighed ruefully. "A *semper paratus* lesson. No tackle again. I can see I'm going to have to get a boat, too, if I want to do some serious fishing."

Pleasant time passed with the gentle rocking of the canoe. A breeze sifting down the inlet kept off the bugs, and the smell of ripening blueberries drifted from the peaty hills. They were worlds away from raucous music or roaring boats, only the lonesome cries of seagulls in the distance. Belle stared mesmerized at the cliffs, matching the geometric holes to the massive pieces below. As she rotated a hunk the size of an elevator in a familiar mind game, an idea occurred to her.

"Charles, do you know much about collectibles?"

He met her eyes with a helpful expression. "I have that Toby jug. Or do you mean stamps and coins?"

"Not so ordinary. Have you ever heard of a market for puzzles? Jigsaw puzzles?"

A quizzical expression crossed his face. "As a matter of fact, yes. When I was wedded to cable in the city, I used to watch a show on the FX channel. Ran the gamut from Elvis memorabilia to cigarette lighters to antique banks. You name it, and some fool'd have a passion, and speaking of passions…"

He pulled out a bottle, along with two mugs, pouring with aplomb. "This is one treasure I brought from Ottawa. Quinta de Vargellas '55. Unblended, of course. It is said to have the essence of, well, can you guess?"

Sherry again, from the description and colour. That binge at Anni's was fresh in her mind, yet she couldn't refuse his thoughtful gesture. Belle reached for the mug reluctantly, but found herself inhaling its promise, a light and ambrosial spring bouquet. "Could it be violets?" she asked.

He nodded like a satisfied mentor. "But here I am interrupting you. What were you saying about puzzles?"

"Just remembering a hobby of Anni's. She collected jigsaw puzzles. Framed them on her walls."

"Is that so? I had one of Buck Rogers," he confessed with a chuckle. "Used to be a card-carrying member of his fan club."

"A few older ones might be valuable. Her nephew Zack's starting out in business and might appreciate the information."

The sun had dipped behind the hills, leaving coolness in the air. From far away, small bursts of fireworks began. They looked toward the marina, where fountains of red and white sparks showered from the sky. "Time to go, I guess." Pushing off, she pulled the starter cord. An ominous click made her wince. "It's stubborn sometimes. Never failed me yet, though." A harder yank brought only a spastic chug. Uttering a generous selection of Miriam's minced oaths, Belle adjusted the choke, checked the gas, and jiggled the cord before trying again. Finally a roar broke the stillness, but she cocked her head. "This motor sounds fun…" Her hand shot forward in a reflexive grab as the 1.2 headed for the bottom. With her arm nearly wrenched out of its socket, soaked to the shoulder, she hauled the motor into the boat, setting it down gently and bending over the gunwale in bewilderment to inspect the wooden bracket. "It split in half. Dry rot, I guess."

Charles was a statue of relieved horror, frozen in his seat.

Then they both started laughing. "Quite the timing. At least you saved your little friend. What now?"

She picked up a paddle and gestured. "Old-fashioned elbow grease."

Thanks to a cooperative tailwind, they made their way back in an hour. Several times Belle was forced to turn the canoe into the wake of a thoughtless powerboater to avoid swamping. Up and down went the prow, soaking Charles with spray. He brushed his eyes and reset his cap, the image of the Old Man and the Sea. Belle could have sworn that he took a slug of the sherry, perhaps in homage to Papa Hemingway, and he insisted on singing boating songs. Her unsteady alto joined his baritone in "Paddling Madeline Home."

As they rounded the final point, a vast and slow-moving craft emerged from the darkness, spotlights crisscrossing the water like a patrol boat. "Ahoy, the canoe. Is that you, Belle?" yelled a familiar voice.

So that was the party barge. Only on Edgewater Road would a rescue party be dispatched so fast. Yet she knew Ed and Hélène caught everything from their deck. They'd never forgotten that summer twenty years ago when their three cousins had drowned, buried in a black storm. "We're fine. Some motor trouble."

"Saw you go by such a long time ago. Barometer's falling. Thought we'd check. Glad you're safe and sound," he called, and the barge moved sedately away, heading for anchorage.

EIGHT

That night Steve called. Before he could finish a sentence, Belle interrupted. "Thanks for telling me about arresting Anni's murderer. I thought you were going to keep me posted."

He sighed and muffled the receiver, though Belle could hear him call out with an apology in his voice. "I won't be long, hon. Start Heather's bath." If he could drag his feet on filling her in, perhaps she wouldn't be as forthcoming in the future.

While she seethed, a chair squeaked, and he continued. "Don't blow a gasket on me. Here's why I didn't bother telling you. Sure, the paper reported a confession, but it's a dud."

She lifted a dubious eyebrow. "A dud? You mean you can't make the charge stick?"

"If confession were good for the soul, Chris Ralston would be in heaven by now. Give him the IQ of a smashed pumpkin or a duffer's golf score, same difference. "

"But it all fit. Skead's just across the lake. And that Seniors' Centre. Maybe Anni had visited there. Word gets around about old ladies living alone. What's the story on him?"

"Sometimes he gets into trouble on his own, or sneaks out after dark to meet friends. On their daddies' quads, he and his buddies cruise the roads looking for entertainment. Got probation for some mischief with a closed-up cottage this spring. Broke a window and guzzled the rye that was left. Place was pretty well hidden by trees, but they got seen by a wildlife photographer bushwhacking. Other times he hears a few details of a crime and makes up the rest. When his parents question him, he breaks down and bawls. Then, like good citizens, they call us."

She snorted in disbelief. "That's a new one. So what tied him to Anni?"

"Day after the murder, he started bragging to some Grade Nines at his school like he was living in a television show. Stupid, eh? Luckily one of them told a teacher. Guess teenagers aren't all bad."

"But you don't believe his story?"

"Can't. His parents have an alibi for him a mile long."

"First they turn him in, now an alibi. How credible is that?"

"Sure as Salvation. His mother's a preacher, and they were all in their pew at church that night singing 'Amazing Grace.' Iron clad in the Lord." He paused. "Sorry you got confused by the paper. I warned the reporter not to print it, but she was a gung-ho rookie fresh out of Nickel City College."

So cancel the easy answer about Anni's case. Back to zero, square one. The more she thought about the hunters, the less she imagined that the moose perch belonged to a murderer. Who would be stupid enough to return to the scene and pot more game? Her thoughts turned back to the house, the puzzles she had discussed with Charles. Blessing the technology that had linked her isolated Northern community to the outer world, Belle went to the computer room and logged onto Ebay, selecting "Collectibles." Maybe this was the place to advertise those Royal Doulton white elephants her mother had left her. Gracious ladies in flowing gowns didn't belong in Belle's cosmos, though the impressive St. George and Broken Lance could stand guard. Postings covered Fritos chip racks, Jackie O catalogs, and the elusive bakelite bird napkin rings, so she wasn't surprised to find a heading on "Nineteenth-Century Toys." The seller was offering, among metal banks and china head dolls, a jigsaw puzzle of the Crystal Palace during the Great Exhibition of 1851. A thousand dollars, and Anni's picture pre-dated that by a good fifty years.

Belle picked up the phone again. "Charles, I need your discriminating eye. I want to check Anni's collection. And by the way…" She explained about the boy's false confession, realizing as she spoke, that Zack was back in the picture.

When she reached him the next day, Zack was cooperative about the visit. Why not? As the heir, he had a selfish interest in adding to his auntrimony, or whatever it was called. He met them that evening at the lake, sighing elaborately. "I swear those lawyers delay things deliberately to pad their fees. Probate's still not completed, but the police have given me permission to stay here. Some question of keeping the property safe. It's better for the dogs, too." As he opened the Firefly's creaky door and they pounded out after a chipmunk, he stroked the shiny van with a fondness that made her cringe. "Too bad I'll have to wait on this beauty."

With footsteps hollow on the polished wood floor, Belle felt that the proud house's spirit seemed to have withered in the absence of its owner. All but the hardy cactus plants lay brown and sere. Anni had helped Cece fashion this home, woven herself into the very fibres. Now the slow ticking of a shiny brass century clock marked time where measurement no longer mattered. Or perhaps it did. That was why Belle had come.

"Never thought twice about those puzzles," Zack said. "I just checked for the stereo system, the boat motor and stuff. She didn't own any guns."

"The Internet quoted a thousand dollars for a good

Victorian example. Even portraits of Shirley Temple could finance a vacation in Bermuda," Belle said.

"Aunt Anni had something like that?" His uneasy look lacked credibility. "I knew some were old, but I thought she collected them as a kid."

Step by step, they examined the puzzles on the walls and those boxed in the spare room. Nothing caught her attention. "I'm pretty sure that's all," Zack said, sneezing at the dust as he pulled his head out of the closet. "She wouldn't have kept any in the shed where the damp might have ruined them."

"I'm no expert," Charles observed quietly. "You would likely have to take the collection to Toronto or Ottawa, but there might be some money here from the right buyer. I wouldn't mind that delicate Japanese one myself as a curio."

Zack's eyes lit up. "How much would you..."

His voice trickled off as Belle drew close to the wall, looking at an ordinary framed print of Paul Peel's "After the Bath," youngsters standing naked in front of a cozy fire. Innocent pre-pubescence rendered in chiaroscuro. Probably get a child pornography rap today. A light margin around the picture indicated that a larger object had been removed. "Where's that Pilgrim's Progress? That was her prize. It was here over the sofa." She wheeled accusingly. "Zack?"

He sat down with a gasp as if suddenly asthmatic. "It's at my place. I need money to buy stock for my store." His voice grew petulant, like a querulous squirrel deprived of a juicy nut. "Aunt Anni left everything to me anyway."

"Since you profess to be such a novice, may I ask why you chose that one in particular?" Charles said sharply, in a credible imitation of Frederic March in "Inherit the Wind."

Zack reached across the coffee table and swiped at some dust. "She boasted that it cost her a month's pension. I was going to cruise the antique stores in Toronto. A couple of them expressed interest over the phone. Sure it was wrong, but I couldn't lose out a second time. Even a thousand dollars would give me a start on a bunch of used CDs. I have to be ready to roll. Liquidation opportunities don't come along every day." He agreed to return the puzzle if they kept the matter private…and he promised to water the plants faithfully.

"We're probably doing the wrong thing, letting him off on a judgment call," Belle confided to Charles over coffee on her deck. "He's such a jerk, almost pitiful sometimes. I'm revising my dog lover theory."

"Yes," he said, the mellow glow of fire in the sunset reflected in his kind hazel eyes. "It is hard to imagine the callow fellow as a suspect. From what I've learned of Mrs. Jacobs, she could have juggled five characters like him. What a sad excuse for a nephew. Family ties spelled only a source of money. That disheartens me."

Belle hadn't heard him speak so frankly of personal concerns. "Sounds like family is important to you, Charles. Do you have relatives up here? You've never mentioned anyone."

"Mother and Dad are gone now, of course. My older brother was killed at Dieppe. Just turned nineteen. And my only sister died years ago. Leukemia. As for friends, I've always been a private man." He spoke so softly that she had to strain at the words. "Not that I seek isolation, though. The worst punishment in the world is being cut off from family and friends. But that's a different idea entirely."

"Like prison, you mean. I'd hate to see us get like the States. Building bigger and better jails seems to be fueling their economy."

"Sometimes vengeance seems so belated that it's purposeless. What about those ninety-year-old remnants of the Third Reich

82

sent back to Europe to stand trial?"

She paused at the idea of law vs. justice, her usual argument with Steve. "Dragged out of nursing homes. They deserve punishment, but at their age, it seems a useless exercise." A change of subject seemed in order. This was getting too morose. "What was your profession, Charles? You came from the capital, so I presume you might have had a government job like half the town."

"Just a boring old auditor for a paint company. Nothing romantic or exciting. But no one wants to see him coming to check the books, you can bet on that. *Persona non grata*, even for the innocent ones." He clucked and shook his finger. "Quaking in their boots that I'd make a mistake. Never did, though. Numbers are ruthlessly amoral, but they never lie."

She gave him a ride home, noticing as she turned that a lilac Cadillac had pulled into the lot next door. The Rogers family, Sophie and Earl, used their camp in summer for the occasional weekend or holiday. Though heavy bush separated their place from Charles' quiet refuge, Belle winced to see a passel of dogs leap out. Last year there had been three, helter-skelter blends of collie, shepherd and lab. Now she counted six.

The next morning's unfinished chores found her at a shop which specialized in assistive devices, the endless varieties of canes, walkers, wheelchairs and scooters which were multiplying exponentially along the streets and in the malls of graying Sudbury. Doncaster Medical sold a gel cushion the nurses had suggested for her father. So many consecutive hours even in a padded chair was hard on old bones. For $150 she received a square plastic pillow filled with the space-age ingredient that plumped bicycle seats. "I can give you a good price on a hospital bed. Special rates for nursing homes," the young female clerk said with an expression as mild as buttermilk.

Belle's heart turned over at the pathetic image, and she whispered, "No, not yet." Call it short-sightedness, even denial, but why rush the man to complete helplessness? Soon enough he might be sentenced to an official Procrustean hospital bed, the system in crisis, institutional pap meals trucked in from Ottawa, rumours went.

Parcel under her arm, she walked several blocks back to Brewster Street to find her van happily intact. Every town had a dark and musty basement, collecting the trappings of failures in an evil seine, those poor souls who didn't have a shack of their own to celebrate Welfare Wednesday. All their slender needs were met within a few hundred yards. Shabby hotels and rooming houses, cheap apartments, pawn shops, check-cashing outlets, fly-blown restaurants with bargain breakfasts, and, of course, bars for every lowlife preference.

A tall man shambled towards her, head bowed, long black hair matted with grime. Despite the ripped jeans, stained leather vest, and filthy T-shirt, he reminded her of Steve. Undercover work? Should she speak to him? Belle cleared her throat pointedly, but he walked past, tripping scuffed boots on a piece of lockstone pavement lifted in the winter frost. As he fell to his knees with a grunt, she turned instinctively to hold out a hand, but he lurched off, covering his ears as a train blasted by, his mouth a frame of silent pain like Munch's screamer's. Quite the thespian. Steve had never mentioned acting in high school plays or amateur theatre. Unshaven for days, too. Poor Janet. And that ratty hair looked so real. Then she detected raw fumes of rum. What the police suffered for verisimilitude.

On the weekend, it was time to keep her promise to Anni. That moose stand's hours were numbered. Having set her clock for an eye-opening five on Sunday morning and fueled up with hot coffee, she went alone into the woods to Surprise Lake, crowbar and flashlight under her arm, realizing with some trepidation that poachers liked early hours, too. As for Nick, how could he have been involved in setting it up? Moving a thousand pounds of moose quarters was too much of a job without a quad or a game trike.

Once shielded by the hills, she flicked on her flashlight, eager to slip in and out as fast as possible in the role of eco-saint. Dawn was an unusual time for a hike, a new sensory experience with eerie, unidentifiable noises of nocturnal animals. Fortunately they sounded small, skunks or weasels perhaps, maybe foraging rabbits. Feet tuned to the familiar bumps and roots of the path, she slipped the cumbersome flashlight into a loop on her coat when the first rosy glints of sun broke the dark.

Kaleidoscopic shards of light were penetrating the forest as she reached the perch and started dismantling the boards. Hastily erected, one nail where two should go, it fell apart quickly under the crowbar. Breaking into a sweat, she took off her coat and hauled the lumber into the woods, biffing it into a small ravine to lie concealed under thick cedars. Then as she turned, wiping her hands, she was startled by a strange movement. For a moment she couldn't make out the shape in the shadows. Then as she approached, the picture cleared. Over a branch someone had draped a moose hock, which dangled in the rising wind, hair clinging to the scraps of skin in an obscene parody of Claudette Colbert's shapely hitchhiking gam in *It Happened One Night*. A grotesque mockery? A drunken joke? Gingerly she removed the bones and buried them under leafmeal.

Halfway back, satisfied at her demolition, moving as quickly as her thoughts, at one open stretch she stopped for breath at the bottom of a hill. A soft pounding made her turn her head. Looking up, she gasped. Two cubs were rollicking toward her, eight paws hitting the ground in three-quarter time. Emergency advice flashed across her brain, all ignored. Nowhere to run, nowhere to hide, nowhere to climb. And bears climbed well, too, especially agile cubs. A mere fifty feet from her, a bark stopped them, and they turned to look at Mother, appearing over the ridge. With disappointed bleats, they followed her into the deep bush. Belle fell to her knees, still holding the crowbar like a useless sword, and forced herself to wait until they had cleared the area. Then she limped home on a prayer.

NINE

Steve had invited her for lunch at the new Szechuan place downtown. With Janet and Heather on an all-day bus trip to Canada's Wonderland, perhaps he was lonely, or better yet, had information about Anni. As usual, he was late, so she entertained herself with the drink menu. Its tempting pictures brought back a childhood in Toronto, the occasional treat of a Chinese dinner at the elegant Lichee Gardens. Her mother would let her choose an exotic cocktail and try a clandestine sip. Feeling sentimental and expansive, Belle ordered a zombie. Valuing time over manners, she gave the waitress their order.

"Don't choke on the paper parasol," Steve said minutes later, shedding his leather Sudbury Wolves jacket and easing long legs into the padded booth. "Another salt mine like those margaritas at Pepe's?"

"A zombie. Self-explanatory. Anyway, how's Heather? All of our conversations lately have been about murder. You haven't filled me in on the joys of parenthood."

"She's fine. Remember how we sweated about the possibilities of fetal alcohol damage? Too young for the definitive tests when we got her. But scratch that now."

"What do you mean?"

He flashed a two-thumbs up reply to match his grin. "What's to test? She finished at the top of her class."

"They rank them in junior kindergarten? Poor babies." She

sipped her expensive experiment and grimaced at the syrupy overkill. Heather had been adopted at three from an abusive family. Now she'd have more love and attention than Belle's first pup. Some things were right with the world. "I'm really glad. When I babysat for you and brought Freya, she seemed happy and confident."

"You were right about the bonding. Once she saw that Janet trusted me…" He gave her a resigned glance. "Don't sweet-talk me to disguise your agenda. You want to know if we've made any progress with the Jacobs case. The answer is a big no. All the leads except Zack have petered out, unless somebody talks, which has been known to happen."

"Except Zack?" Had Steve found out about the missing jigsaw?

"Claims he drove to Detroit to check out CDs, but the store he visited is closed. The owner went to South America for a month. And of course our nephew slept in his car. Too poor to spring for a motel." He turned in surprise as the waiter set down a platter. "You ordered? Pretty nervy."

The hot-sour soup arrived, followed by spring rolls, roast duck with winter melon, braised pork and celery and sizzling shrimp. A large glass of ice water cut the sting, but her tears flowed. "Why do we do this to ourselves?" She was sure that Steve was summoning all of his macho to keep up. Maybe he had prepped with Maalox. No chiles remained on his plate while on hers they formed ziggurats.

"How about the MNR? Any reports on bear mutilation?"

He looked at his plate. "Glad I've finished eating. What I learned made me lose my taste for bear meat. Dick King in Kirkland Lake found four or five carcasses already. He's had some luck tracing connections to herbalists in Toronto or Vancouver. Wouldn't mean much, though. You could FedEx a package anywhere in a day. And guess what? It used to be legal in Ontario to possess bear parts, but not sell them. Makes some sense, eh?"

"I shudder to ask, but what do they use the paws for?"

"A gourmet soup. Especially a tender cub."

Coughing, she covered the last egg roll with her serviette. "Hunters are still in the area. I found a moose stand down by Surprise Lake on another trail. Lumber fresh enough to indicate that it was built this year. The big guys aren't in season yet, but that makes no difference." She paused and cocked her head, feeling a bit disloyal. No use leaving a turn unstoned. "And, there is this strange guy on our road."

Steve listened patiently to Nick's description. "Worth a try. Can you get the number of that truck? I'll check the registration with motor vehicle authorities and see if there's anything to follow. Seems to me that he overstays the season. Suspicious for a young guy. All that first-rate gear, the Rolex and no apparent means of support, you say?"

"Look, he seems like a decent person. I don't want to get him into trouble." Belle poured cups of steaming green tea to settle the meal. "One other thing. You weren't doing undercover work on Brewster the other day, were you?"

A dark cloud crossed his face as his large hand reached unsuccessfully for the tiny cup, splashing tea onto the linen tablecloth. "What are you talking about?"

"I saw your *doppelgänger*. Your double. Maybe I shouldn't have…"

He tossed the serviette onto the mess. "Just like me, but drunk, right? Dressed like a bum."

Belle held her breath and counted to ten. If people were books, Steve read like a large-print thriller. "Did I ruin a set-up? Were you undercover?"

The tone of his voice assumed the burden of bitter resignation. "It's my brother."

"You have a brother? You've only mentioned an older sister in the Sault, the one who helped you find Heather."

"I don't like to think about Craig, much less talk about him. I'd say he's da black sheep of da family, but it's not a joke like the song." His strained humour couldn't disguise the conflict.

"Sorry, Steve. It's really none of my business," she said without conviction, wishing that she could summon magic words to ease his pain.

"You might as well know. Simple enough on the surface. Craig's an alcoholic. Menial jobs back and forth across the country, far as I ever learned. I thought it was a good sign that he finally came here, even if I saw him panhandling."

"Sounds like he wanted to reach out. What went wrong?"

"Maybe I tried too hard, playing social worker. I gave him the numbers for AA, the shelters and a couple of places for casual labour. No use. He's lost, Belle, but…" Steve looked out the window to where a mother pushed a triple stroller. "When I left home for the navy, he was nearly twelve. What a smile he had, like a sunflower." Near poetry for Steve, a solid man with little use for the trappings of language.

She swallowed around a hard lump in her throat that no tannic tea would dissolve. "He was gone when you got back?"

"Ran away from his school my first year in the navy. Didn't like the formal discipline, I guess." A happier recollection brought a slight smile to his face. "When I was his age, I lived with my Uncle Eddie in the bush working his trapline. Taught me to read and write with an Eaton's catalogue."

"And you were out of touch all these years?"

"No word, nothing. Once in a while a relative out west said that he'd been by, so at least we knew he wasn't dead. But he never came home. Not even for Mom's funeral."

"How can you help him if he won't let you?"

He picked up the discarded parasol and twirled it absently. Suddenly the frail stick snapped in his massive hands. "If I see him on the street, I pass him a few bucks. That's all he'll take. Won't even come over for a meal. He's so broken, a shadow in the night. I hope to God he gets enough food at the soup kitchens and maybe some medical attention. TB's on the rise again, especially with our people. That's how Mom died. She was only forty-five."

"You must feel helpless. But there are support groups, counselling."

"Not for him. I don't even know where he sleeps, how he lives. Maybe that's why I spend so much time with Big Brothers, because I can't rescue my own." He massaged the back of his neck as if to knead away an ache, then checked his watch. "I'm due at headquarters." He flipped down a couple of twenties. "My turn this time, I think."

"And for the last five. I'm soft on public servants."

"Stay out of those woods for a while," Steve yelled over his shoulder as they left. Good thing she hadn't told him about her recent sabotage. He was wound up enough about his brother. What had started as a friendly chat had turned into an emotional roller coaster ride. Just as things were working out with Heather, the spectre of Craig was stalking the gray areas of Steve's black and white life.

At the office, Miriam had booked an appointment for Belle to take the Balbonis from Toronto out to the Kalmo property. They were in their early forties, junior managers at the Taxation Centre, one of the government transfusions which had injected new blood into the community as the mining base shrank with the increase in technological efficiency. Mark

Balboni wore a crisp beige summer suit which made Belle wonder where she had last seen her iron. His wife was fresh and bouncy in a Laura Ashley shirtwaist and low-heeled pumps. "The house is close to the city," she said as they drove. "Down 69 through the Valley and you're there in half an hour."

"No more Metro gridlock. That's one of the reasons Joanie and I jumped at the chance for a transfer."

His wife gave a tinkly laugh like ice cubes meeting ginger ale. "Our friends couldn't believe that Mark and I would agree to move to a …" She paused, pulling out a compact to arrange a few stray hairs.

"Mining town?" Belle asked with a wry smile. "Sudbury just cracked the top ten in the best cities in the country according to *Canadian Living* magazine." Next week she would apply to the Chamber of Commerce for a grant.

"We passed that big old stack. It doesn't smell so bad," Joan said, craning her neck, remarkably free of chicken skin for a woman her age. No lip lines. Collagen? Belle kept quiet, knowing that air quality in Sudbury was downright ethereal next to southern Ontario where a perpetual haze coiled over the Big Smoke like the wreath from Santa's pipe in an old Coca Cola ad.

Now that the owner had eaten the cost of the access road, the house was a bargain. Beamed ceilings, a California kitchen with island, expensive cabinets, quality ceramic tile, and easy-care Berber carpets. Two bathrooms, one with a Jacuzzi. A heat pump and air conditioning. Down south even on a puddly lake, double the price.

"Looking good so far," Mark said. "The boys would love the water. Make a great hockey rink, too. How's ice time for youngsters up here? Are there many leagues?"

"Sure thing," Belle answered. "Midget, bantam, any age

you want. And don't forget our Sudbury Wolves. They could probably beat the Toronto Make Believes."

He frowned, scraping mud from his wingtip. "Did you read about that scandal at Maple Leaf Gardens, for Christ's sake? Trading sticks for sex. That place was like a shrine to youngsters." Over sixty victims had phoned in already, with three men in jail. Too bad the ringleader had died ten years ago.

Despite the gigantic lunch, she cooked up one of the frugal gourmet's recipes that night, fried bacon and onions, adding canned baked beans, a chopped apple, and a *soupçon* of maple syrup from the local *érablière* or sugarbush farm. Hearty French Canadian fare. Cheap, simple, packed with carbos for red-belted voyageurs who broke down at age forty packing two-hundred-pound loads for the Hudson Bay Company. Unable to decide what wine complemented maple syrup, she chose Dragon's Breath beer, one of the many microbrews and exotic imports elbowing Labatt's Blue to the side.

On television, Spencer Tracy as Father Flanagan was insisting that there was no such thing as a bad boy. What an idyllic world, Boystown. The mailing campaigns with those heart-tugging pictures had created one of the world's richest charities. Now anti-monopoly laws were demanding divestment of its holdings. Spencer would probably have gagged at the commercial monster his character's noble efforts had fostered: "He ain't heavy; he's my brother." Belle thought of Craig. Did he live on the street? What would happen to him when the icy winds of November shrieked across the Cambrian Shield? Unlike in Toronto, where people slept over heating grates or huddled with their loaded buggies in sheltered alleys, in Sudbury no one could stay outside in the winter, clear suicide at -40°C. What if she had a brother in trouble? Hard to imagine. Her parents had needed seven years to construct her before immaculate conception technology, too weary for a second try.

"No such thing as a bad dog," she said as the movie finished. Then before taking Freya for a walk, she checked her answering machine. Zack had left a message about a memorial dinner for Anni, so she headed down the road. As she approached, she could hear the whap-whap of the weed cutter over the ear-splitting burp of its motor. "Watch those feet," she yelled as he mowed down a patch of tenacious ragweed. "Friend of mine ripped his toe off."

He tapped one steel-toed boot in answer. The dogs roiled around the corner in a mass of fur, arousing Freya's herding instincts. Zack motioned her inside to the living room, where he disappeared for a moment and returned to pour from a dusty bottle. "Uncle Cece's wine cellar. Says white burgundy. Thought it was all red." He passed her a glass, then pointed to the wall. "I returned the picture."

Belle felt that the wine deserved a slight chill, but she glanced up in satisfaction at the scene. "It belongs there."

"I'm not a crook," he said, giving the Nixon salute. "Just short on cash. Anyway, I know you like wildflowers, and I thought you might enjoy having Aunt Anni's Peterson guide." He reached into the bookcase and presented her with the memento, almost too eager to please.

"Thanks. I'll take good care of it. Anyway, about that memorial service. I'm not surprised that Anni wasn't formal about religion. She wasn't one of those who drove faithfully to church each Sunday."

"Think she'd gotten a bellyful of it somewhere. She read the Bible, but more as literature. Stories with lessons. Those…" He scratched his head, searching for words.

"Parables?"

"Sounds like it. Anyway, she said the woods were her cathedral. Sort of paganistic. A stuffy funeral would be the last thing she'd have wanted. Probably come back to haunt me."

Belle squelched the urge to correct his terminology, then laughed. "My mother never wanted a service either, only 'Onward, Christian Soldiers' on my trumpet. She died down in Florida where my parents retired. Later I played it on the deck, listening to it echo across the lake."

"Well," he said, looking more serious and confident, "there won't be a minister. Just a friendly meal. I reserved a banquet room at the Caswell, asked a few of the neighbours she mentioned, some woman at the Canadian Blood Services. Uncle Henry's coming in from Montreal, poor old guy." He showed her a small list. "Anyone else you can think of? That man you brought over? Charles?"

"Charles Sullivan. I'll give you his number. She might have had other friends in town, too. Were you using her address book?"

He scratched his head, leaving a grass stain on his temple. "Don't know where it's gone. Always was by the phone. Little gold heart-shaped clasp. Mom gave it to her."

"Could the police have it?" she wondered. "You know, Zack, nothing in the present makes sense about her death. Maybe we should look to the past. Did she have a career?"

"Quite a long one. Didn't marry until her late forties. Back then she was a dental assistant. Gave Uncle Cece a cleaning and he came back for more." He winked.

"In Manitoba?"

"Winnipeg. But before that she spent a year in western Ontario helping a dentist. Pretty rough conditions. She used to tease me about it whenever I complained about the weather. You'd think she had lived in a sod hut."

Travelling to the wilderness for a job was a familiar story in Canada. Belle's mother had gone straight from normal school, the old-fashioned term for teachers' college, to Prince Albert, Saskatchewan, boarding with a Ukrainian family and carrying mashed potato sandwiches in her lunches. The limitless vistas of the prairies had made her so uncomfortable in a mountain setting that even one night on her honeymoon in Banff left her breathless.

Belle tucked the book under her arm, whistled for the dog and headed home. How odd that one conspicuous item had disappeared from the house. An item with names and places. Had Anni misplaced it in her recent forgetfulness? Such problems weren't the exclusive terrain of the elderly. Once Belle had stored a container of fishing worms on the pantry shelf. Not for long, though.

Going home, she met Ed on his all-terrain quad, tooling around in hopes of borrowing a screw gun for drywall installation. "Hey," he said, tapping his cane to coax Freya to jump. "See you lost that flashlight."

Belle gave a comical smile and tapped her head in an absent-minded gesture. She hadn't thought about it since she had returned from her Seek and Destroy mission. Probably fell out of her jacket when she took it off. "Did you find it on the trail to Surprise Lake?"

"Don't have no time for picnics. Hélène's on my butt to finish the basement. A young guy knocked at the door with a yellow model with a nick like yours. Thought you'd dropped it on the road. I gave him your name and house number. Didn't he stop by?"

An icy dagger tickled its point down her spine, despite the warm night. "You told him my name? Jesus, Ed."

"What's up?" He looked sheepish.

"I tore down a moose stand the other morning. Must have dropped the light."

"How come? Moose hunting's legal in the fall. Maybe someone's getting ready."

"These are people's backyards. Let the hunters go up to Bisco or Shining Tree. May not be against the law to build a perch on Crown land, but no one can stop me from wrecking it."

"Sorry, Belle. He seemed OK. Guess I didn't think straight about a woman living alone. Should have knowed better after what happened to Anni." Adjusting his cap, he squirmed in the distractive method that dogs used to disguise guilt or embarrassment.

"At least tell me what he looked like." She glared at his demeanour, honest and helpful, but when it came to women, a few solar panels installed on the north side.

"Well, it was only a minute. About our boys' age. Thirties. Couldn't see much hair because of the hat bill. Just regular clothes. Nothing special. Dark pants, red sweatshirt like I…"

"Right. Like we all wear. Did you happen to notice what he was driving in case another body turns up, namely mine?"

He brightened into a grin. "Help you there. It was a dark blue Dodge truck. Late model. But one thing, Belle." He looked up hopefully at her sceptical face. "The truck cap was ugly as sin. Some homemade paint job. Red with white trim. Bugger looked like a Yank flag."

An ugly truck cap. Every other person in Sudbury owned a truck. The Big Three automakers were balancing their budgets on the sales. Belle went to bed with an uneasy feeling, despite the hairy guardian angel snoring by the bed. In her sanctuary she didn't even lock her doors. No sirens pierced the night, no screams or screeches of burning rubber on pavement, just an occasional boat ferrying home a load of pickerel. She was more likely kept awake by the treble trills of the loons, or a scrabbling raccoon trying to finger the top from the garbage barrel on the deck. Except for a dull carving knife, her only weapon was a twelve-gauge shotgun in the downstairs closet, shells in an underwear drawer. Now she regretted not telling Steve about the perch. Suppose that… She rolled over, punching the pillow. Surely she was blowing everything out of proportion. Now if only an apple-cheeked young boy scout chewing Juicy Fruit gum would rap on her door with that flashlight, she'd offer him a cold root beer. Maybe he had decided to keep it. Damn thing cost forty bucks.

TEN

Belle groaned as her slippers encountered a pool of water. Either the dishwasher was leaking under the fridge, or vice versa. She tossed a mound of towels on the mess to mop up the spill. Impossible to have a bad hair day with her elder elf cut, but this wasn't a pleasant start. The plans included desultory banking chores, namely depositing the commission from the Balboni sale into her thirsty account and a peek-in at the Canadian Blood Services. Anni had gone there once a week for years.

Outside, the cedar deck was festooned with tiny footprints crisscrossing the dew. Raccoons again. They scooped seed from the bird feeder, tossing it around in festive abandonment, and grabbed the hummer feeder to chew off the little flowers and suck sugar water from the holes. A mousetrap would pinch their larcenous feet, or would that be too cruel? Belle took her portable coffee cup to the van, contemplating the cost of seed.

Suddenly her eyes grew wide with disgust as she traced an ugly scar weaving down the passenger side, the old key trick, senseless and deliberate vandalism. Or was it? Someone, no casual urban barbarian, had skulked down her driveway, leaving a wicked calling card. The flashlight man? From where she stood, she could see two zucchinis uprooted in the garden, given their fecundity, more favour than crime. She hunched her shoulders, imagining eyes amid the thick leaf cover. No wonder stalker victims got paranoid. Several properties down, Christakos had installed motion sensor devices to detect quivers within two hundred feet. Problem was, his siren blasted away at squirrels, birds and even hapless walkers. Had Edgewater Road come to this? A microcosmic collapse of society, the rich sipping chilled Bombay martinis, barricaded behind broken-glass-topped compound walls? Freya was still the best protection. No barking house in the area had been robbed. Then she calmed down, rationalized to restore a sense of security. When was the last time she'd looked at that door? It could have been damaged in a parking lot. And coons might have disturbed the garden.

The scratch could line up behind other duties. She headed into town and parked on Elgin Street, fishing out a loonie for the hungry meter. Giving blood always seemed like a good idea, and certainly she had signed the organ donor form on her driver's license. Why hadn't she ever rolled up that sleeve? Perhaps the idea appealed more than the reality. She might faint or be unable to drive home. Maybe this would be a milestone in her life, the conquering of an unreasonable and selfish fear.

The office on Cedar Street was nearly deserted as she walked in, measuring her steps like consequences. An enthusiastic young man in a T-shirt with a giant red drop ("Give blood. Starve a mosquito.") nearly snatched her up bodily and completed the screening process. At one of the curtained cubicles, a strawberry-blonde nurse stood, folding a blanket. Belle's blood pressure dropped several points at the familiar and appealing young face. "Melanie, what a surprise. So you graduated from Shield?"

The woman nodded, pulling up a metal footstool for Belle.

"Sure did, but you know the hospital cutbacks. No jobs. Half our class went to Texas or California. Just call me a sucker for the North. I'm volunteering to keep busy, make some contacts. Extendicare might have an opening by the winter."

"I remember you were specializing in geriatrics. And how's that therapeutic touch coming?"

"Great! Holistic medicine, massage, relaxation techniques, aromatherapy, all these alternatives have finally become respectable. If I can't get hired, I might start my own business. Hard to get loans, though."

Belle climbed onto the padded table and closed her eyes. She wouldn't, absotively, posilutely would not, watch the blood fill the container. The mind was powerful, but it could be tricked. Ignorance was bliss. "Did you ever meet Anni Jacobs? She used to help out here."

"I just started last week. But tell you who'd know. Maureen Murphy." She set up a Secretariat-sized needle, while Belle calmed herself by thinking of the stalwart Queen, her usual procedure for injections and punitive dentistry, and when that failed, an old song of her mother's. Pass the blood to me, Bud. Shoot the juice to me, Bruce. What were the other verses? Crimson? Jimson? Suddenly she became aware that she was humming frantically.

"For heaven's sake, relax. You're impeding your energy channels." Melanie was laughing, adjusting a tube for the bubbling blood, no doubt.

Belle's right arm began stinging, then the left one joined in sympathy. "So is Maureen around today?" Her voice sounded unnatural, disassociated, coming from some distant place where she would prefer to be. Papeete, the Virgin Islands, Hamilton.

"No, only Tuesdays and Thursdays. Who's Anni, anyway?"

"My neighbour." Belle inhaled slowly, held her breath to a

count of ten, then exhaled slowly. Sensing a sudden pressure on her arm, the stick of a bandage, she opened her eyes tentatively. "She was killed."

Melanie's smile vanished, a tiny frown crossing her brow. "Oh, my. That's who they were talking about. Sorry to be so dense." With a few efficient disconnections, she bounced out with the bag of corpuscles as Belle sat up like a zombie, testing her balance, expecting the scene to swirl into a dark vortex as Dracula's pal Renfield murmured, "The blood is the life. The blood is the life." When nothing dire happened after a minute, she kicked her feet gently against the table, coltish and relieved.

Melanie returned bearing a small glass. "Here's your apple juice. Compliments of the house."

"Juice," Belle said, pooching out her lip. "Where's the rum?"

The girl grinned. "That was a long time ago. An old British military custom. Health fanatics caught up to us. Drink up. You need to restore those fluids."

Like a sailor returning to land, Belle made her way to the van, settling into the seat and blinking. Feeling a bit weak on a minute-by-minute appraisal, she stopped on Notre Dame, calculating that two Big Macs might compensate for the trauma, fries and chocolate shake added for gluttonous good measure. Donating regularly might be useful to curb the pounds. Her generation found it hard to shake off the "no fat chicks" mentality. 130 for blood pressure and weight seemed reasonable at a scratch under five feet four inches. Fit counted more than fat. A few more visits, and her name would be in the paper as a Gallon Club member.

On her way home, the first miles of her road skirted a swamp, a desolate stretch, though a paradise for water lilies. Once she had been stuck with a zapped alternator for two hours waiting for someone to pass. So when she saw a slender figure leaning against a green Escort with one door patched with duct tape, hood up, the radiator steaming, she had to stop.

It was Patsy Sommers and in the car, bawling in a cappella, were three small children. Why a single woman with no apparent job had moved to the remote road had been a mystery. Perhaps the cheap living expenses were a factor, the ancient cabin with only the bare essentials she rented from a snowbird landlord. Now and then she'd disappear for six or seven months, returning with another baby, her learning curve too steep to master.

Dressed in a pair of Capri pants and a tanktop, jelly sandals on her feet, her concave belly sporting a golden navel ring, the woman raised her hand in a half-hearted gesture which moved Belle to a rare sympathy for one who lived off the public purse. "Need a ride?" Patsy nodded weakly. "Get the kids and hop in."

"I'm Belle Palmer. Down the road from you." She hoped that they were well-diapered. Regular vacuuming for dog hair was bad enough.

"Patsy Sommers. And these here are Lisa, Joe and baby Susie. Appreciate this." Into the rear seats with the toddlers flew bags with mega-boxes of cereal, jars of peanut butter and a bulk container of powdered milk. Barely thirty, she wore coral-red hair in a straggly ponytail, her face mottled and pale, perhaps the result of recent slashes to the Ontario safety net. One controversial Minister for Health, "Mr. Tuna Fish," had suggested that welfare and Mothers' Allowance recipients comb shelves for dented cans and bargain with shopkeepers to accommodate the ninety-nine-dollar monthly menu printed in *The Toronto Star*. Spartan fare, it didn't include margarine, nor sauce for the pasta.

Belle made small talk about the weather. As the van passed

Anni's, she glanced at her passenger, noticing a black rose tattooed on her white arm. Some sinister motorcycle club? "I guess you heard about the murder," she said.

Patsy stiffened, hardening her slitted mouth over clenched teeth and hugging the baby fiercely, its whimpers like an irritating radio alarm with no snooze button. "Can't say I'm bawling all night over that nosy old bag." She muttered the last two words like a curse.

"Old bag. Old bag. Nosy, posy, rosy old bag" came a chorus from the rear.

Mother was right. Some people aren't made for kids, namely me, Belle thought, as they arrived at the shack and Patsy marshalled her brood, the older ones waving good-bye with a smile. Would dinner be cereal? Profuse dog droppings lay in piles ready to be washed into the lake, and garbage accumulated for opportune coons and bears to sort. In a discordant note, two lines of laundry hung in the breeze, perfectly graduated from baby to adult sizes. Patsy opened the creaky wooden gate and closed it behind her. Two Rottweilers pushed blocky faces through a broken screen door, barking fiercely as they scratched at the frame, giving occasional yelps colliding with each other. "Dummies. Wouldn't hurt a baby," she said, working her bundles inside. "Come pet 'em if you want. I know you like dogs. Seen your shepherd. She's a pretty one."

"Uh, maybe another time. Got to go now." Boy, it was ripe, Belle thought, speeding up to clear the air. What was the innuendo about Anni? She lived only a few lots over. Had she reported Patsy to the Children's Aid? Everyone on the road suspected that the kids were left alone on short trips to town. It must be tough stuck in the bush with three small children, no babysitter in miles even if she could have afforded one. Even getting them up and dressed would take hours. As for security, the dogs would keep anyone from the yard. But there was one fly in the proverbial. What if something happened to her and she couldn't get home? Calling Dean Koontz.

Belle took advantage of the hour before dinner to run over her list of chores, choosing the last first for a psychological advantage. In a sub-minimalist cleaning system, vacuuming hovered near bottom, just above windows. But with a long-haired shedding machine, it waited for no man. Whether the central vac was a blessing or a hassle, she still hadn't decided. Grunting, she hauled the serpentine tubes up and down stairs, nicking paint at the corners as usual. Yelling at Freya, who pounced at the droning power head like it was a small beast, she directed her to the hall. "Saw a show on making sweaters out of dog wool," she said. The enterprising woman had carded and spun the stuff, touching corners of prehistory where females provided the comforts of warmth and food while males clubbed the meat. Suddenly a paper clip or something more sinister clattered down the tubes into the far reaches of the basement.

As she coiled up the hose, the phone rang. Charles sounded distressed. From the halting tones, she could imagine him unfolding an ironed handkerchief to wipe sweat beads from his noble brow, refolding it precisely. "Belle, you didn't tell me about the dogs."

She hesitated. Maybe it was unwise to befriend clients, like selling them used cars and then commuting together. "Next door? The Rogers' mutts?"

"It's a madhouse. There are a half-dozen over here. Peed on my porch, dug up the dahlias and deposited pyramids of all sizes. I nearly ruined a pair of shoes by stepping..." He mumbled something unintelligible.

"Did you call the family?"

"Immediately. There was this woman, the wife, I presume. Do you know what she said?"

"I couldn't possibly guess."

"Picture innocence. Picture vacuousness. Picture fractured logic: 'Reeeaaally, Mr. Sullivan, why in the world do you think they would want to go over to your place?'" A Churchillian "harumph" caused Belle to stifle a giggle. "Can you imagine? As if blaming me. I rang off. You can't have a discussion with that inanity."

"Any ideas?"

"Plan A begins with moth balls around the garden and buildings, then a pest repellant I saw at Canadian Tire. Cayenne pepper or something harmless. Nothing too rash to start."

"That's not going to work. Tell you what. I have a large live trap left over from a battle royale with feral cats."

Charles' tone notched up several notes. "What would I do with a trapped dog? Call the Animal Control people?"

"You're not in Ottawa now. Take Bowser straight to the SPCA shelter on Notre Dame. 'Duh, I don't know who it belongs to.' Rogers will have to pay fifty bucks each. Money talks. They'll get the message."

He mulled over her suggestions, declining the "duh" part but cheering up at the systematic offensive. "Sounds fine. Let's give it a try."

Minutes later, as she rounded the turn for his drive, a pack of all persuasions and proportions lunged out of nowhere to snap at her tires. It wouldn't even be a challenge to dispatch the poor idiots. But suppose someone were walking, or an oncoming car jumped the odds? A swerve and an embrace with an uncooperative birch tree might result. Braking for animals was safe in theory only.

"Here you go," Belle said, hoisting the three-foot metal cage out of the van. "Now get me a pork chop. I can still smell them from your grill." She baited the trap, which they positioned under a wilting forsythia bush. Then heaping plates of chops and potato scallop appeared, and the pair talked strategy like a couple of Yalta generals, gesturing with forks and pausing for gulps of Maudite, an excellent Quebecois overproof beer.

"Now we'll see what happens. When do they usually arrive?"

The evening was hot and still, heavy with humidity from the predicted rain. Charles fanned himself with a rhubarb leaf the size of an elephant's ear. "Around dawn and then after supper. Thank God they have other pastimes during the day."

"Are they vicious? Getting bitten's great leverage."

"No luck there. Friendly as pups. It's just unconscionable that their owners don't seem to care." He gestured toward the thick greenbelt between their properties. "My place is fenced in back. Suppose I could extend down the line, but that would make it look like a concentration camp."

"You can't fence into the lake. If animals want in, they'll get in." She rolled her eyes in sympathy. "Just another feud. Happens all the time out here."

"My lord, what else can I expect?"

"Start with wind chimes that rattle your brains, someone aerial-spraying bug poison on their trees or removing your survey stakes to better locate their new garage. Teenagers and quads seem to be multiplying lately. Luckily you're at the end of the road, not in their path."

Charles had been listening attentively, but as his gaze returned to the yard, his face brightened. "While you're here, I want to show you the sauna. Won't claim that I did it all myself. A couple of workers laid the foundation and set the frame in no time flat." The size of a small garage, the building boasted a change room with a shower, cedar panelling and rows of shiny brass clothes hooks. Inside the steam room were graduated benches for four people to sprawl in comfort. A bright red enamel stove with a container of lava rocks on top, the imported kind Belle didn't even bother pricing, sat on a tile floor, wooden water bucket, loofah and soap nearby. The place smelled like a sprucy corner of Scandinavia. It had been a long time since she'd enjoyed a sauna.

"I'm a bit reluctant to try it out alone," he said.

"Why?" she asked. "It looks as if you've followed the code."

Charles patted his chest as a small wrinkle worried the bridge of his nose. "Nothing to do with construction. Just my high blood pressure. Keep it under control with pills, but perhaps I need a stronger prescription. Sometimes I feel a bit faint." He sounded embarrassed, so she nodded in mute understanding.

"Charles, even at my tender age, many of my friends have hypertension. Don't worry about it. Ask your doctor."

"Haven't been able to get one yet," he said, rummaging in his pocket. "Only a few take new patients, and choosing the right physician is very important. Anyway, I also wanted to give you a key to the house for safekeeping."

"Sure," she said, tucking it away, flattered by the confidence. "It's a good idea in case you leave town and forget something. Half-way to Toronto, I thought I had left the woodstove door unlatched and drove back two hours to check."

As they walked to her van, she saw a neat stack of greenish scrap behind the sauna. "You're not burning that stuff, are you?"

"Why not? Just short pieces. I don't want to waste it or haul it to the dump in my car."

She raised an eyebrow. "Ed burned treated wood in a stove one year, nearly didn't wake up. The fumes gave him one hell of a headache, but it could have been worse. Even outdoors it's toxic."

Poor Charles, she thought, zigzagging through the dog pack on the way home. He'd better master the rules of rural living before they killed him.

That night Belle's nose was stuffed from a change in weather. As the rain arrived, charging the air with ions, she tapped an ash into a brown ceramic mitt holding a ball with a hole, another cottage curio. The glass top on her bedside table pressed an assortment of wildflowers: the tiny pink bells of the rose twisted-stalk, a blue-eyed grass and a yellow marsh marigold, spring's announcement. She picked up the Peterson's guide Zack had given her. What exotica had Anni found over the years? A rare red trillium? A delicate orchid? It was hard to discover new species in a limited ecosystem. She opened the book and raised an eyebrow at a check beside striped coralroot, a saprophytic plant, waxy, without chlorophyll, thriving on forest wastes. According to the scribble, her mage friend had found it beside her boathouse. As she leafed through, a piece of folded paper fell out.

"*Dear Anni*," it read. "*So many years. I was surprised to get your letter from Sudbury. So that's where you went with that handsome engineer. How did you ever chase me down in Saskatchewan? Through dear old Verna? Can you believe Bell Canada wanted the earth to string a line through the bush? Life's simpler without it. Sam sold the grocery and here we are out west. You ask about that place, and I remember your suspicions. Shortly after you left, I saw something disgusting that made me go to the police. The children were sent away and the school boarded up. The town was in shock. I only hope THAT ONE was locked up and the key thrown away.*

"*Edith*" was the only signature, with June 20th the only date. Had it arrived the week of Anni's death, or years earlier?

ELEVEN

The letter pointed toward the past, but Anni had other enemies in her present. The very hostile Patsy Sommers, for one, even though that pathetic stockpile of cereal would have tugged at the black heart of the coldest futures speculator. A client, Dottie O'Neill, worked at Children's Aid. She had appreciated help in getting a quick sale on the family home after her mother returned to Newfoundland to nurse an aunt with Parkinson's. "I need a favour about a situation your office might have handled recently. And I promise not to compromise you," Belle said.

Dottie laughed like an overloaded potato trucker arriving at an unmanned weigh station, her Newfie accent a hearty Irish transplant frozen for centuries. "Lard dine Jaysus," she boomed, a signature expression from the redoubtable Rock. "I could use some compromising, but first get me some Viagra for the old man. What is it you need, my girl?"

When Patsy had reappeared after Christmas with yet another baby, its needs had pressed her abilities to cope. Belle had seen the woman make more than one fast trip to town without any sign of heads bobbing in children's car seats. "Can you tell me if one family, who shall be nameless, on Edgewater Road was investigated recently?"

A cackle broke the silence, then a flutter of paper. "That's a doozy. Don't you live out that way?"

"Five years now. Finally tore the cottage down and built. You'll have to come out for a dip."

"And turn into a popsicle? Everyone knows how cold that bugger lake is. Anyway, that visit nearly led me to early retirement. It was a circus from first go. We were responding to an anonymous complaint about children left alone. A pair of black devil dogs charged the rickety fence, spitting and snarling. Looked like animals had been at the trash. Diapers dragged across the road, even baby bottles in the ditch. The mother denied everything. Was she mad! Repacking garbage cans, swearing like a Hell's Angel. I wanted to check inside, but we didn't have just cause. All I could do was warn her to clean up, or I'd notify the Health Unit. Haven't heard anything since, so maybe the visit kept her on her toes."

"She's still driving alone now and then. And I'm sure there's nobody minding the kids. Too bad we can't charge her with cruelty to animals, but they're just crazed by being penned and fat from no exercise."

"Isn't that just like you, my friend? Bet you'd have reported dog abuse fast enough. Children pay the price for community blindness. Look at that boy's death in New Brunswick. Failure to thrive, doctors said. No wonder, chained in the closet all of his miserable life. Four years old and twenty pounds? Little legs like sticks and bruises all over his body. Parents should be licensed."

The dart about dogs made Belle wince. "So lay it on with a moral trowel. And don't worry. I'll keep an eye on her...for other reasons."

"There is more. Tell all."

Belle cut the details to the quick and dirty, wondering if her bias was showing.

"As I said, the call was anonymous. We had some temporary summer staff. No way I can check if it was even a woman. Since Mrs. Sommers wasn't charged, sounds like more a nuisance than a motive for murder. Still, I wouldn't want to face that banshee riding a PMS flare."

Alone with her thoughts, Belle turned director. Patsy looked like a scrappy brawler. If Anni had confronted her about the kids, it would have been no secret who had called the authorities. Perhaps one night, she had gone to Anni's to have it out. Would the old woman have let her in? Harped at her further in that self-righteous tone she could wield? Patsy wasn't sharp with words. A few choice, acerbic shots could have turned the moment ugly in seconds. One blow from a mother defending her cubs, no matter how misguided.

And then there was still Nick, the man without a source of income. Before she left for town, she primed the bread maker with tomato-basil mix. On return, she'd have a tempting piece of bait to troll. It was time to see inside that little camp.

Later that day, at the Imperial Body Shop, a wizened Finnish gnome paced back and forth with his estimate book, checked the paint number and made a few calls. "Ship-shape tomorrow if you can leave overnight, Missus. Important to give her a bake, like a dry sauna." His distinctive accent, another delicious ingredient in the Sudbury melting pot, sounded like "Rupperpoots," a local newspaper column in syllabic dialect: "Vuns der vuss a liddle gurl…" Belle took a taxi home, appalled by the thirty-dollar charge. It might have been higher, except that the driver knew he could loop by the airport afterwards to wait for arriving planes.

A savoury breeze was drifting through the house when she opened the door. Mother's little servant. She wrapped the loaf in a paper bag and hiked down the road, the dog sedate as an old maid. Anyone in the bush who needed to leash an animal shouldn't own one, if "own" was the right word. An occasional dip and flip was necessary, though, since a perverse gene made Freya select the exact middle of a driveway with the precision of a surveyor's transit. "Not there! Go further, I mean farther. Ooo. Too late," she said, grabbing a thumb-thick branch sliced from the winter plowing and catapulting steamy piles into the brush. "To you it's a registered letter, but humans don't read with their noses." The response was a gambol into a muddy ditch. Just like a kid.

Nick's truck sat at the schoolbus turn just before Charles' place. Short of a pencil, blending mnemonics with math, Belle memorized the license: 851 RTM. In (19)85 I (had a Mustang) R(egistered) T(o) M(e). That sporty red devil with its useless rear wheel drive and tendency to fishtail in winter hadn't lasted long in the slippery North. She peered into the rusty box. Only a couple of sandbags for weight and two cans of oil. The doors were locked. The usual rubbish cluttered the dash, junk flyers for pizza and dry cleaning. She shielded her eyes against the glare of the window. A Royal Bank deposit slip for five hundred dollars, chump change even stacked into a miserly pile of loonies.

Along the trail, she paused to look for mushrooms. Every week brought a surprise: blewits, fly agarics and yellow boletes with spongy bottoms. Many old-timer Italians, Finns and Ukrainians prized the fragile fairy rings and the luscious velvet foot, the latter cultivated commercially as enotake, but why risk poisoning when the market was carrying portobellos and shiitakes even at ten bucks a pound? The CBC had reported that a couple in Bracebridge had gone to bed in philosophical resignation, leaving a note: "We ate mushrooms." Something poking through leaf mould caught her eye. Speckled dark brown and cream, fresh-birthed from the rich peat like a reluctant egg. The rare panther, as transfixing and deadly as its namesake. Picking the beauty would break Anni's unwritten rules, ruin the brief perfection. One of these days she would buy a decent camera.

She passed a favourite pair of wooden lovers, Ontario's answer to the holly and the ivy. A tall golden birch, king of the forest in its girth, reached skyward, embraced by a smaller sinuous maple, the smooth gray skin contrasting with its silvery-amber companion. Stopping for a moment to drink in the quiet, Belle was surprised to notice the forest open far and away for a change, nearly to the bay. Usually the hardwood stand was dense with undergrowth. What had happened to the leaves? She examined a branch and swore at the sickly lace shred in her hand. Something hit her neck, and she swiped at it absently. Dropping onto the path were tent caterpillars, green with brown and black stripes, harbingers of another cyclical invasion. How long before they crawled across the road? Would the trees survive? She squashed a few underfoot, yanking down their cottony nests with singular malevolence.

Belle was so disgusted that she nearly missed the turn to Nick's camp. Left to weather naturally, the boards on the trapping base shack had turned a delicate Cape Cod gray. Cheery impatiens decorated a flower bed constructed painstakingly with thin rock shards. Under the post-and-beam construction, a plastic waterline headed for the lake, likely run by a hand pump. By a shed, an axe and bow saw leaned against a pile of pine splits, Nick's hard sweat instead of a quick chainsaw fix. Satisfied that the dog was amusing herself by crashing around with a stick, she knocked on the door.

A minute later the edge of a curtain moved, and she brandished the bag with a friendly smile. "Could you use some homebaked bread?"

Nick's face was red from more than sunburn. "Let me get

my pants on. Had to sew a rip."

They were both laughing by the time she entered. The single room was simple but comfortable, reminding her of sweet, uncomplicated days in the cottage. A tin woodstove for summer use, dresser, pine table and two side chairs, a Swedish style daybed with futon and pillows. Two kerosene lanterns provided evening light. The kitchen corner had a dry sink with a bucket, cupboards and a Coleman stove. For entertainment, a portable radio. On a small shelf near the water bucket, a pharmacy of prescription bottles lined up.

"It's tomato-basil," she said, placing it into his hands, the fingers strong and graceful, capable of hard work but perhaps something more intricate. On the window sill she spotted a cup of pencils.

"Smells wonderful after 1001 pasta recipes. How about a slice with some tea? I've got butter cooling down at the lake."

One boiling pot later they munched and drank in quiet contemplation of a squirrel on the deck outside methodically dismantling a pine cone and stuffing it into its mouth like a woody artichoke. Since the camp perched twenty feet up on a rock face, the view was spectacular, nothing but the long lines of the unbroken wilderness. "So peaceful here without the boat traffic," she added. "Do you know the bluff on Wapiti a couple of bays past the island? I call it Raven Cliff."

Nodding brightly at a personal connection, he pulled a thick sketchbook from a drawer. "One of my paths leads to the big lake. Fishing's perfect there on a cool morning before the bugs wake up." He opened to a page and turned it toward her. "I have special names for places, too. Bear Inlet. Saw one checking the blueberry bushes yesterday. Big, lazy boar. Something odd about his nose."

Nick had been reading the landscape with pens and

pencils. Belle traced the image, the moment returning like a warm embrace. "What fine lines. Art's not my forte. I can't imagine the hours of patience. Even my stick men need crutches."

The next picture showed a huge hump of aged granite surfacing from the forest floor like a leviathan sounding. "Moby!" she said, clapping her hands.

"Whale Rock. This was done in Rapidograph pens." Then in a charcoal drawing, a golden birch twenty feet high struggled to plant roots in a shallow cleft no deeper than a suitcase.

"That's by the creek. Old Yeller."

"I call her Golden Girl."

"Do you ever work in pastels or watercolours?"

"No," he said. "I prefer the subtleties of black and white. More of a challenge with texture and light."

"True enough. Films are my passion. Even the silents fascinate me. I'll take the starkness of *Nosferatu* or *The Blue Angel* to the washed out messes from the Fifties and early Sixties. The actors have turned pink and brown."

As she turned to leave, Nick razored out the page with Raven Cliff, inking in the name, and offered it to her in a gesture humble yet proud. "I can always make another. Every hour of the day brings changes to the landscape if you have a sharp eye."

Belle studied the fine work with clear pleasure and then met his shy expression while she pointed to the sketchbook. "You could sell these, you know. If you ever want to, try Sudbury Paint and Custom Framing on Elgin. They promote local talent."

She rallied the dog and left Nick beaming over her just praise. Now she knew how he spent his spare time. No stolen stereos, no dope lab, no pornography studio, no canvas bags with stencilled bank names. Just the evidence of a soul. Maybe he laboured out of town in winter to afford this solitude. Maybe he got help from his family. From the numerous pill bottles, there might be serious health problems not evident at first glance. Who could know?

Feeling disloyal if not downright ungrateful as she placed the drawing in a folder where it would be safe until framing, she called Steve. "I have that number. British Columbia. 851 RTM," she said, fulfilling her promise with little enthusiasm.

"Great," he said. "I'll get on it."

She drummed her fingers on the table in a restive tap dance, steering the conversation in another direction. "I'm getting strange ideas about Anni."

"Like what? Shemale intuition?"

"Stop that, Mr. Chauvinist. One week she's broke, the next she buys an expensive van with cold cash. And she said some weird things in the weeks before she died." To test his reaction to her efforts, Belle related her conversations with the car salesman. Should she tell Steve about the paint scratch...or the letter...or Patsy? She couldn't run to him with every fragmented suspicion.

His sharp tone convinced her to keep quiet. "What in hell are you up to now? Stay out of my case."

"You said to stay out of the woods. What's wrong with a few questions?"

That flip approach was a mistake. From the heated tones on the line, she could imagine steam seeping from his ears. "Keeping your eyes open is one thing. Making the rounds like some vigilante is another. I'll handle police work. That's what I'm paid for. You, however, have another source of income, or are you so rich that you're retired now at, what, fifty?" The added years scored a mean jab. She narrowed her eyes like a frustrated cobra and hung up none too gently. Sometimes Steve needed a lesson in manners even if a date with Celebrex was around the corner. Maybe indigestion was getting to him. Rarely did his day go by without an apple fritter from Tim's.

On his way shopping the next morning, Charles dropped Belle off to pick up her vehicle. "Call me the Pied Piper, or maybe Porker," he said, humming along with a tape of Gregorian chants. "I collected two chop fiends. That little spotted one didn't want to leave me. Licked my hand all the way to the shelter and gave me the most sorrowful look."

"Sounds like Dog Day Afternoon," she added. "Anyway, you're on the right track now. Don't weaken."

No charge, her Finn pal at Imperial Autobody said, a case of comprehensive damage. Feeling suddenly rich, escaping retribution from the five-hundred-dollar deductible option she'd used to tether down ballooning insurance costs, Belle spent the afternoon with a cheery face even for paperwork. By the time she left the office, it was obscenely late to cook, so she hit Pizza Hut for the all-you-can-eat. An hour later, smug about having tiptoed past the dessert bar, she was burping home in a light rain, just enough to grease the pavement. It was an easy trip once past Garson, skirting slurry monsters pulling out of the Falconbridge Mine, giant linked vats on wheels, throwing up stones to chip windshields. A few miles from her corner, she cruised twenty klicks over the limit on a deserted stretch, with one turnoff to a helicopter business and another to a thriving gravel pit operation. The hills of scrub made a bleak landscape, yet in the Fifties a sizable forest had flourished there, as black stumps a metre in diameter bore witness. A lightning fire had wiped out hundreds of acres, contained at a swamp which had sheltered her road like an asbestos blanket.

She squinted at shadows fading into the dusk while drizzle smeared bugs under the wipers' swish. Groggy but satisfied from the carbo blast, she slipped in a tape and listened to Lucille Ball croak out "Wildcat." Couldn't carry a tune in a carton of the Pall Malls she hawked on her television show, but she conquered Broadway through sheer guts. Born the same year as Belle's mother, who painted on Lucy's shapely candy apple lips and made fun of Loretta Young's "hen's patootie face." Miss See-the-USA-in-Your-Chevrolet had passed on recently, joining Clark Gable, the father of her "adopted" child, according to revelations from the middle-aged daughter. MGM must have sweated bullets to protect its virginal goddess after the King-before-Elvis had issued The Call of the Wild.

Then a dark shape moved up at warp speed in the mirror, and her pupils widened. A drunk driver? Not the first time she had seen someone weaving along in an area police never bothered to monitor. Did the idiot want to pass? She edged to the right, but the huge hood only drew nearer, so close that she braced for a bump. Adrenalin pumped in, sharpening her senses like razors. From the height, she guessed that it was a truck, but what action to take? Her blocky van wasn't a sports car, loaded with power and dime-slicing control. Around corners and up and down the hills, they tangoed like estranged lovers. Luckily no rock cuts loomed ahead although there was a particularly wicked drop-off at the next sharp curve, flanked by a row of posts and steel cables. Something quirky about the banking angle, though. Last month, several rotten posts had been knocked over and never replaced. At the bottom of the hill, a small pile of rocks topped by a white wooden cross and a wreath of plastic flowers had appeared, a "descanso" tradition born in the American Southwest.

The truck had the advantage. Whatever testosterone game he was playing would leave her the underdog, and one wrong move might flip her. Primed with Dirty Harry movies, she half-expected gun blasts to echo and the rear window to shatter, showering her with broken glass. Lucy belted out encouragement: "Who is the cat with more pounce to the ounce?" as the bass thumped. Belle switched off the stereo to concentrate. Through the wiper sweeps the red reflectors of posts winked. Sloping into the turn, inches over the centre line, out of desperation she tried a high school trick for tail-gaters, flicking her lights in an illusion of braking. Then she tromped hard on the gas. A screech sounded, and in the mirror she watched the truck skid on the slick asphalt and barrel down the hill, jerking a line of cable behind like a cracking whip.

Belle eased onto the berm as a distant horn blared a killer migraine. Her legs were shaking spastically from the rush, knees bumping the dash. Good old fight or flight, the primitive protective response that had kept Palmer primates paddling in the gene pool. The spasms passed after a couple of deep breaths, and she dialled 911 on the cell phone. Then armed with a tire iron and a brush-trimming machete from the trunk, she got out and walked back to the accident site. To her horror and satisfaction, the truck lay upside down in a peat bog dotted with grassy hummocks. A crazy logic borne of fear made her wonder if the driver might wrench open the door and charge out like an indestructible alien. She eased down the embankment, sliding on the slag, then walked on cat feet across the mushy terrain. Ooze soaked between her toes and rain began spilling down her glasses, blurring her vision.

The vehicle fit Ed's description, dark blue late model Dodge. License MTN CT. No cougars around here, except for the two-footed variety. And as for the cap, their power painter must have jammed. At a cautious distance, she sat down on a stump. The horn had finally stopped, the engine silent, so a fire seemed improbable. Call her a bad Samaritan, but she wasn't getting any closer. Though the dark was pressing in, she could see two figures flailing inside amid guttural moans and lively curses. Unless service cutbacks were more grievous than expected, the police and ambulance should arrive within ten minutes. "Help is on the way," she called in a sarcastic tone, "even though you don't deserve it." A rank smell of liquor and vomit floating into the rainy night made her gag. Didn't excuse their murderous behaviour, even if the recent "Drunken Defense" had acquitted a sixty-five-year-old man accused of raping a woman in a wheelchair.

"You say this vehicle was trying to run you off the road? Was there damage to your van?" asked a young officer shortly after, pencil moustache twitching as he wrote up the report under the cab light in his patrol car. He'd cast an amused eye at her arsenal.

"He didn't hit me, but he came close. You couldn't have slipped a piece of paper between us." The officer nodded, grabbed a yellow plastic parka and left to supervise the rescue. Belle sat quietly, the chill disappearing under the dry roar of the heater, but her stomach protesting at the heavy digestion of pizza overload. Attendants were transferring the men on stretchers, their floodlights weaving ghostly slices though the fog. Oblivious to the drama, a white-throated sparrow sang a goodnight, "Old Sam Peabody, Peabody, Peabody," one note up and four notes down.

It was black by the time she pulled into her yard, triggering the automatic floodlights. Freya bolted out in grateful trust, shaking off the rain. Ten hours was a long time, but the dog had a bladder like a whale's. Forget watching Bette Davis in *Dark Victory*. Wiser to knit up the ravelled sleeves of care. She selected an Ofra Harnoy cello recital, resonant and soothing, and poured lemon balm oil into the bathtub. The bubbles concealed her body like the simple facts around Anni's death. If these were Anni's killers, why not get out of town? Did they think Belle knew something? And how long had they been trailing her? Easy enough to follow her movements in a small community, driving to work, to Rainbow Country. Steve was not going to be a happy man. Methodically, weighing honesty on one side, prudence on the other, she arranged her scales.

TWELVE

The placid lake reflected no signs of the harrowing night before, shooting up on demand a psychedelic sunrise of red, orange and burgundy streaks. Hardly had Belle trundled herself downstairs than Steve knocked at the door, depositing carrot muffins and slathering them with chunks of butter from the table. "Help you get your strength back. I read the report on those fools," he said, talking with his mouth full. "Blub, I mean, blood tests are positive for driving under the influence. Broken bottle of rye on the floor. Too bad they didn't actually bump your van, or we could have laid an attempted murder charge." Her withering look earned a grin. "But not to worry. A couple of leg casts will put them out of action until the snow flies."

So he hadn't guessed her complicity. This would have to be played with delicacy. She spread out one hand to demonstrate the tremor. "Bad joke, Steve. I was shaking all last night, even after I turned into a crêpe, marinating in a tub of hot water. They could have killed me. Who are these bozos?"

He leafed through his notebook. "Go by the names of Jack Birchem and Barry Coil. Good old boys laid off in the uranium mine shutdowns at Elliot Lake. Retraining at Nickel City College, when they bother to show up. Heavy equipment mechanic or something. Probably get turfed out by Christmas. Here's the best part. Rifles, unregistered, and illegal hollow point bullets in the cap."

She gave a thumbs-up gesture. "Our hunters?"

"You bet. That gave us cause to search their rathole apartment downtown. Freezer chock-full of fresh moose meat and eight bear paws, assorted sizes. Inside a wrapped up skin, ten galls. Their pictures were recognized by an agent who arranged last month to make a buy from them, except that they didn't show up."

"So what do they get? A slap on the wrist?"

"Hardly. With the new laws, they could be facing two years in jail and a fine of $100,000. They named a few names to plea bargain, including some geezer in Chelmsford who calls himself the Godfather of Bear Gallbladders."

"The God. You must be making that up. So what did they say about attacking me?"

He shrugged his massive shoulders, his expression mimicking their innocent stupidity. "Just arsing around. Wouldn't pull over to let them pass. Don't know you from a scroll in the ground."

Lies or truth, their stories were keeping her escapades a secret. "But we've got a match with the mutilation? And a solid link to Anni?"

"Forget it. Those bear carcasses are long gone. Best I could do on that score was bluff and tell them that their truck had been seen. Then they admitted only that they'd scouted that path by the turnaround. The one to Surprise Lake, I think you call it?"

"Scouted. Sure," she said, recalling that moose hock and the platform. "And the night she was killed?"

"They don't keep appointment calendars. Once beer six slides down, every place and face is the same. We're still making the rounds of their watering holes, but it would be hard to make a case we can prove. Tearing down a baiting spot is a weak motive for murder, even for these jerks."

"Doesn't seem like you're trying very hard." She felt like pouting.

"I saved the best for last. They're left-handed."

"And I supposed Graveline concluded that a right-hander dealt the blow." He nodded quietly.

"It sounds pretty flimsy. People can be ambidextrous." Her desperation was annoying, even to her own ears.

Backed by a logic she couldn't deny, he shook off the protests. "I never liked the idea of hunters as her assailants from the beginning. Those slippers. The house so neat. You know, Belle, that there's no way she would have let them in, so stop giving me evil looks."

"They're not evil, just discouraged. Anni's memorial dinner is tonight. Will you have anyone there?"

"Ten plainclothes persons and a hidden videocam in the potpourri. Your tax dollars at work." He paused conspicuously, as if a thought crossed his mind. "Say, why don't you act as unofficial liaison? Make the rounds. Tell me what you hear. You're good at that."

That was a new one, she thought, Steve enlisting her help. Sounded more patronizing than sincere. At least MTN CT and its teeny brains were plaster casters, no longer cruising for something defenceless to blast, namely a short red pelt fast turning to gray.

The distraction of the evening was welcome, the only problem what to wear. Sorry for once that she had decided to stay retro and foil the fashion industry, she bulldozed her closet, decade by decade. The image of Miss Boggs, her fourth grade teacher, who had worn the same suit September to June, materialized like a pea green ghost, raised appliqué welts on the wide lapels. Teachers had all been "Miss" then, forced to resign if they married. With a wisp of a smile, she selected a light mauve linen pantsuit the colour of wild clematis.

Belle drove in with the DesRosiers. To her disappointment, Charles had said that he had declined Zack's invitation. "Only met the lady once or twice, my dear. Might appear as if I were cadging a meal." Parking at the Caswell, they saluted a few more old timers from the road, the Maenpaas, the Cleroux and the Perths. At least the hotel was renowned for the best prime rib in town. She was ravenous.

The banquet room was well-appointed, one end cozy with sofas and easy chairs clustered in front of a fireplace, the other with a table set for scarcely a dozen. Was that all a life deserved? Yet, better a few sincere mourners than a hall of hypocrites. Cece's older brother Henry wasn't hard to spot with his distinctive Montreal tailoring, despite the gravy stain on his tie. A frail man in his eighties, he recalled Anni with the discontinuity of radio static. "Grand gal. Just got in. Rough flight. Air Canada broke again? Cece bagged a winner all right. Remember their wedding. Those noisy prop planes. Briggs and Stratton painted on the wing. They make better lawnmowers. Turbulence the whole damn way. Downtown Winnipeg in a blizzard. Charged together across Portage and Main like a herd of buffalos. Ever seen a buffalo coat, young lady? Keep your knickers warm at fifty below." After burbling into the whiskey and soda she brought him, he fell into a coughing fit which propelled him into a nearby chair. Anni's life before marriage was a closed book in that family library.

Seeing room on a sofa, Belle joined a pleasant-looking woman with a pink tint to her hair, applying what looked like homemade lip balm from a doll-sized pot. "It was pure luck that I read the obituary. Happened to be at the library to catch up on the Sudbury news. We went back a long way."

Belle placed a hand on her arm, her heart jumping. "Edith? From out west?"

The lady gave Belle an uncertain look. "From Muskoka. I'm Lynda Sidney, that's with an 'i'. Cece used to work with my husband in the labs at INCO."

Belle was in no mood to sort out which name contained the "i". "Sorry to confuse you. I'm Belle Palmer, a neighbour. Zack and I have been trying to contact a woman called Edith, but Anni's address book disappeared."

Lynda raised one threadlike eyebrow and shook her head slowly. "That doesn't sound like Anni. She was so organized."

"It is odd. Are you the friend she visited earlier this summer?"

The memory must have been warm, for her eyes misted over. "Our place is on a very small lake. No motorboats allowed. It was so quiet that evening. Anni and I took a canoe out to watch the sunset. Had a grand time catching up." She pulled a handkerchief from her purse and collected a tear which smudged her cheek, papery as a faded blue hydrangea. "Then she told me about how they put out bait for bears and what she had done. Sounded dangerous, I said, but she just patted my hand. Couldn't tell Anni one mortal thing. She was all for causes. NDP, of course." The New Democrats perched on the far left in Canadian politics. Though never in power nationally, this "Conscience of the House of Commons" had spearheaded such social welfare programs as universal health care and the Old Age pension.

As the last seats filled at the table, Zack tapped his glass lightly, only a quiver in his voice revealing his emotions. "Thank you for coming tonight. Aunt Anni wasn't a formal lady. She would be happy to be remembered by a gathering of friends." Belle was relieved that he wasn't getting lugubrious, sinking into guilt about his debts, moral and financial. Instead, he dwelt nostalgically upon boyhood summers with her and mentioned the volunteer work with modest praise. Later that week Anni would be cremated, and according to her wishes, the ashes scattered among the many floral beds she had loved.

Asked unexpectedly to say a few words, Belle rose with trepidation, taking a sip of water, focusing on Hélène's sympathetic face for encouragement. When was the last time she had made a formal presentation? A senior seminar on Jacobean Revenge Tragedy? Keep eye contact, don't use filler words like "um" and "uh" and remember that sincerity smooths the worst gaffes. She tossed aside the sterile rules and spoke from the heart. It was difficult not to feel frustrated at a killer still walking free, but bitter observations didn't belong in a eulogy. Their meeting amid the fragile blossoms kick-started her, and she pursued the nature theme. Anni's celebration of the wilderness, her forest paths, the gardens which crowned her property, and...she paused for effect, her devotion to animals. Finally the ordeal ended, and she resumed her seat in great relief to quiet nods from all and sniffs from dog owners, especially Hélène.

The savory roast beef was ferried in, medium rare, she noticed with approval, duchess potatoes, asparagus, salad and fresh blueberry pie to crown the meal. Zack had not scrimped in his tribute, so perhaps probate had been settled. As coffee cups were refilled and dishes clinked on trays, people began to rise for departure, clasping Zack's hand or patting his shoulder. A white-haired woman across the table had been hard to ignore, her thunderous voice dominating the conversation. After pausing at the liquor table, she sailed up to Belle like a colourful galleon, taking as ballast great gulps from what looked like a double Gibson. Maybe a triple. Under a fluffy yellow silk print dress with scalloped neckline were the shoulders of a wrestler,

Marjorie Main gone the route of Sly Stallone.

"I don't think we've…" Belle said, holding out her hand.

"Eh?" The woman adjusted a small device in one ear. "Maureen Murphy. Call me Murph. Liked your words about our girl. Did her proud." A healthy seventy-plus, she looked as if she could squeeze blood from the most wizened customer, and her grip confirmed the impression.

"I was at the Canadian Blood Services the other day," Belle said. "Melanie mentioned you as one of Anni's good friends."

"Siphoned enough red stuff together to float a ship. Served on one in my navy days," Murph answered in a gravelly voice tempered with a toothy grin from an era before orthodontia. "Knew Anni for donkey's years. Quite a shock. No accident either, I gather."

Belle stifled a smile. Was the woman speaking in abrupt fragments like some preposterous Colonel Blimp in the Pinewood Studio films? "Apparently not, yet they haven't made an arrest. You might say I'm prospecting unofficially for clues. Even something casual you talked about might lead to a breakthrough."

Murph pursed her lips, crumpled foil creased with animation, the lightest dust of face powder making peace with age instead of disguising it. "Just chewed the fat in slack times. Still trying to win back support after that damn tainted blood scare. Bunch of twerps. Can't get AIDS or hepatitis from donating, for Lord's sake." She drained the drink, popping the onions into her mouth like peppermints. "Now the Mad Cow fiasco's started."

"Was anything bothering her lately?"

A batwinged arm swept out in a casual gesture, barely missing a ducking waiter. "Usual old lady gab. Weather. High cost of living for seniors. Damn government wrecking our health care to balance the budget. Letting our water go to hell and sending us tax rebates to buy Naya. Never voted for those—"

The room had nearly emptied, and the DesRosiers were waving at her from behind a potted palm. Belle interrupted. "What about her new van? She must have been pleased."

Murph squinted in reflection, a bulldog ruminating over a problematical thigh bone. "Odd thing. Waltzed in out of the blue a week after our '78 Suburban went belly up at 400,000 klicks. Said she'd got it to drive donors and run errands. Damn handy timing."

"But that van cost a fortune. Where could she have found the money?"

"Beats me. Stretched the pennies like yours truly. Boosted that car all winter for her. Carry heavy duty cables. But…"

"Yes? You remembered something?"

"Different that last day. Teasing her about the van again as we left. Air conditioning, power whatzits. Asked if she'd nabbed her a sugar daddy. Know what that is?"

"Sure do. Along with rumble seats, bathtub gin and flappers. I learned my slang from classic movies." She cocked her head, interested in the repartee between two opposites. "What was Anni's answer?"

"'Bitter fruit,' she said. The sly old cat. How do you like that?" Proving that she could complete a sentence, Murph plucked the last unopened wine bottle and shoved it into her massive purse with a wink.

What had Anni meant by that famous radio signature: "The weed of crime bears bitter fruit"? Clearly reverse gear from the impression she had given the salesman about an ill wind bringing good. And after the good, why remorse? Tainted blood in the gift of life? Why had she changed her mind? Only the Shadow knew.

131

THIRTEEN

Tuesday, Tuesday kept rolling around again, time to collect her father's lunch. Maybe she could catch Zack to discuss the letter. It had been in her briefcase for days, but the dinner hadn't seemed like a politic moment. Belle headed for the restaurant, surprised by the lopsided grin which greeted her. Fred, Maria's second best customer, commandeered a pot from the counter, escorted her to a chair like a maître de, and straightened his tie, emboldened with a large beaver. "Complimentary coffee all week," he said, taking special effort to master his diction. "Guess who's the new owner?"

Belle shook his hand, newly strong and confident. She should have guessed from his hints about plans. "Now those marketing courses will come in handy, but don't juggle any books, just the dishes. Say, though, you have to maintain standards. Did Maria toss in her recipes?" Luscious homemade gravy was the elixir which elevated the simple café meals to nirvana. With bitter winters and chill nights even in summer, Sudburians needed arterial transfusions year round.

"Big Mama gave me lessons before she left. Boil up a ton of bones late Sunday's the trick. Ten pails do her." He set his mouth with pride, rubbing a freshly-shaved chin bearing a few nicks. "The usual order? I know how you like your dad's shrimp. Hold the seafood sauce. Fries and lots of cole slaw. Hey, cherry pie today."

"New staff, too?" The coffee was hot and robust, a good sign.

"My sister Fran's our waitress. Just broke up with her husband and needs a job. The cook's a pal from my rehab therapy. Gosh, we're a real support group."

Cadaverous and waxen, her hair in a lacquered bouffant draining strength from her small frame, Fran moved timidly around the restaurant. Thick makeup couldn't disguise the mottled colours of a bruised eye. Back in the open kitchen, a strangely familiar figure pushed a broom. Belle took a second glance. "Who's your helper?"

"That's Craig. He sweeps up for meals and the odd buck. Washes supper dishes to spell Fran before closing."

"He passed me once on Brewster Street." She tried to be discreet, but he looked even more like Steve now that the beard had been trimmed to a neat goatee and the long hair gathered into a shiny ponytail.

Fred learned forward and lowered his voice. "Might have. Couple of weeks ago I saw him dumpster-diving in an alley downtown. Booze is his problem, nothing special up here. Helped him find a rooming house around the corner. It's pretty quiet in Garson. No biker bars or dope deals. Best way to straighten out is stay away from bad habits, 'friends in low places,' as the song goes. Got to start fresh, get out of the ruts."

Belle followed his facial expressions and body language, occasionally asking for a repeat instead of patronizing him with non-committal replies. "You should have been a psychologist, Fred. Breaking new paths is important." She recalled her depression over her mother's death from cancer and the distractions she had used to heal, namely the purchase of a sharp-toothed, inquisitive shepherd pup. Would Steve welcome good news about Craig? Maybe she should stay out of family business after witnessing the raw nerves behind his feelings.

From her window seat, she watched Craig ply his way in methodical deliberation to the front of the restaurant, twisting the broom expertly to snare every dustball and crumb. His brown work pants were unpressed but clean, with a denim shirt buttoned to the neck. Even the scuffed boots gleamed with a spit shine. He cocked a thumb toward the door, and when Fred nodded, went outside and lit a cigarette, leaning against a post and staring at a buxom babe in shorts and a swimsuit top scissoring herself out of a Miata. A teenager in a Marilyn Manson T-shirt leaving the Mac's store next door seemed to be badgering a young child, snatching at his package. It seemed like harmless teasing until the bag fell, scattering the contents and spilling open a milk carton. Sinking to his knees, the boy scrambled for the groceries while the grinning teen stuffed fallen candy bars into his own pockets. Suddenly Craig flipped away his cigarette and grabbed the youth, holding him firmly and whispering into his ear until he handed back the candy and ran. After helping the sobbing child rise, Craig opened his wallet and pressed a blue five-dollar bill into the youngster's hand. Saturday Matinee without a ticket. Prince Valiant's got the real moxie, Belle thought.

When he returned to the broom, she caught his eye. "I saw that. Good for you."

One corner of his mouth rose to reveal a missing tooth, then lowered in apparent embarrassment. "No big deal, Miss. Don't like to see kids pushed around, that's all." He straightened his shoulders and walked to the kitchen like a knight in denim armour. Was that a soft whistle she heard?

Fred was helping his sister wrestle mammoth hot turkey sandwich platters, three pounds of food per serving, including fresh-cut fries and vegetables. "Craig's a hard one to talk to. Do him good to make some friends, though," he said, nodding like a concerned parent, despite their similarity in age.

Belle collected the meal and drove the few blocks to Rainbow Country as the Statler Brothers celebrated Thomas Edison, for "giving us the best years of our lives." She and her father had loved playing that song's game on long car trips. The first person named a film, and the opponent had to start another with the last word. No simple *Caine Mutiny* and *Mutiny on the Bounty*, *Rio Grande* and *Grand Hotel* stuff. This was expert territory. *All About Eve*, *Eve Knew Her Apples*, a musical version of *It Happened One Night* with leggy Ann Miller. Or *Hunchback of Notre Dame* which her father countered with Busby Berkeley's *Dames*. She ceded him that round because of its lead tune, "When You Were a Smile on Your Mother's Lips and a Twinkle in Your Daddy's Eye." Since his cumulative strokes, their contest had faded to a poignant memory.

"Lunch day?" Cherie asked from the desk, sniffing the rich seafood aroma. "You are a sweetheart. Never miss a week. Were you close when you were a child?" Her warm brown eyes looked sincere and motherly rather than inquisitive.

Belle recalled toddling along to private screenings as soon as she could walk, receiving a nickel for the ancient red Coke machine between features. Often alone in the little theatre in his office building, she sprawled in the front row with him one row behind. "I guess we shared a love of films more than anything else," she said. "Maybe it's genetic. But one thing for sure. Whatever I did was right. Can't ask more than that." Besides, she thought, his unconditional love balanced the demands of her mother, who frowned at an A minus.

A bit groggy that day, perhaps from a change in medication, her father ate slowly and seemed to want to nap after lunch, so she helped him to his bed and cleaned up in record time. When she stopped later at Zack's to return the letter, he was hammering new boards onto the deck. The bushes and perennial beds were freshly nipped, and a brush pile sat by the lake ready to be fired, garden hose nearby. The tantalizing smell of roasting meat reminded her that the chicken intended for dinner was as icy as the lake in February. Captain and Sam were clearly expecting largesse, parking themselves downwind and minding their manners for a change.

"A white bleeding heart," she said, tracing a finger along one delicate row, from the embryo stage to the full drooping bloom. "Hard to find up here."

"Take one. Seed themselves, Aunt Anni used to say. And how about a hot dog and a beer?" he asked, pointing to a sizzling grill with buns and trimmings on the side shelf. "Later we can play Boy Scouts and burn that brush pile."

"Not unless you have a permit, Zack. And only after dark." In forest fire territory, a wisp of smoke during the day and a contingent of planes or helicopters based at the Sudbury Airport would descend on the naughty cottager like a black and yellow wolf on the fold.

"Thanks for the warning, and for speaking about Aunt Anni at the dinner. I'll get you a bag for that plant," he said, heading for the house.

Belle never turned down a free meal or a free perennial. After preparing the shoot and its earth ball, she bit into the sausage he offered, appreciative of the fiery mustard. "You did a fine job yourself. But I came with a question. A letter fell out of that Peterson guide…and I read it. Shabby ethics, or what?"

He waved off her confession and unfolded the paper she presented, shaking his head as he scanned. "Maybe you had the right idea about her past. The scary part is what's left unsaid. Know what I mean?"

"I thought so, too. No date, of course, but it doesn't look that old. From the reference to marriage, I'm guessing that the letter came fairly recently from someone who knew her in western Ontario. Where exactly was she?"

He frowned, sucking on the beer for inspiration. "I was just a kid. Some animal name, that's all."

"In this country, only 1001 places. South Porcupine, Caribou Lake, Whitefish Falls, Marten River, Heron Bay."

"Maybe I'll have a brain wave. Anyway, it was some god-forsaken spot."

"This mess seems to have taken place years ago. Sounds like she had gone to some trouble to find this Verna. Written for information. Or called. Did you keep her long distance bills?" His vacant look answered. "We have to track down this place, Zack. Tell me everything she said about that town."

"Aunt Anni was pretty serious, not one to gossip. I think I told you that she assisted a dentist. He was nearly retired but did charity work with poor kids. For sure, she loved those youngsters. Never could have any of her own, Mom said." He wiped mustard from his mouth. "Guess that explains why she spoiled me."

"What about the dentist? Any hope of finding him?"

He shrugged, then shook his head. "Never said his name. God, he was decades older than she was. That's a dead end unless he's a hundred."

"Did she mention an Edith?"

"That's a name I'd remember." He threw up his hands. "Nada. Zip. And the address book's still missing. I asked that guy, Steve, but he said that it wasn't on their list of evidence."

"Damn," she said. "This is the first break, but there's no substance."

Snapping his fingers, he excused himself and returned a

minute later with a black and white photo in a shiny silver frame. "Think this might be the place. Aunt Anni wasn't big on photos. Luckily it's one from Mom's album, a special keepsake I brought over with my things. Nothing written on the back, but the time looks right. About twenty-five or thirty years younger, wouldn't you say?"

Belle considered the snapshot, disappointingly amateurish with its sun flares. "Scrub bush. Black spruce. Must be the dentist beside her, and you're right. He's quite the fossil. Nothing else except…" She turned it around, wishing that she could sharpen the focus. "That curious steeple sticking up in the background. An octagon with a timber spire. A little piece of England in the brave new world."

The next morning, after settling the white bleeding heart between two clumps of sea pinks, Belle took Freya to the turnaround, rescuing a nine-inch earthworm crawling across the road by placing it on a bed of humus in the shade. "Sure you can have sex with yourself, don't even brush your teeth, but you don't have the sense to stay off the gravel." Then she spied an ominous striped shape inching toward the lakeside. How many feet a day could an army of tent caterpillars advance? Gleefully she stomped on it, one less potential cocoon to spin destruction.

At the Rogers' camp, six dogs sat on the property line observing her quietly, the spotted pup among others apparently redeemed from the pound. Only cars interested them, or perhaps a German shepherd kept them in line. At their first meeting, Freya had raised her hackles, given tongue and chased them howling back to their property. As Belle turned to dance a tarantella on a few more 'pillars for good measure, Charles called her down to his gate, lifting a small basket. "Funniest thing. This present was left hanging here with a card. 'Welcome to the Neighbourhood.' From a Mrs. Ben Drummond. Does she live nearby? I haven't heard you mention her." He rubbed Freya's ears with an intimacy she rarely allowed strangers.

With a hundred properties lining the shore, several were bound to change hands each summer. Usually Belle got the first call, but a quick swap between friends might have sneaked by. "Drummond doesn't sound familiar. It might be a visiting relative, some coffee klatsch gossiping over the new bachelor," she answered with a hint of humour feathering her mouth. It was a fun to play turnabout, after the teasing she had experienced as a single woman on the road.

Blithely innocent to the game, he unwrapped a red-flowered cloth to reveal a dozen delicate yellow-orange mushrooms, distinctive funnel-shapes. A delighted smile warmed his face, as if Christmas had arrived early. "Chanterelles, if I'm not mistaken. I've had them in Ottawa restaurants, very dear indeed," he announced. "She's a generous lady to share her wealth. They'll be scrumptious in a scramble with a sprinkling of fresh chives. Sure you can't join me?"

Belle fingered the bright material, a high quality linen, then shook her head with reluctance. "Work calls, you lucky retiree. Rain check." At his insistence, she poked one into her sweatshirt pouch.

Something mumbled in a distant corner of her mind all the way home, a cynical little imp, or was it a caution from Anni's lessons? Why shouldn't some kind woman have thought of Charles? Garden produce often got passed around, especially the scandalously fecund zucchini, scourge of August. Still, it wouldn't hurt to check her fungi book.

At the shelf in the computer room, she leafed through several pages. Then her hands started shaking. Across from the picture of the succulent prize sprouted a tempting double. "Jack O'Lantern. Very close to the edible chanterelle, but oranger and poisonous. No pleasant apricot smell." Reading the next heart-stopping line with widening eyes, she pushed into the storage closet, elbowing aside her huge down coat like a truculent mammoth and pulling the folding doors behind her. In the dark, this mushroom emitted an eerie green glow, just as the text warned. In an instant she was on the phone, only to find a busy signal. Was that a good sign? Could he be eating and talking at the same time?

Her van rounded the corner at Rogers' place, narrowly missing a strolling spruce grouse. Down Charles' lane she screeched, dodging a lawn tractor and nudging three potted fruit trees. Without knocking, she charged into the kitchen to the marshalling beats of the "William Tell Overture" on his stereo. He looked mildly astonished, as if she had suffered a fatal lack of manners but poured her a coffee without blinking.

"Just cream, isn't it?"

"Sorry, Charles. No time for niceties. Your line was busy. You haven't tasted that gift yet, have you?"

He pointed to a sizzling pan, the air rich with butter. "Why? What's wrong? I was calling the weather line, or as they call it, da wedderline. That dialect tickles my ear."

She flopped into a chair, her breathing returning to normal, noting the chopped mushrooms still on the counter. "Oh, nothing. Just gastric upset possibly leading to convulsions. Probably survivable, healthy man like you. Jack O'Lanterns aren't as deadly as the infamous amanitas or the corts."

"Jack...my God." He sat down heavily, mopping his brow with his apron, colour bleached from his face. "The poor soul must have made a dreadful blunder. Do you suppose she gave them to anyone else? We should call her immediately."

Belle picked up a phone book and traced a few columns, snapping it shut with an irritated frown. "There's no Ben Drummond listed. Let's see that note again."

He gestured outside at the smoking sauna pipe. "I burned it starting the stove. A test run."

"And the basket?"

His expression showed a momentary sign of relief. "That, I saved. It seemed handy for collecting my raspberries. Looks like a bumper crop's coming." Out of a closet he lifted a typical two-quart cardboard basket with a wooden handle.

Examining purple stains on the bottom, Belle sighed hopelessly. "Ubiquitous. A million of them every blueberry season. The note might have told us more."

He rubbed at his hands, shrinking for the first time into the pose of an old man. "I'm not sure I follow. What are you implying?"

Belle sipped the coffee, unable to avoid noticing that his machine was the purest white, instead of all-concealing black plastic like hers. The tablecloth looked freshly ironed, and infinite pasta varieties sat in clear graduated canisters on the shelves. What a wonderful wife Charles would have made. "How's the dog situation?"

"What? Oh, I see, but that's unthinkable. People don't poison neighbours over dogs," he said, his face a mirror of righteous indignation betrayed by a tic which rustled one eye. "Or do they? Should we call the police?"

Charles was such a baby. She resisted an urge to laugh at his naïveté. "Remember my van? I didn't tell you that the damage might have been done in my yard. Didn't want you to worry. Somebody comes down this road at night, they can get away with...anything. First, let's be sure about this Mrs. Drummond. I'll check Ed's list of property owners."

"The plowman?"

"Ed's President of the Road Association, a dubious distinction. Just an ad hoc group we formed to keep government on its toes. Bring in those Neighbourhood Watch signs, make sure the garbage collection is regular, dump asphalt into the potholes before they swallow smaller children. Anyway, this could be a very vicious prank, so as they say in gangster films, watch your back. And since you're a regular at the pound, you might think of adopting a nice junkyard dog. The old 'can't beat 'em, join 'em' rule." As she rose to leave, he shook his head soberly, dumped out the mushrooms and began scouring the pan with religious fervour.

The roar of a chainsaw greeted her as Belle pulled into Ed's drive. He was slicing birch while Hélène held the log on the battered sawhorse. Looking up, his wife ran her finger over her throat so that he cut the throttle and turned around. "God in heaven," Hélène said, removing her ear protection. "I can't hear, and the sawdust is killing my eyes. The old man's half-deaf anyway."

"Time for a break," Ed said, hauling them to the kitchen table.

Belle refused the offer of more coffee, looking in consternation at her watch. Would she never get to town? "I need to check your list of property owners."

"What's up? Are you ambulance chasing? Didn't hear of no one dying lately."

She bristled at his jibe but decided to dismiss it in good humour. "Very funny. And if you mean Whitman's place last year, his daughter called me. It might interest you to know that Charles Sullivan was given a basket of poison mushrooms."

Ed plumped out his apple cheeks. "No kidding! The new guy? Is he from Toronto or something? We don't eat no funny fungi don't come from the supermarket," he said, stuffing a piece of banana bread in his mouth and walking his fingers toward the butter.

Hélène tapped his arm in mid-motion, and he drew back like a chastened kid. "We love Cousin Berthe's mushroom stew, Ed, but she has her patches on the farm."

Belle narrowed her eyes. "Maybe a mistake, maybe not. There was a note saying that they were from a Mrs. Drummond. Charles has been having trouble with the Rogers' dogs. I wouldn't put this stunt past Mabel Joy."

"Mabel Joy?" said Hélène. "This is starting to make sense. Her grandmother, bless her soul passed on now, was a famous one for wild mushrooms. Mabel Joy used to carry her pails. Snotty kid she was, too full of herself for our boys."

Ed came back with the list, scratching his stomach where his Expos shirt hiked up. "No Drummond. Didn't ring a bell, and we've been here forty years."

"Listen," Belle said. "I'll take care of Mabel Joy. As for Charles, he needs a friend. You like fishing, and so does he. He doesn't have a boat and might appreciate knowing about a place where he could fish from the bank. Why not take him to that kettle lake by the Airport Road?"

FOURTEEN

Miriam pasted on a stamp, licked and sealed the envelope and placed it on a small pile of mail. She rubbed her thumb and index finger together and shot a mischievous grin across the room. "With six sales this month, you can afford to give me a raise."

A mental close-up over the balance sheet made Belle grimace. A bonus was a kiss, a raise a commitment. "Listen, Madame What-Have-You-Done-For-Me-Lately, we had to share the commissions on three. And even if this is the peak season, you know our ups and downs. A strike at INCO or Falconbridge is always around the corner." She selected the cream-filled morsels from a box of Timbits. Who said something couldn't come from nothing? The enterprising doughnut chain fried the scrap holes into moneymakers. Maybe Zack should get into recycling. All those tires dumped in the bush to avoid disposal fees could be sliced up and woven into blasting site mats. She munched for a moment, then got up and went to the window, sighing mournfully.

"Where did I put the address of that food bank?" Miriam plucked the last chocolate rounds from the box, then watched Belle pace. "For heaven's sake, what's wrong with you? Settle down. You're making me nervous."

"Well, to run with the food metaphor, I love a full plate, but not full of worries. Anni, Zack, now more problems.

Remember Mr. Sullivan? He was invaded by a pack of dogs."

"Wild dogs?"

"Of course not. They belonged to the Rogers next door. Anyway, with no cooperation from them, he took a couple to the pound. That's when he received a warning."

"Sounds intriguing. What kind of warning? Dead seagull tacked to the door?"

"Oh, a friendly note and *eine kleine* poisonous mushroom in the innocent Canadian night." She hummed a snatch of Mozart.

"Do we have a Lucretia Borgia here? Poisoning's a feminine art. Women have always been the experts in what's edible and what's not." Miriam narrowed lizard eyes in juicy contemplation. "I can see her now. Smooth as chocolate chiffon pie. And speaking of…" she poked into the box. "There's only cinnamon left, and we hate those. Next time ask for our favourites. You're assertive enough about refusing raises."

Belle refused to continue sparring. "I have a suspicion Mabel Joy Rogers is the culprit, but he burned the note. A fake name anyway. Just another annoyance to the police. I've got to drop a few very strong hints, without just walking in cold. She's not smart, but she's shrewd. Much more dangerous."

"Do they have a place in town? Offer her a free appraisal. Say there's a buyer interested. It's a foolproof temptation, especially for a big house." Miriam winked. "Good time to look around, too. Check out her rings for flip tops."

"The pellet with the poison's in the chalice from the palace." Or was it? Danny Kaye had her head whirling. While Miriam got Mabel Joy on the line, Belle pictured her neighbour. "Chiffon" to the last atom, all fluff and no substance. In their few chance meetings, she had taken an instant dislike to the pretentious puppet. Five minutes of conversation picking roadside berries had dangled the names of the Shield University president, the Mayor, local MPs and MPPs along with barbs about welfare mothers, immigrants, gays and aboriginals, all under the guise of "what was right for society." That lethal old bromide covered every personal prejudice, as dangerous now as it had been in the Russian pogroms, the McCarthy era, or the Attack on America which had levelled the Trade Towers and galvanized Canada's best ally into a state of wartime alert.

Her husband Earl ran Rogers Concrete, a blue-collar success his wife never forgave, though she inhaled the profits like Royal Bank stock dividends, the license on her lilac Cadillac reading "MY WAY." From pointed comments about local bumpkins and cultural drydock, it was also obvious that she hated living in Sudbury. The two kids were in their twenties, both provinces away from Mommie Dearest.

After listening for a long, uninterrupted period, gesturing theatrically at Belle and making encouraging faces, Miriam finally hung up. "Showtime. Oh, she mentioned a condo in New Mexico. Work that angle."

Earl and Mabel Joy bedded down in fashionable Northern Lights, an upscale development dozed over blasted rockface. No triflers at under 300K, please. The megamonster houses squatted like designer toads on their minuscule lots, dominating the landscape instead of harmonizing, overpriced suburban sprawl from Orlando to Los Angeles to Vancouver to Halifax. 1200 Orion Crescent rose three blocky storeys with a triple garage. Taupe brick, Spanish tile roof, an antebellum portico and English Tudor windows. An architect on Prozac? The salmon lockstone pavement, which clashed with the Caddy, was bordered by mugho pines and spreading junipers along the walkway. Standing like an encyclopedia hawker in front of the double doors, etched glass and shiny brass, Belle pressed the buzzer while chimes clanged "The Sound of Music" and a fierce yapping developed inside, followed by leaping scratches like chalk on a blackboard.

After a well-timed pause, one door opened and Mabel Joy appeared in a silver lamé jumpsuit better for ogling than for exercise. With a theatrical smile, she swept back a honey-blonde mane and executed a leg movement worthy of Margot Fonteyn to shove aside what appeared to be the fattest Lhasa Apso on record. A self-actuating dustmop.

"So soon? I'm impressed. Business must be slow."

Behind a closed-lip smile, Belle clenched her teeth together before answering, a few dental isometrics to manage a professional tone. "Not at all, Mabel Joy. I was volunteering at the soup kitchen and just ladled out the last of the minestrone." Some day I should do that, she thought, remembering Fred's support group.

Mabel Joy's face didn't twitch, thanks to Toronto's premier nip-and-tuck surgeon, or just mighty good practice. "Such a worthy cause. Before I became allergic to cats, I was Vice-President of the Homeless Persian Society." She checked her watch with thinly disguised impatience. "Let's get started. Your girl said that you'd do a thorough appraisal, and though I don't believe for a minute that you have a buyer lined up, Belle, such a stale old ploy, I have been thinking of using the house as collateral for a condo in Santa Fe," she said. Then she retreated as if on wheels into a marble foyer leading to a spiral staircase perfect for Rhett Butler's famous climb and Scarlett's equally famous fall. The air reeked of lemon oil.

Belle followed the brisk tour, jotting notes to match Mabel Joy's staccato delivery. The classy touches were as expected in newer, high-end homes built during the Nickel Capital's last boom, distressed oak floors, a gas fireplace in the sitting room and a master suite large enough for beach volleyball. The kitchen rivalled a set for a television cooking show. "I'm very proud of this," the woman added, flipping open whisper-quiet doors to reveal custom-made spice racks and appliance hutches amid acres of light blue-grained oak shelving. She tapped sequined fingernails on a tiled island framing a Jenn-Air grill. "So convenient in the long winters, if you must spend them here, that is."

Belle could have blinked back icy tears recalling her stubborn efforts at barbecuing on the deck during blizzards. They cruised by five bedrooms, four bathrooms, a combination library and computer room, and a cedar sauna in the basement. On the recreation room wall, Mabel Joy pulled down a screen which served as a giant television via satellite connection projector. "Saves so much space." In the exercise room sat every apparatus in the history of body building: weight-lifting centres, stair-stepper, treadmill and a twisty torturer she described as an ab machine, patting her flat stomach with an annoying smirk. Belle sucked in her gut all the way outside.

The back yard butted against a rock outcrop, framed by tall redwood fences. A graceful pool with waterlilies and a bronze cherub spouting water from a questionable place made a peaceful setting for garden furniture of white wrought iron. Scant privacy, though, since from the second floor vantage of any neighbouring house, all properties gave free shows. Belle's eyes followed several golden shapes swimming in leisure around the pond. "Beautiful koi. I used to have an aquarium. You must need a big tank to keep them through the winter," she said.

Mabel Joy flicked a pebble into the pond, startling the fish into a frenzy. "They're cheap enough. Give them to the cats next door every freeze-up and get new ones in May."

Stifling an urge to make an anonymous call to the Royal Society for the Protection of Carp, Belle tallied up the juicy additions which would add bucks to the value, making a note to learn what nearby houses had sold for lately to add credibility to her appraisal. Looking at this conspicuous consumption, it was hard to comprehend how mean-spirited, not to mention murderous, Mabel Joy was acting at the cottage. And where were the animals? Other than the obnoxious scratching machine, there was no sign, not a kennel or dog house, and no dark hair floating around the creamy leather sofa and chairs.

Finally the last chandelier had tinkled and the final eat-in closet had been shut, the gas heat extolled along with the low-e windows. Mabel Joy seemed to grit her pearly caps as she offered Belle a cup of tea, banging down a box of Twining's Earl Grey and boiling water, hauling open drawers for napkins and spoons to complete the token gesture as quickly as possible. Her notebook full, her bag of ideas empty, Belle was ruminating on how to deliver her message without seeming a fool.

Suddenly a red flash in a cabinet caught her eye, and she moved quietly into a chair beside a withered pothos, a plant nearly impossible to kill. "You're considering a condo in the States?" she asked.

With a bright smile, Mabel Joy skipped the warm-the-pot stage and plunged the stainless steel tea ball into the boiling water like a bathysphere cut loose. "Have you been to the Southwest, Belle? It's heaven in the winter. Theatre, quaint little art studios, conversation with more than two-syllable words. And the restaurants. I get so tired of our options: steak, spaghetti and chop suey, not to mention the 'wattleyousehave' mentality. So lovely and dry there, too. A godsend for those of us tormented by allergies."

"Florida's the only southern state I've visited. My father reti…"

"Oh, Florida's just a tourist trap now. Maybe fifty years ago it was a decent spot before all those doddering retirees and then the boat people. 'Castro's dumpsite,' my friends who left Miami call it." Her lips pursed, revealing vertical age lines sucking back fuchsia lipstick while she flapped a bejewelled hand in derision. No compartments, though, just blinding diamonds.

Belle drank quietly, controlling her temper by savouring the smoky tang for a moment. Then she spilled her cup with a clumsy motion. "Oh, darn, don't get up. I'm closer," she said, reaching for a nearby drawer and pulling out a familiar red-flowered cloth. "I forgot to ask. How are you getting along with your new neighbour?" she asked as she blotted with vigour, giving the table a finishing polish and flapping the cloth like a flag.

A flush lit the ivory coast of Mabel Joy's face. "Whom do you mean?" Her little finger trembled as she raised her cup. That pose belonged with the mannered films of the early Thirties. Constance Bennett? Good grammar, though, probably lectured poor Earl about saying "anyways."

"Why, Charles Sullivan, that charming man. You're lucky he bought Brown's place instead of a family with teenagers and noisy Seadoos. He's done wonders with the property already." She added a pregnant pause and looked around pointedly. "Say, where are the rest of your dogs? I'm always…passing them on the road. Awfully friendly, aren't they?"

Mabel Joy cleared her throat, fixated on the cloth as if it were the Shroud of Turin. "Well, except for Fluffhead, my baby, they stay at the plant unless we're at the camp. Earl built a fenced run behind the mixers."

Poor mutts, she thought, inhaling cement dust twenty-four hours a day. Meanwhile her hands examined the serviette, searching for a tag. "What fine linen. Did you buy it in Toronto, or is this something extra special from the States?"

As she left, Belle felt that Mabel Joy had gotten the message, clunky or not. There was a satisfying expediency about simple social dynamics before governments added complications like jury trials and expensive prisons. Medieval communities policed themselves quite nicely, discounting a few witch burnings. What would they have done to a poisoner? Something poetic, no doubt. She pictured Mabel Joy pressed to death with bags of Cartier tennis bracelets.

Rain began to splatter on the pavement as she drove back across town, and a traffic jam made her detour along Brewster Street. Slowing for a light, she thumped the steering column to the beat of Leonard Cohen's "The Future," the apocalyptic lyrics an ironic comment on urban life: "I've seen the future, brother: it is murder." Then the door of a shabby hotel opened, and Craig lumbered out, burdened by a suitcase fastened with rope and a cardboard box on his shoulder, frowning as the rain hit his face. Perhaps he was shifting his belongings to that rooming house Fred had mentioned. Rolling down the window, she yelled, "Care for a ride? I'm going through Garson."

He squinted for a moment, then gave a ghost of a smile in recognition. With a grunt, he unloaded his baggage and slipped into the front seat, wiping his eyes. "Thanks. I remember you from the restaurant. Craig's my name."

"Belle Palmer." She turned off the radio.

He nodded and shook her hand in an oddly old-fashioned

gesture. They travelled a few blocks in silence, past an underpass infamous for muggings. At the petition of women's groups, safety mirrors had been erected at each end. Belle paused to let a stooped form with a grocery pullcart jaywalk across the street. Bag lady or just a baba heading home to cook cabbage rolls? Poverty was well-clothed in North America, invisible from a distance. A boy, a young man, it was hard to tell in the growing darkness, leaned against a wall of graffiti and moved his slim pelvis suggestively while a Volvo station wagon lingered at an alley. As Belle stepped on the accelerator, an arm motioned from the wagon's window, and the boy started towards the car. "Stop!" Craig yelled suddenly.

Startled by the command, she slammed on the brakes, and he jumped out, running to the Volvo and pounding on the hood. The driver, his face contorted with fear, screeched away, while the young boy lit a cigarette and turned to leave. Craig touched his shoulder, gesturing more in frustration than anger, but the boy tossed back wet blond hair, yanked a sweatshirt hood forward and ducked into the underpass as the wind picked up and sheets of rain lashed the pavement.

Craig climbed back into the van, shivering, his head in his hands. Belle looked at him in dim confusion, marvelling at how easily fiction blended with fact and how distant this lowlife scene was from her wilderness, though barely twenty miles separated them. How had she survived in Toronto?

"Sorry," he said, straightening up. "Thanks for waiting."

"And drive off with your luggage? I could never show my face at Fred's again." She laughed to break the tension, juiced the heater to dry him off. "Who was that guy?"

"Never told me his real name. Calls himself Jedi. That's how they operate. No two the same. Helps clients find who they want."

"Clients. I should have guessed. You mean male prostitution." Predators and prey on the pavements. She was surprised to imagine a meat market outside of large cities, but perhaps she had grown naïve, returning each evening to her sanctuary on the lake.

Craig's voice was gravelly, strong with contempt. "They make me sick. Did you see that station wagon? Fancy kiddie seats in the back. Probably told his wife he had to work late, the bastard."

"Can you help…Jedi?"

"I'm no social worker. And even if I was, he likes his freedom, or thinks he does. Anyway, how can a fourteen-year-old make a living?"

Belle dropped him at a large old building around the corner from Fred's restaurant. A tattered Canadian flag hung from one window, a gutter broken above, spewing a deluge of rust stains down the cracked stucco façade. Yet hanging by the front door were two pots of geraniums. A young girl sweeping the steps gave Craig a winning smile. As Belle drove away, a devious idea whispered in her ear. If she told Steve about the two-for-one hot turkey sandwiches on Wednesday nights as a special lure, perhaps he might meet his brother there.

It was later than usual by the time she turned down her road and noticed with some dismay that Patsy Sommers' car was missing. As a rule, she made her shopping trips in the early morning. Visiting relatives? One of those long disappearances nearly every other year? Belle heard the dogs barking inside at the sound of the van. The brief rain had only added to the stifling humidity, yet windows and doors were shut tight.

After a late dinner of pasta salad made with black olives, red peppers and salmon, Belle called Charles to tell him about the impromptu play at Mabel Joy's. "And you're really convinced that she was the guilty party?" he asked, dismay in his voice. "A woman of her position? It beggars belief. More like a cheap tabloid."

"You're a babe in the woods, Charles. Clearly it galled her to ransom the dogs at the pound. Maybe she stewed about it. Then she remembered Grandmother's hobby and banked on your naïveté. It's easy to poison people. I've ripped up deadly nightshade in a field by my father's nursing home. Purple monkshood looks spectacular in perennial gardens. Potato sprouts can be chopped into a pretty salad." He remained silent as she continued. "We didn't stand a chance at pinning her down without the note, and with her shrewdness, she probably wore gloves. Doesn't matter now. I think you're home free."

"On that happy turn of events, I'm off for a dip," he said.

Turning out the light, Belle went to the bedroom window for a final commune with the lake. On the second floor, the heat was becoming oppressive, despite her ceiling fan. A thump resounded on the glass, and the dog nosed slobber on the patio door screen. Dragonflies were back, chomping up the mosquitoes. Warily she eased out onto the narrow deck, a builder's decoration useful only for blessing crowds Papal style. Not a bite, she cheered, thanks to the helicoptering insects. One neon marvel landed on her hand and sat as content as a trained bird, its isinglass wings catching rainbows from the reflected sunset, all twelve billion eyes surveying her in an information overload. Across at the Reserve, familiar lights winked, the first greeting each black winter morning. Who it was, she hadn't a clue, but she welcomed the kinship of all those who enjoyed the lake, like Anni, her friend who was probably pretty damn mad. The end of July already, and no one had the faintest idea who had killed her.

FIFTEEN

It was hellish hot at dawn, but the waterbed thermostat hadn't gone berserk. The annual heat wave had begun, an all-too-brief experience. Tossing on a madras pantsuit from her historical collection, Belle checked a calendar for appointments, then realized that she had pencilled in an open house for Tuesday. Father's lunch would have to hop a day ahead, but he wouldn't mind. Driving to town shortly after seven to get an early start at work, she slowed at the Sommers' place. No car, and still the dogs sang in chorus. Patsy was probably gone with the children, leaving the poor beasts to roast inside, despite the disgusting ramifications. Meddling or not, she should call the SPCA.

The office was quiet. Belle flicked on the air conditioner, stood in front of it for a moment flapping her arms, then charged up the coffee maker. At her desk, she sat down and pulled Anni's letter from her briefcase, reading it for the umpteenth time. If only she could find out where the woman had worked, over what Godforsaken place that curious octagonal steeple presided. Might Edith write again? Too Good to be True usually was.

Miriam banged through the door with a box of office supplies and started loading paper into the fax machine. "The last air conditioner north of Barrie has been sold, Sears said, Canadian Tire, too. Sat up half the night with a bag of ice on my head. I came to work to get cool. Can I rent a cot here tonight?"

"Be my guest. No charge." Belle watched office workers in shorts cross the street, water bottles in hand. Part of her wished that she could bed down here tonight instead of trudging home. "The heat's going to make tempers short. Steve says crime jumps in the summer. But even if pushed to the limits, can you imagine killing someone?"

Her eyes were red and swollen, but Miriam's expression was hard to read. Dead pan funny or drop dead serious. "Yes."

"Are you joking?"

"I said yes. Why do you ask?"

An unusual abruptness. A bad night's sleep made anyone crabby. Or perhaps Miriam was having problems with her daughter. Belle pursed her lips and sat back in the chair. "Anni's death is becoming a cold case, so I'm grasping at straws. This was a deliberate murder of a decent woman."

Miriam spoke evenly, sharpening a pencil with calm deliberation, adjusting the wheel for maximum point until the tip pleased her appraising finger. "Perhaps she was. Perhaps she wasn't. Once upon a time the most decent man in our family was Uncle Phil. Took the collection at church, kind to animals, devoted to kids. Everyone loved him. The best disguise in the world. Always is. That's how they get away with it."

That explained Miriam's face when they had been discussing the abuse movie. What words to say? No matter how old you got, life always served up a custard pie to catch you off guard, Georgy Girl. She felt her pulse quicken in the silence. Comparing a tragedy like that with dessert. "I never imagined. You're always so…I mean…did he…" She bit her tongue.

Her friend gave a dark laugh. "Don't jump to grubby conclusions, Belle. You know me. I settled his hash. Even at twelve I had spunk. But I never opened my mouth. Not until my daughter told me what he tried with her. I was still married to Jack then, and he nailed the old man a good one. No one talks to him now. He's isolated and lonely as he deserves to be. I'd have him rotting in jail, but Grandma would have died."

Belle knew Miriam, and no weeping and demure patting of backs was expected. With no further words, they turned to their respective chores, plastering welcome smiles on their faces as a client walked in.

Later, during her father's meal, and he would insist on the usual hot food, Belle was preoccupied, not only by the brutal temperatures as the day wore on, but by the Sommers situation. The phone line at the SPCA had been busy all morning. She flapped his *National Enquirer* and nibbled in desultory fashion at a tuna salad sandwich, getting up to adjust the fan and close the curtains against the relentless sun. Air conditioners weren't standard in most Sudbury homes, much less in an older building like Rainbow Country. Madame exercise lady looked more chipper than ever, and why not, since chipper was her business?

A college student on placement came by with a metal carafe of ice water. "The nurses want everybody to drink as much as possible," she said. "He'll get an extra sponge bath before bed."

Belle glanced now and then at the old man, mildly dismayed at his swelling cheeks. "Swallow now, Father. Take some cold water." He reached out a gnarly hand for his glass while she read an article about shark cartilage as a possible cure for arthritis. They could be right. Years before doctors confirmed the link, the tabloid had revealed the connection between stomach ulcers and that peppy pylori bacteria.

The last shrimp sat on his plate as the noon news began,

flashing scenes of a wicked five-car accident on the heavily travelled Falconbridge Highway the night before. A slurry truck had jackknifed, and the spillage had complicated rescue efforts. Ambulances were arriving from all directions. "All finished?" she asked without looking. There was no answer. "Are you fin…" A red chipmunk cartoon had replaced him, cheeks pouched to capacity, eyes rolling back in his skull. Worst of all, he made no sound.

Belle threw aside the paper and fled down the hall, yelling for help. With two husky aides hauled from the lunchroom in mid-spoon, Cherie unlatched the lap seat, and they tried to hoist the old man to apply the Heimlich. A dead weight in their arms, he slumped towards the floor, his legs buckling like limp twigs as his slippers dropped off.

Watching their efforts, Belle stood to one side, helpless, crazy thoughts rushing through her head. "Well, if he dies now, in full sail of his favourite meal, without pain, at eighty-four, it's not a bad way to go. Lose consciousness. A quick heart attack. And I paid his rent last week for the whole month." She pounded the back of her head against the wall. What monster would remember his bank balance? Shouting commands to each other, the trio had placed him on the floor and was trying to pry open his mouth, teeth clamped in paralysis, his face plum purple.

At that point Belle surrendered all objectivity and stepped outside, closing the door and sinking into a crouch as her heart hammered. A tiny woman pushing a tripod walker on wheels inched by, bobbing her head like an inquisitive sparrow, a bib dangling from her stringy neck. "What's his name?" she asked in a weak and tremulous voice that drew out the syllables.

That question threw Belle for a minute. All his life he'd

gone by Norman, Sir Norman his girlfriend "consort" called him, with their jokes about the Royal family. But the nursing home used his first name, so he changed back without a fuss. "Uh, Norman, I mean George."

Three more times did the wizened gnome roll by with the same question while Belle answered in a patient ritual, forcing down fear like a coiled spring. Every silver-haired doll might have been her mother had she lived. Would the old man soon be a memory, too? Like Zack with Anni, she hadn't told him that she loved him. Not lately.

Finally the door opened, and a sweating Cherie took her arm. "We got his airway open. He's off to St. Joseph's by ambulance." The front door slammed, and footsteps pounded down the hall behind a squeaking gurney. In seconds, a blanketed form swept past, leaving Belle like a character in search of an author, muddling around the scene of destruction to retrieve van keys, mindlessly collecting the unopened pie and ice cream box from the dresser.

"You saved his life. Will he be all right?" she asked the aide on her way out.

The affable giant with a nose stud, who shaved her father with a surprisingly gentle hand, gave a reassuring nod. "They can be stronger than you think, if there's the will to live."

"Have you seen this before? What will they do at the hospital?"

"Oh, just routine. He might have aspirated food, so they'll want to check his lungs. Pneumonia is more dangerous than the sore throat he'll have."

After presenting him with the pie as a meagre reward, Belle navigated downtown, weaving through traffic in a trance, running full speed from the far reaches of the hospital parking lot. Sudbury's three health care facilities had been ordered by the Ontario government to consolidate. Meanwhile the system was in chaos, only one emergency room in use, a Megahospital the size of Manhattan under construction at the newest site.

"George Palmer," she said to the Intensive Care head nurse, only to learn that her father was in X-ray and that a couple of hours would pass before all the tests were evaluated. "In the waiting room is a direct line to our station. Call about his condition any time."

Half an hour later, a can of tasteless iced tea sweating in her hand, Belle fidgeted in an uncomfortable plastic chair. Her eyes felt gritty and her skin greasy. People came and went, mostly in families, picked up the phone for a moment, then spoke to each other in hushed tones. "Gran's allowed one five-minute visit an hour," a thin blonde woman said to a sniffling boy and girl. "We'll go at two, and Aunt Kelly will come tonight with Daddy." She gave their hair a quick brush and spit-wiped a smudge from the boy's cheek.

Then Belle was alone with her thoughts. Another problem of being an only child. Nobody to share the pain. Nobody to share the inheritance either, her evil half added. She leafed through tattered magazines dealing with cooking or clothes, interests far from her concern, more restless and jumpy as the clock moved on. Finally she focused on a simple cross on the wall. This oldest hospital, formally the General, had been run by the Sisters of St. Joseph, "nunbuns" her Catholic friend from college called them. Perhaps a prayer would help. Surely there was some dark and quiet place. The light was bothering her eyes.

At Reception a helpful volunteer lady pointed the way to the Chapel. In her fragile and almost giddy state, now that some hope had appeared, she thought of the song, "Going to the Chapel." But this small nook was a peaceful, non-denominational shelter for meditation, even for agnostics and lapsed Anglicans. Stained glass windows scattered iridescence across the rows of oak pews, vases of fragrant Oriental lilies scented the air, and a wisp of incense lingered, or was she imagining it? Belle approached a side altar heaped with candles in graduated sizes. Her mother's father had been French Canadian, the only Catholic in the family. She would choose the biggest candle she could find, and ask for, what was it called? Intercession? Funny how these terms from distant confirmation lessons lingered.

She dropped a twoonie into the box and took a thin stick, lighting it from another person's prayer. As she pressed her knees to the velvet cushion, the candle kindled a small warmth. He was an old man in a nursing home, one tremulous step from the final humiliation of bed care. She would not wish life in name only upon him should his last energy drain from his diminishing capacities. Her favourite Shakespeare play had the best advice: "*Oh, let him pass,*" Kent said of Lear. *"He hates him, / That would upon the rack of this tough world / Stretch him out longer."* If he wanted to live, even for his game shows, her weekly lunches, memories of dusty films, let him live with dignity, or not at all. The finality brought a lump to her throat, and she heard a sob though she had thought herself alone. Crossing herself in a ritual strangely comforting, forgetting whether right preceded left, repeating the process three times, she rose and turned. At the door stood a small figure in white haloed by the bright lights of the corridor. A nurse? Were they looking for her? Was it all over?

"I hope your prayers are answered. I will say a rosary for you," said a nun in an old-fashioned white habit, stroking with wrinkled fingers a set of blood red garnet beads as much a work of art as a symbol. Belle wiped her eyes and nodded. Something odd, she thought, as the woman disappeared into the shadowy light of the chapel. Was that a humpback?

Finally she was allowed to see her father. "The tests are fine. He'll be going back to Rainbow as soon as we can get another ambulance. You know the delays," the nurse said with a shrug. "Have a few words with him, but go on home if you need to. I'll keep an eye open."

Belle hadn't even thought about home, about Freya, her other family. "I'd appreciate that. You've all been great."

She moved over to the gurney where he lay motionless, eyes closed, like a stylized knight atop a marble vault, folded hands ready to clasp a broadsword. Another battle won, perhaps the last victory. She adjusted the twisted plastic identity bracelet, tucked the sheet over his bony shoulder, once so muscular. His hair was neatly combed, and his face pink and smooth. Suddenly the blue eyes snapped open, the brilliant cornflower colour that had courted her mother when Canadian troops were marching off to fight Hitler. Bushy white eyebrows furrowed as he looked up, his eyes struggling for focus. Minutes passed. Was he medicated? Had there been some neurological damage from the asphyxia? "Where's my pie and ice cream?" he demanded in a gruff tone. She laughed so hard that she had to close her legs.

With her father dozing, Belle walked the long row of critical care beds, glad that the ordeal had been brief. He could have ended up like that poor soul, she imagined, passing curtains fluttering around a patient on multiple support systems, a ventilator, heart monitor, tubes and bags filling and draining the still form. Man, woman, age, it was hard to tell. A bustling nurse moved a corner of the sheet to take a pulse. Stark against the flaccid white arm was a tattoo. Belle stopped, still wiping tears from her eyes, working her memory.

An Amazon in a lab coat, her thick silver-blond hair plaited in one long braid, picked up the chart. Dr. Evelyn Easton, Sudbury's premier surgeon, an infallible diagnostician with a pair of magic hands. They had met, if one could call it that, over a routine colonoscopy years ago during which Belle had sniffled but never budged under that roto-rooter, she recalled with uncomfortable pride. Suddenly the tattoo came into focus. A black rose. Belle's blood grew icy, though the room was warm and humid. She heard nothing but pounding waves in her ears. "Pardon me. I might know that woman."

SIXTEEN

Easton scanned the chart with approval and made a few notes, then rubbed at her neck as if she hadn't been to bed in days. "A dreadful accident on the Falconbridge Highway last night. She hasn't recovered consciousness." She looked up and stared blearily at Belle. "Are you the sister from Montreal we've been trying to contact? All we had was a name in her wallet. A family member at the bedside can make a difference."

"Family." The last words trailed off like a fading stereo. The floor seemed to move closer. Light shrank into a small white circle in a distant corner. Belle reached for a table, struggling to make her legs cooperate. "My God. Her children!"

With a quick hand, Easton grabbed Belle's arm, and swept her onto a wheeled stool, shaking her gently, her voice level and demanding. "Children? Small children? Are you saying they're alone? Wouldn't they have gone to the neighbours?"

I'm her neighbour, she felt like screaming, but after a hard swallow, she related what she feared.

Calmed by the quiet efficiency of an emergency room surgeon, Belle worked with Easton to alert the police and put the Children's Aid on standby. "I've given them the address and told them about the dogs. Better go home now," she said, pressing a cool hand to Belle's cheek. "You've done all you can." The doctor turned to respond to the urgent wave of a young nurse, who was breathing heavily, a splash of blood across the shoulder of her white uniform.

Belle fled the hospital with renewed respect for overworked health care workers. Even so, she knew that she was heading into another nightmare. It would be impossible just to drive past Patsy's. The air conditioner was set to polar, but she was flushed and wet. This was the fatal convergence, the terrible chance a careless mother had taken to steal a quick trip to town for milk or bread, some inanity, trusting that she'd be back in a hour. How many parents acted with the same bold-faced impunity every week? The papers had enjoyed a field day with the couple who had left for a Caribbean vacation, locking their ten-year-old in the house with a freezer of TV dinners. Patsy's kids weren't even in school yet. Dottie had been right about that fine line between meddling and social responsibility, a line easier to ignore by remaining silent. Perhaps Anni had paid the price for that act of conscience. "And the current temperature is 36.6 degrees centrigrade, folks, that's 100 degrees, a new record for Sudbury," said the radio. "Enjoy it while you can. Here's 'Frosty, the Snowman' to blow some white stuff your way."

When she finally pulled up at Patsy's, she felt reassured to see police cars waiting. Apparently the dogs were still alive, for she could hear them barking furiously. "I'm the neighbour who reported this," she said to the officer in charge, Hal Cooper. "The Rotties may not have been fed for a day or two." She paused, thinking of another nauseous possibility.

"Christ, I hope kids aren't in there. We've tried the door. It's open, but we're not keen on passing those dogs. Dirk has five minutes to get here with his gear. Otherwise…" Fingers brushed over his sidearm, reassuringly snapped Canadian style into a leather holster against the temptation of a quick draw. He let out a breath of relief at an approaching dust cloud.

"Here's our man," he called to his crew. "Let's move!"

Another cruiser pulled up, and Belle turned to see a man dressed in a padded suit, two muzzles and a stick with a noose in his hands. Hal introduced them. "You know the dogs? Are they vicious?"

She gestured with despair. "Owner says not, but that doesn't mean anything."

"Could be tricky. I'm going to open the door easy-does-it and see what we have." He edged in as flashes of dark fur jumped in the doorway. Then the barking stopped, and she could hear his voice talking in low tones. With surprising docility, the Rotties were led out muzzled and placed into the police van. "A giant bag of dog food was broken open in the kitchen," Dirk said, taking off his heavy suit and accepting a soda. "Got water from the usual porcelain bowl. Dogs are pretty instinctive. Kids must be in the bedrooms. I can hear one crying, not very loud, though."

Hal vanished into the house, returning a moment later. "They're in the back. Look OK at first glance. Can you go and stay with them, Miss? Uniforms are scary for kids sometimes. No woman on my crew today. I've got to radio again and find out where that damn ambulance is. Friggin' cutbacks."

Belle wiped sweat from her face. "I think they might be comfortable with me. We met once."

"They'll need some water, not too cold, though," Hal said.

She inched into the house, breathing through her mouth. The window fan was broken. One giant sauna. Any more delay might have brought a triple funeral, dogs notwithstanding. Excrement was smeared over the rug in front of a ripped couch; a few toys lay scattered through urine puddles in front of a giant television and matching VCR. Patsy's priorities again.

Still searching her mind for their names as she picked her

166

way across a floor littered with toys, she saw a colourful height chart beside a doorway, each child's progress documented by a clown holding rising balloons. Down the short hall she followed the whimperings, entering a small room with bunk beds and a crib. On the floor were two children, the girl apparently sleeping with a teddy bear, the boy barely sitting up. Where was the third? She fumbled with the blankets in the crib, retrieving an empty plastic baby bottle. The boy blinked at her, eyes struggling for focus under a shank of wet hair. She smiled, modulating her voice, trying not to sound panicky.

"Hi, Joe. I like your Batman shirt." She turned to the girl, naked except for a pair of panties. "And you must be Lisa. I'm Belle. Remember me? Your mom can't come home for a while, and I've come to take you to a nice cool place where you can get a good supper. Are you guys hungry?"

"Uh-uh. Thirsty." Joe pointed to an empty box of Cheerios, his face pale from dehydration. "We didn't go out. Mom said she'd be right back. She always is. Susie's in the closet. She was sad and I got her out of her crib and played with her and I couldn't lift her back."

Belle's knees grew weak as she turned to the closet to stir what looked like a heap of clothes. Please not a head injury. Would he have told the truth if he had dropped her? For a moment she thought the baby was dead, so still, the skin clammy. Yet its diapers were soggy. Perhaps that had kept it cool.

Hal brought in bottled water. "Drink slowly, kids," he said, resting the girl against his leg. Her hair was done in meticulous braids, a cornrow design that must have taken hours. "Hey, what have you got there? Another one?"

"I hope so," she said. As she handed him the bundle, an ambulance siren sounded.

"About bloody time," he said with a growl, cradling the baby as he left. Belle rummaged in the drawers for a change of clothes to send, surprised at the neatness in the drawers, even the tiny sox pressed and folded. Patsy was an ace laundress, if nothing else. She tossed the small pieces into pillow cases along with a couple of teddy bears, then put shorts and a top on Lisa. Joe took her hand as they left, and on one shoulder she carried the girl. Funny how little kids weighed. Light as a doll. Odd that none of the kids had their mother's flaming red hair. Jet black, every one.

"Ambulance held up at the tracks by a hundred-fifty-car freight. We'll take them to Emerg for a check, and then Children's Aid can take over." Hal glanced at Belle with a grin. "Sure you don't want to go along in case there's a delay? You did pretty well here, Mom."

She laughed in relief, accepting a lukewarm swig from his can of Coke, happy to have helped but wishing she were loafing on her deck with a glass of wine poured over a thousand ice cubes. It had been too long a day. "Not tonight, darling. I have a headache. Last time I took a couple of dogs, and that's my limit."

Washed with sweat, still shaking after the close encounter, Belle did no more than remove her slacks and shoes, let Freya out and race her to the lake. They strolled into the sheltered bay, then swam to the rockwall, the dog pawing at her as if she needed rescue. "Stop trying to herd me," she said. Once past the wall, she floated in the icier temperatures, bearable only in mid-summer. She paddled over her water line fathoms below in the crystalline depths. Weighed down with a succession of cement blocks, it sat on a tripod, foot valve well off the silty bottom, safe from fluctuating water levels and ice pressure.

Back in her bedroom, as she toweled off, her answering

machine was beeping. As Dorothy Parker said, what fresh hell? Steve reported that the license check on Nick had turned up a drunk driving offense in Kamloops five years earlier, about the same time he'd appeared in Sudbury, she recalled. Maybe by sequestering himself far from temptation, he was building a better life. Now that she knew his pastimes, she felt mean-spirited about having suggested him as a suspect. Her gentle friend had nothing more than a wish to live with his talented pen. As for the rest, Zack didn't seem distressed that his alibi hadn't been confirmed. The Godfather of Bear Gallbladders and his team were out of business. Of course there was still Patsy. Was there ever Patsy. She was in for a blast tomorrow, if she lived.

The evening nurse at Rainbow Country took her responding call, assuring her that George had returned in such a lively condition that it took their entire supply of ice cream to satisfy him. "Lord knows we couldn't begrudge him that small pleasure. I heard the man was a whisker from eternity. Don't mind telling you that we've lost some before."

"Guess it's minced from now on," she said, hanging up, grateful not to get a lecture for carelessness. Shrimp and french fries weren't the easiest foods to chew. She should have changed the menu a long time ago. He'd adjust. That was one of his happiest traits. Food was food, the ampler the better, and ice cream always slid down well.

Decompression time. After a makeshift antipasto of sliced Black Forest ham, Swiss cheese and salad greens, Belle climbed up to bed, cursing with each step. 20°C in the basement, 25°C on the first floor, and 30°C (nearly 90°F) in her master suite. Should she opt for the cool but hard leather sofa below in the living room? Blow up an air mattress and bunk in the basement? Easier to tough it out, set up an extra fan, place a glass of ice by her bed and use her emergency procedure, several cold bath dips, blotting on sheets, trusting that the plastic liner on the waterbed would protect her from electrocution. It was absolute insanity flying in the face of science to drink Scotch, but she was a creature of habit, convinced that she would not sleep unless nicely medicated. Jagged little pills were dangerous dragons, nowhere near the fun of liquor.

So she drank, and smoked, and reread *Frankenstein*. Few people raised on the movie versions realized that in Shelley's original, Victor Frankenstein pursued his creature to the ice floes of the Arctic. Her sympathies lay with the Monster, born like a giant child, reviled for his ugliness and abandoned without even the benefit of speech to walk an ignorant world. "I will quit the neighbourhood of man, and dwell...in the most savage of places. My evil passions will have fled, for I shall meet with sympathy," he said in pleading for a mate. But the concept had been too grotesque for his creator. No Elsa Lanchester with her lightning bolt hairdo would share his bed.

Freya, voting with her feet, was bivouacked on the cool tile floor in the basement, so Belle went down to let her out for a final pee. The night was palpable as blackstrap molasses. Deathly quiet, as if every living thing felt too ponderous to move. Bank this memory for thirty below, she thought. Yet heat was so enervating. Maybe Canadians did have thick blood. She clumped reluctantly back to her room, wishing she had pitched a tent on the lawn. Her camping gear was in the boathouse probably getting eaten by something hairy, rabid, or both.

After prayers, she concocted a sleep scenario designed for summer. Step by step she would snowmobile to a hypothetical cabin north of Wapiti, cataloguing the food and gear, describing the light snow starting halfway across the lake, building to a blinding blizzard as she reached the North River trails at the far shore and couldn't turn back. The atmosphere had to be threatening so that when she arrived at the camp, she would be cozy and protected, kindling a fire to banish shivers, shedding heavy clothes like a carapace as the stove warmed the room, cocooned away from even a radio station. She never could decide whether to take a friend (complicated) or if the place would have power (gas generator? hydro?) not to mention indoor plumbing, and debating these fine points endlessly led to snores drowning out the sounds of the imaginary beans bubbling on the woodstove.

SEVENTEEN

The next morning, Belle found her father eating peach yogurt for lunch, a milk moustache on his lip. "Is this Ronald Colman I see before me?" she asked with an exaggerated doubletake. Then she kissed his fresh-shaven cheek. "How's your throat? Do you remember what happened yesterday?"

"It's fine. Of course I do. How much is this going to cost? Will I go broke?"

He was still thinking of Florida and the outrageous American health care fees which drove many to bankruptcy, or maybe he was remembering the Depression. "This is Canada, Father. We're taxed to the max. It's free. You just have to wait a long time."

"I didn't, though, did I?"

"Quite true. There must be life in the system yet."

Time to find out what Patsy knew. If she could talk. Belle found herself on the Mobius strip route to St. Joe's. "Mrs. Sommers regained consciousness," the nurse said to her inquiries. "She's in 233."

A creaky elevator took her upstairs, where the lack of air conditioning combined with record temperatures made a hospital stay a nightmare. Carts of dirty linen lined the halls, and the acrid atmosphere reflected the staff shortages all over Ontario. Her neighbour's bed sat in a ward of four patients, scant space or privacy except for thin curtains, no personal possessions or colour to warm the sterile environment. Did everything have to be painted slime or oatmeal? Patsy looked weary and drained, though the cumbersome monitors had been replaced by a bag of saline.

"I heard you saved my kids," she whispered hoarsely as she brushed her long, red hair, using her right hand, Belle noted with interest. "I was stupid to leave them, but they were cranky in the heat. Cartoons usually settle them down. The video store in Garson wasn't far." Her voiced trailed off uncertainly, then revived as she frowned at a memory. "Damn that slurry truck that cut me off. Ever get out of here, I'll sue his ass to kingdom come."

Belle gave her a disgusted stare. Since there didn't seem to be much wrong with the woman, she aimed both barrels. "You're beyond lectures, so I won't bother. If you owe me one, tell me about Anni."

In Belle's mother's words, the woman didn't bat an eyelash. "Should have minded her own business. Made some snarky comments to me at the mailboxes. Who did she think she was, Queen of the Road? Probably went right home and called the Aid. Lucky I was there when they came. Bunch of jerks couldn't prove dick."

"Sounds like you hated her."

"No secret I felt like killing her, but kids got to have someone." She turned her blotchy face to the wall.

"Proof is the operative word here. A simple denial won't cut it. Where were you the night she died?"

A dry laugh exploded into a such a bone-jarring convulsion that Belle scrambled for a glass of water. Patsy took a few noisy gulps. "No sweat. Ever have kids? I was in my favourite chair in Emerg from dinner until dawn with Lisa and her earache.

Saw in the paper the next day someone nailed the bitch."

A slap might have been worth the assault charge. But at that moment, a white-wimpled face peeked into the room, and Patsy waved her over in familiarity. Sister Veronica, as she introduced herself to Belle, placed a gaily blooming violet on the night table. "It's one of my loaners," she said. "For some cheer." Patsy nodded, then closed her eyes.

With a gentle nudge, the nun pantomimed their exit. "I'm so glad you came. Not one other visitor," she said, shaking her head in the busy hall. "The doctors say she should recover completely. Your prayers must have been answered."

Belle frowned at the irony. "Not exactly, Sister. She's a neighbour. When my father was brought in yesterday, I recognized her. He's the one I was praying about, and luckily, he's fine."

"I see." The nun kept discreetly quiet, her gimlet eye inspecting a gold watch pinned to her habit. "Would you care to take peppermint tea with me? My office is around the corner. It has a lovely view of Lake Ramsey."

Seating Belle in a padded wicker armchair, she heated an electric kettle in a cozy nook decorated with pigs in arcane poses, sitting at a poker game, or playing croquet. "I find them comical in a world which could use a smile," she explained.

Belle found herself staring at the woman, not so much at the hump (The "What hump?" scene from *Young Frankenstein* kept flashing through her mind) as at the pristine white habit, the wimple with a curious European flair. "I'm intrigued about your outfit, I mean your habit." She sipped the tea, refreshing and calming at the same time. "I hope I'm not being rude. Most nuns these days wear street clothes."

Sister Veronica smoothed back a silvery rogue hair escaping from one wispy eyebrow. "I guess I'm a happy anachronism.

Though I'm here in semi-retirement at St. Joseph's, my order, the Cecilianists, wore white. A little bit vain, this difference. Perhaps an element of mystique. Another advantage is that the traditional garb seems to reassure people, mixes medicine and faith, a useful combination even in modern times." She placed her palms together, the knobby fingers joining in a fluid motion. "You, for example, crossed yourself in such an unusual fashion in the chapel that I knew you weren't Catholic. But your distress needed something more powerful than the sterility of science."

Feeling naked at the calm perspicacity, Belle shifted conversation to the nun's duties, learning that her job as crisis liaison officer involved circulating around the hospital to facilitate arrangements for patients and relatives, especially in intensive care. She could arrange for telephone calls, child care, pastoral consultations, cots for all-night vigils and occasionally sneak in a special treat from the kitchen. "Mrs. Sommers owes you a considerable debt. If I recognize your name and description, you are responsible for rescuing her children."

That was a dangerous chord. Belle felt herself running on in a passion. "A dog wouldn't leave its puppies in that danger. And where's the father? She has three kids. What does it take for the light to go on?" She tapped at her temple.

The old nun looked back evenly over the imposing panel of her starched habit. "Facts alone don't construct a life. You are too much a social Darwinist, my dear. Rather unbending. Is all life black and white to you?"

"Really, Sister, how can you excuse that kind of neglect?"

Her voice was pleasant and uncritical, suited for a confessional booth. "It's not for me to excuse. Humans behave as their names imply. She nearly paid the ultimate price... and think carefully. Suppose those innocents had perished?" A sparkle entered her eyes. "But perhaps you were fated to be their guardian angel."

Belle squirmed at the compliment, disarmed but not surrendering. "I'll tell you something else. Our road is a little community, often a nosy one. Several of us have been…concerned about Patsy for a long time. Somebody, perhaps a woman called Anni Jacobs, called in a complaint to the Children's Aid." In the bottom of her cup, leaves which escaped the strainer made patterns. The future? Present? Past? "Not long after, she was murdered. They haven't found the killer."

The voice was smooth, unruffled. "And you imagine Mrs. Sommers had the gumption for such violence?"

Belle stared out of the window across the sparkling lake to the handsome complex of Shield University. "Gumption might be her middle name. But she says she was at the Emerg that night. Of course…"

The nun read the implication like litmus paper, scribbling a quick note. "She could be lying, you mean. Don't worry. It's easy to check. Give me your home number."

When Belle left the hospital, she turned down Ramsey Lake Road towards the complex of Shield University. While in the area, she might as well follow the historical leads on Anni's case. How many tiny churches with that curious steeple could there have been in Northwestern Ontario? Despite the punch-a-button-to-locate an Iraqui-germ-warfare-cake-recipe myth, perpetuated by blockbuster thrillers, computer networks had limitations. Some people thought that anything was possible in cyberspace, but databases were only as comprehensive as the modern monks who converted the written word to disk. Shield's lofty metal and glass towers had given her quiet afternoons browsing through the latest magazines or the mammoth literature section. From what Edith had said, the true story had been buried, but that didn't mean the building hadn't been featured in an article for some other reason. One pictorial source for recent Canadian history was the classic old *Beaver*, founded by the Hudson Bay Company in 1920.

In the stacks, she blew the dust off a bound volume and scanned the indices from 1970-75 as a starting point. Too seductive for her magpie mind. Soon she was leafing through unrelated but fascinating articles about the Inuit carving industry, Haida spaghetti made from clover roots, the derring-do of Arctic bush pilots and heart-rending journals from explorers who had starved to death. One account about a residential school in the Northwest Territories didn't spell cruelty for the white editorial minds of the day, but the subtext was poignant. For a girl and her brother, the plane touched down in Cambridge Bay at sun-up, and they were gone with little more than breakfast and a change of socks. Their first day at the school, they were given coal oil shampoos for lice and baths with a chaser of cold water to close the pores. "How little and lost my three-year-old brother looked," the girl thought. "How could so many people live in one building?" She tried hard to learn English, bury her own language and customs. It was five years before they were allowed to go home for the summer.

Belle grew sick at the warped concept of assimilation which had wrenched children from their families and educated them to work at menial jobs, all at the extinction of a collective spirit. What a travesty of collusion between the churches and the government. It was an old idea long before Duncan Campbell Scott, Head of Indian Affairs at the turn of the century, had "celebrated" the concept in his lyrical poetry. Haunted by one of his poems, she rambled over to the PT section and hunted up an anthology. Despite his lauded sensitivity and admiration for the "noble savage," his popular "Onandaga Madonna" contained a sinister line: "*And closer in the shawl about her breast, / The latest promise of her nation's doom, / Paler than she her baby clings and lies, / The primal warrior gleaming from his eyes*." Promise and doom lay in the paler babe, already his blood diluted by his European father's, his heritage swallowed by a larger and more powerful race.

An hour passed, then another, the mesmerizing curse of libraries. Finally she snapped to attention at an article on Ontario missions. Rainy River, Moosenee, Fort Albany. Browsing through picture after picture, she had nearly given up when a familiar wooden octagon tower caught her eye. "Palm Sunday at St. Michael's in Osprey Inlet," the caption said, a small paragraph of a story extolling the virtues of a Sister Euphemia. In the foreground, clearly in charge, stood a tiny creature in a white habit, a very ringabell white habit, stylized wimple and all, in front of a self-conscious group of perhaps sixty children of all ages shepherded by other nuns. Belle searched each little face, bleak and disciplined. Instead of palm crosses, they held what appeared to be dried rushes, snow still covering the ground.

Osprey Inlet, Zack's "animal" name. And that habit. If the Cecilianists had been in charge of this mission, Sister Veronica might know what had happened. Yet wasn't that like asking Al Capone about bootlegging? Could she have been a part of this, Belle wondered, adding up numbers? The good sister could have been anywhere from a hard-time sixty to an easy-ride eighty. She moved to the window, rotating the grainy photograph. No nun seemed to have a hump. Perhaps it was osteoporosis. Wouldn't generalized bone density loss be more symmetrical? She shut her eyes. Definitely off to one side.

Five-thirty. Too late to call the hospital. This was a subject for personal confrontation anyway, Belle thought, heading home. Cruising with the windows down, she met Charles a mile from his house, puffing along in Colonel Bogie fashion. "It's been too hot until today to get in my constitutionals," he said, retrieving a handkerchief to mop his brow. "Maybe I've overdone it a tad."

His colour was flushed, and he was breathing hard. Despite his enthusiasm and activity, sometimes she forgot that he was not a young man. "These hills are no fun, Charles. I stopped jogging when I moved here. Get in, and I'll drop you off."

"A capital idea." He wasted no motions accepting her offer, removing his safari jacket and folding it carefully onto the back seat. It seemed ideal for camping, all those handy pockets and mysterious zippers. "I'm going to have a light supper and try another sauna. The last few days I called you about joining me, but your machine answered so I hung up. Didn't want to clutter your life with messages."

"If you haven't seen me around, here's why," she said, unfolding the episodes with her father and Patsy like a soap opera.

"Your father's fine? Thank God. He must be strong. Just like his daughter," he said, patting her shoulder in a rare tactile gesture. Then he shook his head while his lips set firmly. "And the other story had a happy ending, but call me old-fashioned for observing that a lady alone with children has no business living so far from town."

When they reached his property, he pointed to a handsome sign, routed and varnished, complete with brass fittings: Sullivan's: Paradise Regained. "Just picked it up at the mall. Special order."

"The apostrophe's in the right place, and how about that colon!"

179

"Took the liberty of giving them a grammar lesson. The title sounded somewhat ironic after my dog problems, but it's settled down now. Expect they'll be gone in the fall anyway," he said, brightening. "Say, Ed asked me to go fishing for brook trout tomorrow at one of those kettle lakes, he called them."

"Bring me a big one," she said as he waved a cheery farewell. It was good that Charles seemed to be making friends. He'd find the DesRosiers a lively pair.

The heat had broken at last. Belle enjoyed her first warm meal in days, a chicken breast with rosemary and olive oil on the grill along with roasted vegetables. Red, green and yellow peppers made an attractive medley with sliced leeks and eggplant.

She stayed up later than usual crawling the web. Now she had a name. Osprey Inlet. Hardly a thriving metropolis, unlikely to have its own page, unless for tourism. Google tossed her around with no hits, so she turned to Yahoo. Delayed by an overload on the server, which pumped twenty-first-century technology through nineteenth-century lines, Belle pulled out an atlas and scanned Ontario, tracing a finger far into the northwest corner. The province was massive, sprawled like a legless, upside down kangaroo, snout nuzzling Vermont, ears tickling Detroit, back stretching nearly to the North Dakota border, and belly cold on Hudson Bay, a country onto itself. Osprey Inlet could be reached only by plane, most likely from Red Lake, the nearest town. And Red Lake was the back of the beyond.

To her surprise, the Chamber of Commerce page appeared, probably a group of one. It named the mayor, Dave Assinewe, as contact. Scrolling through Recreation, she hit a few fly-in hunting and fishing lodges, watching squares fill up with photos. Wolverine Lodge. Click on the fish for a tour. Cabin One's pixels arranged themselves into a cozy interior, complete with colourful Trapper Point blankets on the beds and stuffed pike on the wall. Before logging off, she copied the number of the mayor.

As darkness fell, she went outside to inhale the cool air like a tonic. The humidity had been chased by a high front from the Arctic, and a brilliant full moon, a buck moon as the aboriginals called it, brightened a corner of the navy blue stardome. The sound of a car startled her, and she glanced toward the road, not expecting to see anything through the thick leaf cover. Lights did appear, though, one headlamp bumping along with a nervous tic, blinking on and off. Why the view? The vandalizing caterpillars had reached the maple grove at the edge of her property.

EIGHTEEN

On Saturday, the scruffy grass was screaming for attention. Belle gassed up the new self-propelled mower, a costly technojump from the push model, but she had too much acreage, too many irregular slopes, and muscles too middle-aged to begrudge its price. At least the beast was not as self-indulgent as the riding monsters commandeered like tiny tanks, dinging rocks and decapitating toads. With optimism, she switched the lever from the tortoise icon to the hare and began at the lakeside, glancing ruefully at her prize maple. During construction she had thrown herself in front of the gobbling backhoe to save the tree from destruction. Now the bottom third of its majesty hung in tatters thanks to the tent caterpillars. Criminal to poison the lake through chemical spraying, though, and suicidal to drink the runoff, so amoral Nature would do its own landscaping.

On the first coffee break, she called the mayor of Osprey Inlet. It must have been his home number, for he answered the phone himself. Her explanation of twenty-five words or fewer brought a clipped response. "Residential schools are an ugly part of our history. Just leave us alone."

When she became more specific, his voice heated up. "A waste of your breath, lady. No one's talking about it, not then, not now. You're from the city? Sudbury? Might as well be another country. You don't understand something. Most of our elders are still devout Catholics. Even after that tragedy, they believe that only God himself has the right to judge his servants."

Belle felt anger rising at the limitations of a private citizen. "Listen, whatever happened might have a bearing on a recent murder."

"Then it would be a matter for the police, wouldn't it?"

She tried her last card, hoping to trigger a gut reaction. "Can you at least put me in touch with a person called Verna?"

"White woman," he said, "you are out of luck." Then the contemptuous edge turned to sorrow. "Her funeral was last month. Just a great-great-grandmother who ran out of steam at ninety."

Suddenly they were cut off, or were they? Could Steve get better results, twist Mr. Assinewe's arm long distance? His resources didn't stretch across the country. Most murders in Sudbury were mom-and-pop affairs, drunken brawls or imaginative combinations.

The coffee was as cold as her leads. Just as a new batch perked, the phone jangled. "It's Ed. Is Chuck there?"

"Chuck. Bet he loves that. And no, he's not here. I don't entertain this early, and he didn't stay the night."

She felt ashamed at the lame humour as Ed explained himself. "Guy was supposed to pick me up at eight. Going after those grandaddy trout at the big kettle lake."

"Philosopher's Pond?"

"Huh? You and your funny names. Anyways, he never showed up. I waited, gave him a call or two 'case he was outside or in the john. No answer. Think he changed his mind?"

A hot, tight feeling spread over her chest like a menopausal blanket. Charles had been so flushed and out of breath the night before. "That's not like him. Normally he's the soul of manners. Go down to his place, and I'll catch up with you. I meant to bring Hélène some zucchini that escaped my eagle eye."

Out in the garden, she shoved aside a jungle of leaves and grabbed a ballbat squash, arriving with Freya at the DesRosiers' in a heart-pounding five minutes. While the dog fenced with Rusty over a plastic banana, she let herself in with the perfunctory "knock, knock."

"For your world famous chocolate zucchini cake," Belle said, placing the monster on the table as she looked out the window. "Ed still gone?"

"Been about ten minutes," Hélène said, her face expressing concern while she put down a half-peeled potato and turned off the country music station in the middle of "Little Skidoo, it's up to you." "Could anything really be wrong with the fellow? We had him to dinner a while ago and were swapping medical stories like a bunch of old women. Ed's hip, my gallbladder operation. Right to home, but a bit of a hypochondriac, truth be told."

"Isn't that the ultimate insult, calling a man an old woman? Why doesn't it work the other way?" Belle laughed half-heartedly, tuning her ears for the sound of a motor. "He does have high blood pres…"

Suddenly the four-wheeler screeched back into the driveway, followed by a dust cloud. "The crazy fool," Hélène said as they ran outside. "Not even enough insurance to make me a rich widow."

Ed clumped to the porch in marathon time, cane flailing wildly, his face white as he collapsed into a creaking chair. "You don't want to know. No, siree, you don't. He was just sitting there."

Hélène gave him a sharp look. "Sitting where? You're not making sense, Ed. Calm down. I'll get some cold water."

"Bring me a beer!" he bellowed until she returned to slam a can into his trembling hand. He popped the tab and spilled foam over his shirt, shivering like a huge child as Belle knelt at his side.

"Has something happened to Charles? An accident?"

"Yes, or no. See, I didn't look that carefully. All's I can tell you is that he's dead as a beached lake trout."

"Didn't you feel for a pulse? Where is he?"

"In the sauna. Listen, I know a dead man when I see one. Open eyes, get it?" He waved his hand in front of his face. "Nobody home?" After he noticed Charles' car in the yard, he had hunted through the house, garage, boathouse, and finally the sauna. What he saw sent him hopping back to the quad, though he stalled the motor three times in panic.

Belle pulled him to his feet. "Call the police, Hélène. Ask for Steve Davis if he's there. Ed and I'll go back and wait."

A few minutes later, they stood in front of the small cedar building looking at each other anxiously. "Sure you want to go in? Something sure was funny about his face."

"An injury?"

"Pretty damn dark in there. Could have been a shadow, or it could have been a bruise. But I'm no doctor."

"Let's look around. You take the outbuildings. We've got half an hour minimum before the troops arrive. Just don't tell Steve."

"What should we look for?" he asked in bewilderment.

She rolled her eyes and shook his arm. "Anything suspicious. Remember those mushrooms? Maybe Mabel Joy's gone off the deep end."

Inside the change room, all looked deceptively serene. Charles had hung framed prints on the panelling, Turner studies of sea and fog. Belle placed a cautious hand on the wooden handle to the steam bath, feeling like a voyeuse, opening the door an inch at a time. Bathed in the light from a small window, in the Mannerism style of Michelangelo, Charles Sullivan sat on a bench, head tilted back and eyes glassy and staring, on the chin a distinct bruise. With a mixture of curiosity and dread, she touched his neck and found it cool.

From some bizarre propriety, knowing that he would have been embarrassed, she turned to scan the room, avoiding his body. A thick white terrycloth robe lay in a heap on the floor. The shiny red enamel stove was protected by a wooden fence, but the fire had gone out long ago. The room was clammy, the sprucy smell antiseptic and sinister. The voiding of the bowel being an unscientific cliché, he had been spared that final humiliation.

Closing the door upon the wooden tomb, she tried the house, heading for the bedroom, the one intimate place she hadn't seen. An antique spool bed, narrow and prim, was tucked tight enough to bounce a penny off the patchwork quilt. On the wall was a painting of Rembrandt's "The Anatomy Lesson of Dr. Tulp." Nothing more than sox and underwear in the drawers, tailored suits and casual pants hanging in the closet. Sheepskin slippers and wingtip shoes sat beside a comfortable pair of trainers. The desk looked like a more fruitful site. Suddenly noises from the yard made her twitch, the crunch of tires on gravel, the slamming of doors. Steve and his cohorts or Dr. Graveline. No more time. Only a truly dishonest and deceitful person would have made Hélène delay the call. Why hadn't she thought of that?

Exiting by the front door by the lake, Belle was shielded from the driveway, so she approached as if she had been waiting by the dock. Ed was shrugging his shoulders in a "nothing" gesture. Steve was walking toward her, and she didn't like the look in his eye, nor his speed. "Called in on my day off. A few more friends like you, and I'll be running the department all by myself. Who is it, Belle?" he asked.

Hearing her response, he sent two officers around the property and directed Ed and Belle to wait for a more thorough questioning after he had made a tour. Graveline polished his glasses with a wry expression. "A dangerous place, this road. Well, let's see what we have. In the steam bath, is he? Could be a heart attack or stroke. Bad for the blood pressure. Damn fool should have kept out of there in this hot spell. Winter's the best time. My Norwegian granddad used to toss me into the snow on my bare bum." From his nostalgic tone, he seemed to find this icy recollection pleasant. Then off he went humming "Give me two pina coladas." What would he make of the bruise, she wondered?

Finally Steve settled into his questioning, all of them facing off in lawn chairs as if at a grim garden party. Yes, Charles had been alive the night before, had agreed to leave at eight for fishing. And he had just moved in, retired from a job in Ottawa. Relatives? No one close. His stomach growling, wearing an XXL natural fleece sweatshirt, Ed resembled a hungry sheep. "OK if I go home for lunch? Wife's waiting."

Steve waved him off and cast a suspicious look at Belle, but she ignored the hint and sat quietly, staring across the lake, hands folded in her lap. She closed her eyes to freeze the view she had sold Charles. What a short-lived paradise.

"Pretty, isn't it?" Mitch Graveline said as he reappeared, tucking away instruments the use of which she didn't like to imagine. "If there is such a thing as a nice spot to die." He cleared his throat. "At first glance, I'd say he was the perfect age for a heart attack. Cyanosis is evident. We'll know more at the autopsy. But there's a—"

Belle jumped in. "A bruise on his chin? Ed mentioned that."

"Curious," he said, snapping the lock on the black bag. "An obvious contusion. Still, I guess he could have slipped and fallen forward, grazed his face on the wooden guardrail around the stove. Or maybe it happened earlier that day."

"The boards were slimy from the humidity," Steve said. "People often fall in saunas. Couple of drinks. It's been known to happen."

"Alcohol couldn't have been a factor. With his high blood pressure, he took all precautions. And that robe in a pile in the sauna itself. That didn't look right. I don't want to get melodramatic, but is it possible someone else was involved?" asked Belle.

"A party? Somebody clipped him one? And then just left? One punch? He has a heart attack over that?"

"It's too coincidental after Anni…" Then she stopped and frowned to herself. Was it paranoia, or was she seeing threads everywhere? "Only connect," the poet said. "What about his house?" She hadn't had much time. Perhaps Steve had noticed something.

"In that place, it'd be easy to spot something out of whack. He was a neat one, obsessive even. Washed up after every glass of water. Even the coffee maker looked like he took cotton swabs to it. Mine is a germ bank." He paused as they all nodded in recognition. "No pictures either. A lonely man. Think he'd at least have a friend somewhere."

One of the officers, fresh shave on his pink cheeks, rushed over, breathing heavily. "Excuse me, sir. I found this by the gate. Behind a bunch of trees." Onto the table went a plastic bag with a cigarette filter.

Steve examined it with a pair of tweezers borrowed from the doctor. "Field-stripped. See the paper still attached? DuMaurier. Fresh. No sign of weathering on the letters." He turned to Belle with a question on his face. "Did he smoke? There weren't any ashtrays."

"Don't think so. And I've never smoked here. Ed chews on a cigar when he's out of Hélène's sight." She sat back and spoke more to herself than to them. "Like someone was watching, waiting. But for what? And why would a thief take chances when the car is in plain sight?"

"Or it could mean nothing. Just a cottager out for a walk. This place is past the turnaround. Dead end, it says, but I'll bet cars come down anyway. Natural curiosity." Steve sighed. "So I don't have to do this later, I'm going to ask you the same questions as I did about Anni Jacobs. Have you ever been in the house? Is there anything of value? Did he keep money around?"

"Yes, I've come here for dinner. As for valuables, you saw everything. An eccentric collection of classical music. Books. He has plenty of classical music. Big deal."

"It's not a break and enter anyway. No reason to believe anyone else was here."

Belle watched a cormorant glide through the bay, identical to a loon except to the expert eye. A slight upturn to the bill, and hidden under the water, black instead of white. If it wasn't a heart attack or a stroke, who could have attacked a wonderful man like Charles? "What are the legal implications? If a heart attack killed him, is it murder? Maybe the assailant doesn't even realize he's dead."

Steve closed his notebook decisively. "Assailant nothing. Stop the fantasy."

"So show off your education. Answer my question."

He exchanged glaces with Graveline. "All right. A case of manslaughter maybe. Even simple assault. Depends if the condition was known. People have been charged for literally scaring others to death. Let's say they want to collect an inheritance a bit prematurely. In the absence of relatives, if that's the case, what about his friends?"

Belle swallowed, dangerously close to tears. The water bird had brought back those first moments strolling the property with Charles, watching his face light up at unfolding delights. How quickly they had become comfortable. "He'd only been here a couple of months. I sold him the place. To tell you the sad truth, I think I was his only friend. Ed and Hélène just got acquainted. As for his next door neighbours, they'd been fighting over a dog problem." Her voice hesitated, gauging his response. One by one these little secrets were going to emerge. "I should mention the mushrooms."

Her story about Mabel Joy brought a scowl of distaste from Steve. "You did what?"

"The note was gone. No proof. I bluffed her, and it worked," she said, daring him to criticize her actions.

Perhaps with Graveline attending, he kept his temper under control, giving her a "deal with you later" look. "A dirty trick for sure. Or it could have been an innocent error." She coughed in derision, and he continued. "What makes you fix on the woman? Earl the Pearl is a big name in this town. Plenty of contacts from his union-busting days. Quite the brawler."

"So it fits, Steve. Mabel Joy opened with the mushroom ploy. Earl added the KO punch. What was next for Charles? A concrete overcoat and a ride on their cabin cruiser?"

Belle walked back to the DesRosiers', passing at the turnaround a brown Ford pickup, perhaps four years old, but in prime shape. She filed away the information as did the regulars. Who else was using the paths? More hunters or hikers or even lovers? Once or twice on star-watching strolls, she had surprised a few determined parkers miles from the eyes of nosy spouses or parents. Turning in to collect the dog, she heard Hélène call.

"Might as well have some lunch. Plenty for four. Ed counts twice. It's leftover spaghetti. Fresh sourdough bread, too, popped out of the machine."

"I don't have much of an appetite. Thanks anyway."

"Worm anything out of your police friend?" Ed asked, coming outside nibbling a meatball skewered on his fork.

"The medical examiner seemed to favour a heart attack but can't decide how he got that bruise. Slipped and fell? Someone punched him? They found a cigarette butt outside his gate."

"Are we talking murder again? What the hell's happening on this road? I'm going to start keeping my twelve-gauge in the bedroom. Got more kick than the old wo…" He scratched his belly and glanced mischievously in Hélène's direction. "You don't suppose Chuck and Anni were goin' at it, and then an old boyfriend of hers…"

His wife's tone was testy. "Have some respect, you clown. How ridiculous. Anyway, Belle, at least take some of this zucchini cake." She presented a fragrant chocolaty package along with an envelope with the recipe.

That night while she had a coffee and dessert on the deck and watched a flaming red sky surrender to black, Belle missed her friend. His patrician smile, eclectic conversations, refreshing embarrassment at suggestive subjects. And his cooking. Oh, yes, his cooking. She toasted him with the last morsel of Hélène's rich, moist chocolate cake. Somehow the lake seemed increasingly lonely now that one less admirer approved it. Two, counting Anni. Then she shivered as the darkness pooled. Too bad they hadn't struck up a friendship. What an interesting pair they would have made, or perhaps not, with their singlemindedness. The relentless charge of a Seadoo driver skirting the shoreline sent her to bed with evil hopes that a strong wind would whip up waves to keep the motors at bay.

NINETEEN

Tying up loose ends through a sense of dubious honour, Belle sent the appraisal to Mabel Joy, boosting the value by five per cent for good measure. Off went a check to *The Sudbury Star* for her father, gathering his life into another three-month package. Long neglected, the garden needed attention, too. What an embarrassment of riches. With a fading heart she counted at least a dozen zucchini sizable enough for a bludgeoning. Next year she would plant four, not eight, no matter how innocent and frail they appeared nestling in their peat pots. If she didn't get rid of these, she might have to commit vegecide, kill the plants before they murdered her.

She sat on her garbage box at the road with an armful as the parade of working folk stopped to chat. "Hey, my zucchini's ripe" turned to "Could you use some zucchini?" to "Just got a few left" to "Please take one," but they were all too wise…and too jaded from designing recipes for their own profligate squashes. Into the van went a large selection of bats destined for Rainbow Country. Townies always considered fresh produce a welcome gift. To accommodate the vegetables, Belle moved a few piles of junk fliers in the back of the van. That was when she noticed Charles' safari jacket. Why send it to the Goodwill? It would be a useful keepsake with all those pockets and zippers and a small memory of a fine friendship.

Scooping up a dish of vanilla ice cream at the restaurant, she trotted largesse to the oohs and ahs of the nursing home staff. All the way down the hall she could hear them discussing dinner plans: zucchini pancakes, casseroles and stews. As an incentive, she had passed around copies of Hélène's cake recipe.

Her father was dozing over a talk show about adults who found playing baby an erotic treat and got off on giant diapers. Not so funny when it's for real, she thought, flipping to a TV Ontario nature program as she tapped his shoulder. "Hey, handsome. Remember when you bought me my first ice cream? I put more on my face than in my stomach."

He blinked and dug into the treat. "Strawberry next time. That's what I got you."

Scarcely had she learned from David Suzuki, Canada's eco-prophet, that eating polar bear liver could be fatal, than her father had licked the spoon clean. The man could inhale ice cream without a whisper of high cholesterol, which boded well for her. Studying his face was like glimpsing the future, except that she'd never look that young. No worries, she guessed, always in the hands of a capable woman, her mother, his girlfriend, and now her. "Solve that murder?" he asked, burring the last word like his Scots ancestors.

"Don't I wish. Now we have another one. Or maybe not. The police think it was an accident." She explained the details of Charles' death. "Something else is bothering me. I can link Anni to a scandal years ago at a mission school. The place was run by a Mother Superior named Euphemia." Storytelling had been one of his other gifts, spinning her tales to put her to sleep, scripted from the Brothers Grimm by way of MGM and Fox.

"An evil nun? Beating the kids? Wouldn't have been allowed after the code the Hays Office brought in during the Twenties. Catholic Church had a big stick with their banned

194

list, too. Selznick had to fight like a devil to keep that 'damn' in *Gone with the Wind*." His shaggy eyebrows wiggled like benign woolly bear caterpillars. "But women are the deadlier of the species, your mother said, and she was always right."

"Or we agreed to tell her that," she said. She hesitated to mention that sexual abuse might be a factor. Whenever the subject came up, he refused to believe that anyone would do such a thing. His was a gentle world where all children were spoiled as rotten as his daughter and scared only by fictional witches.

"Euphemia, was it? An old-fashioned name. Kind of majestic, though. Someone you wouldn't want to cross. Bet she was beautiful, too. *Leave Her to Heaven*. That Gene Tierney was a knockout." As she left, he yelled, "Cornell Wilde was a sucker for a pretty face. You be careful."

After checking errant titles downtown at the Land Registry Office, Belle walked into the spanking new towers of the Sudbury Police Department, part of the Tom Davies Square complex. Explaining herself at Reception, she was escorted to the basement. The damp cold in the corridor made her wonder if Steve weren't a candidate for arthritis as well as food poisoning. She could swear that the same sad triangle of pizza from the last visit festered on a paper plate. He looked up, gave a series of hoarse coughs. "Bring anything to eat?"

"I wish I had. You look like you could use a good meal." The spark in his eyes had given way to dullness, and his voice lacked energy. The recent cutbacks in the justice system had led to early retirements for the lucky and punishing workloads for those remaining. She hoped that he were in line for a vacation. The new family could use a break.

Flinging herself into a familiar scrofulous armchair more duct tape than leather, she covered herself with a Cecil Facer

Youth Centre sweatshirt piled on the corner of his desk. "Before I freeze to death, what about Charles? Anything turn up?"

He pulled out a file and gnawed stubbornly at a shard of crust. "Look, we're not prime time television here. It's shoe leather basics plus gut instinct. Autopsy confirms a heart attack. Seventy-five percent blockage of arteries. He should have been a candidate for angioplasty. As for the bruise, it's slim evidence. Mitch says the time frame is difficult to establish with the sauna heat hastening rigor. At a guess, an hour or two after dinner."

Belle felt a twinge of nostalgia for that last supper. Knowing Charles' love of food, it had probably been a fine one. Then she returned to the present. "The tracks?"

"His car, Ed's quad, ours down the lane. A general mess. Rough gravel like that doesn't tell clear tales."

"Our favourite poisoners?"

"No answer at the Rogers' places, town or camp. Secretary at the business says they drove to New York City yesterday. If they're motelling it, using cash, we may not be able to contact them until they return."

"What about his will? He had plenty of money, Steve. How else could he have put up cash for that property? And there was no mortgage."

"A simple holograph we found in a folder labelled 'Legal Documents.' Dated about ten years ago. No *cui bono* there. Left everything to the Cancer Society. Some sizable investments, mostly mutual funds."

"Makes sense. His sister died of leukemia." She drummed her fingers in thought. "What about that auditing job? Did you contact his employer? He must have worked there most of his life."

He rubbed at his temples with a irritated look, then pulled out his notes. "Look, it was a heart attack, long overdue. I pursued this only because I knew you'd be at me like a blackfly, so listen up and bury it once and for all. Sullivan worked for a paint company, travelled mostly around Ontario and Quebec. Quiet, efficient, but kept to himself." He stopped and ran his finger over a few lines. "The one funny thing…"

"Yes, what?" She shifted in the armchair, artistically rearranging a spring behind her back. "Eureka" wasn't the magic word for discoveries; "that's funny" often preceded scientific breakthroughs.

"Life seems to have started at university, when he was well over thirty. Dropped in out of nowhere. He didn't apply for a social insurance number or any other piece of ID until then."

"Not out of nowhere. You must have a birthplace."

"Mille Roche. Doesn't even exist anymore. One of those little towns flooded by the St. Lawrence Seaway."

"No one gets an auditing job without credentials. Where did he go to school?"

"Sailed right through Queen's in two years. Took proficiency exams for a number of courses. A regular genius, or maybe he was home-schooled."

"I suppose you checked with military records." Belle turned from contemplation of a furry object in the dim corner, hoping that it didn't move.

"Come on, Belle. This is getting ridiculous. We don't have the draft here. Our military is smaller than the Boy Scouts. What's your point? If you have one."

"We had an odd conversation once about old Nazi war criminals, you know, those senile, frail old men dragged out of nursing homes to face a trial."

He spoke in a monotone, sneezed twice, then reached for a tissue to blow his nose. "A summer cold is a different animal. So, what was his take on that?"

"Said that they were as good as dead and should be left alone. It wouldn't change the past."

"All of which means nothing. He would have been a kid at the end of the war. Think he had some Nazi uncles?"

Belle laughed in spite of herself, then caught Steve looking at his watch. No doubt that she was wasting his time. "OK. Forget it. Anyway, what happens if you can't find any relatives? Can there still be a funeral? Just curious."

"Court-appointed executor takes care of that. I guess with his money he can go in style if anyone wants to help make the arrangements." Steve shrugged and doodled a tombstone on the pad. "You, maybe."

"No thanks. Anni had the right idea. Short and sweet. Ed, Hélène, and I will hoist a few in his honour." Rising to leave, she noticed a framed black and white snapshot of two young boys. They were grinning at each other, holding a long-nosed pike which weighed as much as they did. Craig and Steve. She'd forgotten to mention the hot sandwich specials at the restaurant. And this wasn't the time.

Back in the van, a belly level growl drowned out the oldies station she'd located. Just as well. It seemed to play the same ten tunes, especially "Wild Thing" and "Are You Lonesome Tonight?" She hauled herself to Harvey's, a hamburger chain recently melded with the American Church's Fried Chicken, ordering a Crusty Chicken sandwich, a bag of fries, milk to ward off osteo and on a whim, fried okra. Who in Northern Ontario knew the joys of that wagon wheel vegetable, except disguised in chicken gumbo soup? One golden morsel popped indecently into her mouth at the cash register. Sensational!

Searching for a table, she saw Zack finishing a coffee, circling ads in the classified section of *The Sudbury Star.*

"How's business, Belle?" he asked pleasantly, motioning her over to his booth.

"In the chips," she said, waving a catsupy example. "And yours?"

He shrugged and blew out his cheeks. "A used book and CD place downtown folded. Bad location. I had a plan to buy the stock and relocate, but I can't float it. Looks like I'll have to take a job as a taxi driver. Only action these days. Easy enough if you can stand the hours."

"And memorize the pit stops. Listen, I know your aunt's affairs aren't finalized, but when they are, you could sell the house for start-up capital. Interest rates are at an all-time low." She realized how opportunistic this sounded when she saw his wounded expression. "No offense, Zack. Just a thought. The lurking realtor rears her head."

"I couldn't let a stranger have Aunt Anni's place, not with all those memories. When I was a kid, my mom parked me there every summer. If I wasn't fishing with Uncle Cece, I was building a tree house or hunting frogs with her. Did I ever tell you that she invited me to move in after he died? Nearly took the offer, but guessed that she felt more sorry for me than lonely. Lord knows she kept busy." He rubbed at his hands, poking at a blister.

"More manual labour?"

He laughed. "The Valley potato fields. Minimum wage, but free spuds. I'll get used to it. About time, wouldn't you say?"

Maybe there was some hope, Belle thought. Anni had loved him with an affection beyond gene splicing. An hour later, as she pulled into her driveway and stepped out of the van, she noticed a GM Supercab truck parked in the yard. In the box were bags of what looked like instant concrete mix. The door slammed, and a tall, wiry figure in workpants and a dusty sweater came toward her, blocking her way. With eyes blazing in his brick-red face and fists bunched up in his pockets, he didn't look like a Jehovah's Witness. "Yes?" she asked.

"You Palmer?" She nodded, regretting that the dog was inside.

"You've been giving my wife a rough time. I want you to lay off." The voice belied the bluster. It was squeaky, hesitant. At close range, the eyes appeared tearful and hurt. "She's threatening to go to Santa Fe for good, leaving me, she said." He pulled out a huge handkerchief and honked his nose while she counted to ten. "Allergies," he said. It was then that she noticed stencilled letters on the driver's door: "Earl The Pearl."

"Your wife is Mabel Joy?" At his blinks, she stepped forward, raising her voice aggressively. "She nearly poisoned a friend of mine with mushrooms. Your neighbour Charles Sullivan."

"She what? Are you crazy? That old fart who took our poochies to the pound?"

Belle delivered a coup with a satisfying verbal smack that stretched her frame to the max. "The man you're speaking of is dead, murdered, I suspect." Earl sank down heavily on the bumper, struggling for breath.

"Jesus, you don't think that she…" Out came a small vial of tablets, and a shaky hand stuffed one under his tongue. He seemed ill, or judging from his florid face, a drinker.

"Haven't the police contacted you?

He mumbled something about a pileup at Buffalo which had hung them up at the border. "Come on to the deck and sit down," she said, suddenly aware that she might have to test the ambulance system yet again. "I'll get some water." Earl probably would have preferred a beer, but she wasn't feeling charitable.

A short discussion and an examination of Earl's crabbedly-composed pocket calendar revealed that on the night of Charles' death, the Rogers had been at a fund-raising ball for the Nickel City College Special Needs Centre. "Made *The Sudbury Star.* Picture and all. She was real proud of that." Earl promised to erect an electronic fence for his dogs. After he pumped her hand, Belle took his card in case she ever needed an interlocking stone driveway or, perish the thought, a new septic tank at cost plus. He wasn't a bad man, just turned to jelly by his wife. Ed would have used a ruder term involving a pussy cat and a whip.

As she went into the house, the phone was ringing, a distinctive Newfie accent on the other end. "I just learned about Patsy Sommers. Sorry I wasn't there to give you a hand with those kids. Wouldn't that be my week off. You did a great job, I heard. Ever thought of being a foster parent? We're always short."

"Don't press your luck, Dottie. Anyway, if you think it was toxic outside the house, you should have been inside. I had a chat with Mom at the hospital. She's back to consciousness if not conscience. What now? Will charges be laid?"

Dottie sighed. "Sounds open and shut, but the CAS tries to keep families together. Despite the plain stupidity of her actions, it wasn't deliberate abuse. If there's a chance in hell she can raise the kids, she'll get them."

Belle felt her temper rise at the image of that empty cereal box. The persistence of vision. "They seemed happy, and I suppose they got enough to eat. The laundry was clean. More than one neighbour gets his garbage ransacked by coons or bears. Is that all there is?"

"Miss Peggy Lee had it right. With social services funding stretched to the max, the kids will be out of the foster homes as soon as Patsy's released. Regular visitations will be arranged for a while, so there will be some controls. There is something I haven't mentioned, information I received which might soften your attitude."

"About Patsy? Not unless it softens my head."

"She's a patsy of another kind. Those kids belong to her sister in Montreal, post-partum depression. And don't ask me why she keeps having them. Whatever Patsy's doing, it's better than the jeopardy they'd be in down there. Remember the psychiatrist who jumped in front of the subway train with her baby in her arms?"

TWENTY

In the week following, Belle resumed her inquiries into Anni's past, starting with her favourite nun. At St. Joe's, she found the woman sitting quietly in the Intensive Care waiting room holding a young woman's hand while a thin man in a sweat-soaked tanktop paced the floor stoically. Kids having kids, barely eighteen at a glance, though dark shadows framed their bloodshot eyes. The girl twisted one end of her long brown hair into greasy tendrils, then sucked the nipple of a noxious-coloured sports drink bottle. He groaned, reached into her purse on the floor, and set up a small cigarette-making apparatus. As he shook out the tobacco, Sister Veronica tapped his arm, her arch eyebrow more reproving than a slap in the face. "Smoking is allowed out by the front door."

As they walked to her office, the nun's face mixed resignation with fear. "Their two-year-old wandered into a neighbour's pool while she talked on the phone. The child's conscious, but at that age it's difficult to determine neurological damage." She stopped momentarily to touch the arm of a still form on a gurney in the hall outside the Radiation area.

Offering Belle a chair, she pointed out a new addition: a plastic bottle of bubble bath shaped like the Hunchback of Notre Dame. "From a little one we nearly lost from pneumonia. She went home yesterday. Aren't children amazing?" she asked. "They see but rarely judge. It takes a careful upbringing to establish that signal character fault."

Belle stayed quiet, amazed at how Disney could remould such a benign and loopy creature from Hugo's grotesque, or even from Laughton's more sympathetic rendition. She shook her head at an offer of tea, Sister Veronica regarding her coolness with mild confusion. "Mrs. Sommers' alibi, as I think it's called, has been confirmed by records. She arrived at 4:00 p.m. and didn't leave until twelve hours later. Does that fit your time frame?" she asked with a friendly collusion.

Belle felt prickly at yet another display of the woman's helpfulness. That white habit had lost its innocence. How naïve was she? Or how clever? "Probably. But there's another concern."

Sister Veronica shifted forward, her eyes steady, reflecting a nuance of perplexity. "It must be very serious indeed. What's wrong? I heard that the children were safe."

"It's nothing to do with Patsy. Let's talk about Osprey Inlet, north of Red Lake." Belle continued, selecting her words with silver tongs. It was no time to babble. "Have you ever been there?"

"No." The expression was bland, disciplined, hard to read.

"Twenty-five years ago something went terribly wrong at St. Michael's residential school. No one in the town wants to talk about it. Not even today. An old magazine carried a picture of the church, the kids, the religious staff." She narrowed her eyes, tossing the hump an oblique glance. Still off to one side. "A Sister Euphemia was the Mother Superior. Her unusual habit was the same as yours."

In the palpable silence, one heavy eyebrow rose. Sense of entrapment? Belle had the impression of a wise old badger, back to the wall. Yet the voice was too honest, and voices and body language were hard to disguise. Except for true psychopaths, Belle recalled with a nervous twitch. "Are you interrogating me, my dear? I said I hadn't been there, and I haven't. Yet perhaps that was a sin of omission." She sat back, smoothing her habit as she cleared her throat. "I have no compunction about admitting that those stories are true. It was an evil of such malevolence that I almost lost my faith. St. Michael's shrouded the proud name of our order under the blackest infamy."

"Go on." Belle watched the garnets in the chain of beads wink with the light streaming in the window.

"At the time I was at a hospital in the Peace River area in Alberta. What filtered down to us was quite skeletal, merely that the central figure was a nun, a mother superior."

Belle jumped in her chair. "A woman molester?"

"That a woman would sexually abuse is quite rare, but never underestimate the permutations of temptation. Sister Euphemia had a special charisma, as all such monsters do. That is why they succeed for so long. As well, there were rumours that she was protected," she said with a troubled sigh.

"Protected by the Church. Of course." Belle didn't try to hide the disgust in her voice, making "church" a four-letter word.

The nun stiffened, as if taking personal umbrage. "Osprey Inlet is hundreds of miles from supervisory boards and thus subject to few inspections. Have you heard of the term '*éminence grise*'? Someone in the shadows who introduces an unspoken element of fear? But at last the travesty was exposed, thanks be to God."

"Exposed, but apparently never prosecuted. A total cover-up. What about the victims? Crime without punishment. Without any resolution, how can they put their lives together?"

"Even after the most heinous act, healing can begin. All depends upon the individual."

Belle folded her hands. "What do you mean? I suppose you'd free Paul Bernardo?" Canada's handsome serial killer received a life sentence for his murder of at least three young women, including his sister-in-law. Meanwhile, his evil blonde twin, Karla Homolka, was finishing a twelve-year sentence, having plea bargained her guilt by turning Crown evidence against her husband.

"You mock me. I speak of the victims. Every generation has its terminology for a disease of the soul. Early scholars called it simple Christian guilt. Modern psychologists refer to 'baggage.' The victims may feel, as do many, that they were the only ones signalled out for abuse, or worse yet, partially to blame. So insidious, isn't it?"

Belle felt her fists clench. "Sounds like revenge is the best medicine."

"The Old Testament contrasts with the New on that concept. 'Justice is mine,' 'an eye for an eye,' instead of turning the other cheek as our Lord beseeches us. Whatever the path, after a spiritual cleansing such as we have seen in the renewed concept of native healing circles, there can be a return to purpose. Work is the salvation."

Belle shuffled her feet and poured herself a cup of tea as Sister Veronica watched with placid amusement at the small gesture of capitulation.

"Let's get back to the source of the evil? What happened to Euphemia?" Belle asked, sounding out the beautiful syllables of a deadly identity.

"An internal purging. All patently culpable ones were sent to cloistered facilities, and those who wore moral blinkers were pressured to return to the laity, so we learned through quiet channels. But as for the courts, no charges were laid. In those benighted times, I would have been happily surprised had they been. Witness the recent lawsuits dating back forty years or more. Grandmothers and grandfathers trying to redeem their childhoods." She searched Belle's sceptical face. "Don't judge us all by a few sinners."

Even a stone wall would crumble under those sad old basset eyes. Could she trust that the nun hadn't been there herself? "No, but I detest the hypocrisy of the Church taking care of its own, even if every profession has its secret police. Perhaps it deserves the expensive litigation it faces. Now, these cloistered facilities you mention. Are they only for punishment?"

"Oh my, no. Some choose to spend their lives in quiet meditation and prayer far from the secular world. Such a commitment is as true a vocation as nursing, teaching or any valuable community work."

Belle blew out a puff of contempt. "Hardly a prison, then. Food, shelter, books, probably satellite Christian TV channel, no doubt."

"Have you noticed how often you use humour to cloud the issue? Being forbidden to speak is torment for someone who loves the rewards of human conversation, or of power, for that matter." She considered Belle with a cautious assessment. "I'm still unsure how this matter concerns you at present."

"To be blunt, I want to know if Euphemia is alive."

"Still no answer, but I will indulge you." The nun reached for a Rolodex on her desk. "Our numbers have been dwindling as the old ones die and are not replaced. The priesthood as well. The next Pope will have to deal with reality and perhaps revoke the stubborn insistence on celibacy. There is one facility left. Le Coeur de Repos up in the Gaspé. Anticosti Island. Do you know it?"

"The Quiet Heart," she whispered in recollection. A trip to Montreal, Quebec City, and up the North Shore had introduced that breathtaking but little travelled coastline of Canada. "It's remote all right. A ferry from the mainland. Too expensive for me."

"Very few visitors, unlike in modern prisons, if I may borrow your comparison. The Church can wield an iron hand when it chooses. However, residents on a voluntary basis relish the privacy and concentration." She flipped through the cards, squinted at the information with a nod. "My old novitiate friend Sister Margaret bides there in perfect contentment. We exchange Christmas cards."

Belle wondered if Sister Veronica would flinch at a grateful embrace. "Can you contact her?"

"Family calls are allowed once a week. I'll do my best. But I spoke of the here and now, and you have skillfully avoided the implications. What is your role? Are you an avenger?"

"Now you're making jokes." She rotated the cup, wishing that it contained tea leaves. Her grandmother had been famous for divining the future through that companionable art. "My neighbour we discussed, the older woman who was murdered? She lived at Osprey Inlet when Euphemia did. After all these weeks, there's no sign of an arrest. My last hope."

"Could she have been Euphemia? The ages seem to match." A suspicious crease marred her smooth forehead, eyes shrinking into pinpoints as she drew Celtic crosses on a pad. "Perhaps she found some way to leave the cloister. Through an escape, or more likely through her eloquence and guile. The Church sets great store by repentance, the lost sheep rejoining the fold. Suppose that she returned to the mainland and after all those years was brought down by the hand of one she had abused?"

Belle fought back laughter. "Let's see. She sewed herself into a shroud like the man in the iron mask? Swam to shore? That really is a baroque plot, Sister, but they couldn't have been the same person. Anni was a dental assistant." She looked at the pig with the Sherlock Holmes greatcoat, pipe and hat and thought for a moment. "Do you know Euphemia's family name?"

The nun shook her head. "Oh, my dear. Taking a saint's name is like assuming a new identity. She might have been a Betty Jones pleased with something more exotic. Perhaps Margaret can give us a start."

Great, Belle thought. Long distance sleuthing on the cheap. Yet what better network than the Church itself? Canada's first intensive history had been the two-hundred-year chronicle of the Jesuit Relations. Unfortunate connotations for an innocent word.

That night Gilbert and Sullivan rang in the air. Fuelled by fresh possibilities of new paths, her appetite had returned with a passion. A grilled pork tenderloin marinated in Manitoulin honey, accompanied by flower-fragrant basmati rice mated well with spinach, green beans and broccoli from the garden. Two dollars' credit against the nine-hundred-dollar soil bill. A Talus zinfandel kept pace with the spices as she mused over her favourite line: "Skim milk masquerades as cream." No cynic when it came to friends, she took them at face value. Charles and Anni had been *crème de la crème*. Now both were dead. One murdered; the other? Pulled in two directions, she surrendered to one.

A cigarette. A dubious bruise. Feeble clues, if clues at all. Yet someone could have parked at the turnaround, walked in quietly to the well-concealed property. Smoked in the dark while watching Charles enter the sauna. Had the police overlooked some small detail as they had at Anni's, the letter in her Peterson's, her missing address book? What might she unearth about Charles' death with more leisure to search the property?

She eyed the forgotten key, whispering temptation from a suction cuphook on the fridge. If only she had a clear objective. Setting aside the lunatic-out-of-nowhere-in-the-night scenario, she reviewed the small evidence of a lonely life. Charles had money, as much as might have accumulated from a solid career and no children, rather none that she knew of. And he'd left all to charity. A dead end. She started at their meeting and took baby steps. The raspberries, the wine, the cottage, the tool shed, her joke about Jason Brown's treasure.

As she ate mindlessly, a stubborn chunk of broccoli stuck in her throat. She swallowed more wine, bitter with tannin, and her eyes snapped open. Treasure? Brown's nephew had been casual enough, making light of that legendary hideyhole. Had he left something after all, something worth killing for? Or was it the ravings of a senile old man? She'd never seen him at Rainbow Country, though he might be on the second floor or confined to bed. Perhaps he'd already died. "They either go in the first few months, or they live on for years," a candid nurse had told her. But Jason was mute. Couldn't or wouldn't talk. Had her father met the man, she wondered? The nephew's number in Sarnia was still in her computer records.

"Sorry to hear about Mr. Sullivan," he replied as she explained her call. "You said he'd been so pleased with the place."

"If only for a brief time, he loved it," Belle said, filling him in about her suspicions. "This may be a wild shot, but what about that secret room? Could someone have been looking for it?"

His raucous laugh made her yank away the receiver. "In the first place, it wasn't a room. More like a nook. Said he kept a few private things away from his sister, my Aunt Deborah. She acted as his housekeeper until she passed on. Never gave a hint where it was, though, and we kids crawled over every inch of that property. Guess he liked to tease us."

"No jewels or stolen bars of palladium from INCO, then?" Rare and expensive by-products from the nickel process had proved tempting to many employees.

"I'll be honest with you," he added, the least credible words in the world. "It might have been something as simple as a collection of *Playboy* magazines. Or maybe some screech, that raw rum from the Maritimes. She didn't mind the wine, old Bible-thumper, but she was fierce about hard stuff."

"Would you mind if I visited him? My father's over at Rainbow Country."

"He'd probably like that. Ashamed to admit we don't get up there more than twice a year. Ten hours is a long haul. Damn government never going to four-lane 69. It's still a cowpath from Parry Sound."

TWENTY-ONE

So that's why you're here at the crack of dawn," her father said as he buttered a sixth piece of toast. "The Brown fellow? Sure, I know him. Gives the nurses some devil of a ride. What do you want with that old geezer? Aren't I leaving you enough money? Did you flub up my mutual funds? Canuck buck gets any lower you'll need a wheelbarrow to buy a..." His chuckle turned to a cough as he grabbed at his coffee cup.

Belle's heart thumped like a dicky engine. "Take it easy. Another choking scene will finish the both of us. Anyway, Charles bought Brown's property. Could be he had a visitor that night he died. I was thinking of a secret place that the old man bragged about for years."

"Secret, eh? Leave him to me. We've had grand chats. Born the same year, you know."

Belle clasped his shoulder, grinning like a Cheshire cat. "So he can talk!"

"Jason? 'Course he can. Just no one understands him except me. Got to listen, not just hear. Poor guy's got no one to help him either. Remember my trouble down in Florida?" After one particularly potent TIA, he'd been mute for weeks, but a strong will and the coaching of his girlfriend had restored his speech.

"Gets pretty mad when they can't catch on. Darned if he didn't nail Cindy smack on the can with a boiled egg

212

yesterday. Haul me out of this contraption, and we'll try the card table in the dining room. Can't play, but he likes to watch. He's got both oars in the water. Look at his eyes. You'll see what I mean."

Belle unfastened the table of the gerry chair with an urge to weep. How did he stand the confinement? And yet if he fell... She took his arm and straightened him to his feet as he marshalled his resources and sweat broke out on his broad forehead. "Geronimo," he yelled, and they turtled forward. He fumbled at the handrail down the long hall to the dining area. Some residents had returned to their rooms after breakfast while the more interactive ones played cards or joined in a bean bag toss led by the staff.

Jason Brown, a hulk of a man shrunken into a wheelchair, had intelligent, deep-set eyes which seemed to burn with a hatred for his loss of independence. Dressed in a Blueberry Festival T-shirt and mismatched but clean slacks, he followed the deal of the cards, pointing a trembly finger at the occasional move. They'd only met casually at the mailboxes years ago. No chance he'd remember her. Yet if she could interest him in something precious from his past...

"Jason, old man." Her father patted his back before easing into a chair, leaving Belle standing behind. "Daughter of mine here needs your help. Listen up."

When she bent to his level, at first he seemed confused, glancing from one person to the other. "I won't keep you from your game, Mr. Brown. There's a problem. The man who bought your property died under suspicious circumstances. Your nephew said that you had a secret hiding place. Maybe there's a connection. Did you leave anything valuable there which we might be able to bring you?" The promise didn't make sense, but it sounded helpful, a necessary conspiracy of

213

young against old which shamed her.

Suddenly Jason exploded in a series of cackles mixed with unintelligible words, disconnected syllables. The man's breath was no pansy patch, through no fault of his. Dental care was a messy, time-consuming chore placed at the bottom of the list. But he was smiling oddly. Unsure how to proceed, she looked at her father. "He likes you," he whispered with confidence. "Otherwise he wouldn't have paid attention."

She turned from the table and formed silent words with her lips, adding a shrug. "What's he saying?"

Her father leaned forward. "How's that again?" His gnarly hand clasped Jason's. "Go on, pal. Take your time." A garble followed, a spew of consonants and vowels repeated several times. Belle backed off discreetly from the spittle.

"Medicine, he says."

"You want your medicine?" She scanned the room for an attendant, speaking softly to her father, "Are you sure? How 'with it' is this guy?"

Brown shook his gleaming bald head, mottled with age spots, as he pounded the table, blasting out more guttural grunts. "Nope, that's what he means all right," her father said with a frown. "Funny, though. Med time is ten and six. It's only nine."

An owly nurse with pointed ears responded to her questioning. "Of course Mr. Brown will receive his medication at the proper hour," she answered with an annoyed tone as she arranged a tray with rows of tiny paper cups. "We chart everything."

Belle flashed Brown her broadest smile and shook his hand. The skin was cold, but the grip surprisingly strong, as if he were trying to speak through what small powers remained in his charge. "Thanks for your help, sir. Good luck with the game."

"You did your best, Father," she said as they teetered back to his room.

"Med time is ten and six," he repeated.

"Keep pumping him. You never know." She helped him into his chair, locking the table with sickening reluctance.

He beamed and gave a v-for-victory sign. "We'll crack her. Just like Nick and Nora Charles."

"And Puffball can be Asta," she added, patting the resident bichon frisé trotting by in search of a handout. Her father winked as he pointed to a box of Peek Freans on the bureau, so she left him a handful. "Just one for the dog, Father. Remember what happened to Lucky." Treated to butter pecan ice cream and constant cookies, their dachshund had ballooned into a cartoon and died in his sleep on a sunny lanai in Florida.

"Practically a hundred in human years. Hope I go like that," he shot back.

"Medicine," Belle thought as she left. What else would the captive elderly be interested in but food and pills, whose arrivals marked lagging hours for all but the most active few? She was glad her father still had a passion for *Jeopardy* and *Wheel of Fortune*. Yet there had been something in the old man's animation. At this point, anything was worth a try.

At the office, she logged a few inquiries. When summer ended, cottagers would be eager to sell, but who would want to buy as the cold winds of September sifted dry leaves? She left at five still mulling over Brown's desperation. At least she and her father shared their memories.

The blueberry hills on the road past town were dotted with pickers, the air beckoning spicy-sweet through the window. Hot weather and frequent rains would provide a banner crop. Though her favourite fields lay nearer home at Hidden Valley, a half-mile down abandoned railroad tracks, she remembered that in late March her last freezer bag had been transformed into a succulent cobbler. Wouldn't a pie taste great? Or just plain berries? Besides, the experience itself provided a welcome relaxation.

In the late summer ritual for "Northrunners," as people often pronounced it, everyone got into the spirit, young, old, rich and poor. Hélène's philosophy was that picking revealed character. "There's the lazy ones, see. Relax with a beer in the shade and gobble pies later. Others pretend to pick but just eat. That's Ed. Some can't find a good bush and quit after a few minutes." She would pause thoughtfully, shaking her finger for effect. "Now, never waste time on a poor spot with only singletons. Bad for the back. But you know where to look, you'll find as many as the bears."

Belle pulled off the road behind a line of cars and rummaged for a plastic bag. A few minutes later she was climbing the hills, past "Bob 4ever" spray-painted where the glacier's icy fingers had raked the stone. "Not even rocks are forever, Bob," she murmured. Hunkered down in the late afternoon sun, the insistent ticking of grasshoppers in her ears, she missed the panting partnership of the dog. Freya nosed out the berries and roamed around independently until her evil alter ego emerged. Then she plowed into the middle of the best bunches, nudged Belle's hand with slobber, and more than once had the effrontery to munch from an unwatched bowl.

A trained eye helped, the mind judging in a flash the configuration of the bush, the number of berries, size, colour. Large were prized, since they filled the container quickly, but small were often tastier. Under sheltering trees, the berries were tarter, in the sun hotter and sweeter, a piquant combination. Thick, luxuriant leaves meant a good season but hid the fruit. The picker tried to strip five or six at a time, holding the pan underneath, shuffling horizontally on haunches to avoid a slipped disc. Belle gauged the riches by how long it took to glean enough for a pie. Ten to fifteen minutes was standard.

A short reconnaissance provided dessert, discounting the few morsels that exploded the signature of summer into her mouth. As she stood and stretched, familiar complaints broke the stillness. "What are they paying? Only ten bucks a basket? Remember that drought year we got twelve?" Another voice talked about a convoy which had rolled up from Toronto with giant rakes and were nearly lynched by locals protecting their territory. On a flat rock, a wiry man in a straw hat sat and smoked, tapping ashes into a pop can. Smoking was illegal while walking in the bush. A person had to stop and attend to the cigarette, a sensible rule but hard to enforce. Forest fires in the peaty Sudbury area could follow roots underground, lie dormant, then spring up later twenty feet away.

Insulated in the mindless pleasure of gentle industry, wrapped in mental cotton batting, Belle sensed someone talking to her, but couldn't decipher the words until she looked up and wiped sweat from her eyes. "Hey, I said I haven't seen you at the restaurant this week." It was Fred. "We're trying to make enough for tickets to Garth Brooks at Skydome."

She laughed and admired the full baskets in the usual social gesture. They might realize their goal. Many patient pensioners earned over two thousand dollars a season, if their knees held out. "So who's minding the store?"

"Craig's taking charge with Sis. He'll be here second shift soon as I leave. Made over six hundred bucks so far at the Farmers' Market." He flicked a small green worm into the brush and rubbed his back. "Been tough money, though.

217

Tougher than running a restaurant. These hills get pretty dry without trees. Couple more days we'll have to find another spot." Together they walked to the vehicles, where he showed off his pride, a 1967 Camaro. His plan was to restore it as soon as the restaurant got onto its feet. If cars could express feelings, the grill frowned at the dull paint and rusty bumpers.

Belle arrived home in a mood of curious elation, convinced that something lay behind Brown's wild insistence. Charles' place was worth a second look, especially after the cursory examination from the police. Washing the berries and dosing them with heavy cream, giving Freya her share, she grated a large zucchini for pancakes, adding dollops of McIlhenny's green jalapeno sauce while plotting the next morning's search. Maybe Charles hadn't even discovered the hiding place, if in fact it existed, but at least she had a clear goal.

To get an early start and avoid prying eyes, at eight she started to drink and read. The light outside and racehorse nerves made it hard to settle down, but she never scrimped on sleep, an affordable luxury. Didn't Delores Del Rio snooze fifteen hours each night to keep that profile baby smooth well into her eighties? As the last Scotch trickled down an hour later, the phone rang. "I hope I'm not intruding, my dear," a plummy voice said. Sister Veronica waited politely.

"Of course not. Did you reach your friend so soon?" Quite an operative, Belle thought. Speaking of an *éminence grise*.

"Under the pretence of an emergency..." She coughed delicately. "I was able to talk briefly with Margaret, but the news is ambivalent."

What an odd word. "What do you mean?"

"Euphemia arrived at Le Coeur de Repos ten years ago, transferred from a redundant facility in Manitoba. By the time she reached Anticosti, she was a very sick woman and passed on shortly after. With no word from her family about arrangements, she was buried on the island, her goods placed in storage. The shocking part…"

"Yes?"

"So that you may better understand, let me tell you more about Margaret. Psychology is the field in which she took her degree. When the occasion arises, she acts as therapist. In this personal capacity, she spent much time with Euphemia." A long silence made Belle uneasy. Something had shaken the nun's usually maddening sang-froid.

"Go on, Sister."

"I don't know quite how to form the words for this loathsome sin. There was no repentance. The woman claimed divine sanction for a mother-son relationship. Utter blasphemy."

Belle stubbed out her cigarette in a punishing gesture, grinding it to tatters. "Better dead then. I would have liked to have laid hands on her myself."

Sister Veronica exhaled, then her voice strengthened. "And although I am not one to credit a cult of diabolism, a singular malignancy seemed at work. Thank God her timely unmasking forfended further destruction."

Belle poured another finger of liquor against the painful light of these sobering revelations as well as another word to define. Forfend. "That's very helpful information, perhaps all we'll ever learn at this point. What about the victims? Do you suppose they would find solace in knowing that their tormentor is dead?"

"Malebranche says that we are not our own light. In this case I hope he was wrong."

As she hung up, making a mental note to research French philosophers, a bright spear across the lake at the North River caught her eye and she waited for the corresponding crash, counting the seconds. Twenty miles. Somewhere down the line the Hydro was disturbed, flickering the lights on and off. On and off. A chill thought charged down her spine. Like the headlight of the vehicle the night Charles had died. She'd pushed that fragment into a corner of her magpie mind, but it hadn't disappeared. Suddenly Belle realized what she might have witnessed through the ravaged trees. The car of the elusive visitor. That narrowed the scope to seven hundred local "padiddles," as her generation of teenagers called them when looking for an excuse to steal a kiss.

With troubled thoughts and sketchy plans, not to forget the hot sauce, even dreams allowed no escape. Belle was tracking someone through the deepest woods. She could hear bushes crackle but saw no one ahead. The moon cast sickly beams between the scraps left by the caterpillars. As cloud shadows dodged among the rock outcroppings like starvelings, a wolf howled across the distance, answered by another. In the choking humidity, her lungs felt asthmatic, gulping the thick, poisonous air with no relief. When her bare feet met something slippery, she stumbled to her knees. Along a slime trail, chewing at a bunch of leaves, its raspy maw undulating as it ripped the fabric, crawled a metre-long blue-green caterpillar, covered with red, yellow and blue tubercles. The larva of the stunning Caecropia moth, destroyer of maple, birch, wild cherry and lilacs. For a moment she was as fascinated as repelled. Then the creature whirled, spinning a cocoon, only to burst out in winged glory, beady eyes compelling her, antennae banging her face. With a scream, she jerked up in bed, riding the swelling water waves. Thrashing her hands and tossing off covers, she hit the light, only to discover a fragile white moth battered on the pillow.

TWENTY-TWO

Despite her insomniac's rule that the best way to return to sleep was never to check the time, Belle lifted a bleary eyelid. The earlier the better, so at 4:45 by the green glow, she flicked a switch before the obnoxious country station blasted the morning into honky-tonk hell. If only the CBC came in without static, she might have awakened to Mozart. Freya stretched idly, so accustomed to six a.m. reveille that she returned quickly to doggie dreams. Best let her doze or she'd make preparations miserable. Dawn Patrol was the scenario, not Dog on Parade.

The coffee maker wheezed in cranky protest while she tossed back orange juice and glanced out at the lake, the darkness swallowing space and time like a black hole. The storm had long passed, leaving everything green and wet for a change. Surprisingly hungry in anticipation, "nerved up," as Hélène would say, she popped a bagel into the toaster, piling on soft, succulent goat cheese.

Charles' safari jacket hung in the closet, with a light scent of bay rum that made her heart jump as she tried it on, rolling up the sleeves. "Help me, my friend. I should have been there when you needed me," she whispered, tucking her Swiss army knife into one pocket, a mini-flashlight into another, and fixing a screwdriver into a couple of loops. Doing up the flaps and zippers, she felt a small bulge in an arm pocket. A padlock key, presumably for the toolshed since he wouldn't have locked the sauna or boathouse. No need now to play vandal. So far so good, she thought, tiptoeing to the door, only to trip over her garden duckboots. At the crash, the beast awoke and barrelled down in the dark, hitting each stair by sheer faith. "Not wanted on the voyage," she said with forced sternness. "Go back to chasing imaginary rabbits." Literate with tones and gestures, Freya wheeled in displeasure towards the computer room and the solace of her easy chair.

The road was shrouded in Avalon mist, dew sticking to her eyelashes. A cool front was sucking warmth from the lake. Only the sounds of a foraging raven broke the silence, a cry so raucous that Ed's aunt, a skeetshooter in her youth, had taken her shotgun to one who had plagued her mornings. Not that such thoughtless savagery caused her to drive into that rock cut a year later, but it was foolish to anger Raven, the Trickster. He was a faithful companion through the bitter winters, a comical ragman in his tattered feather cloak.

At Charles' gate, a lock confronted her, but she climbed over, bending the wire squares with her weight. Where to start? She squinted through fog as she walked, each building emerging like a separate tomb. Forget the sauna. Charles had built it, not Brown.

The boathouse was unlocked, as she had suspected. Brown's nephew had taken the small motorboat, so likely Charles hadn't even used the place. An old anchor, cracked canoe paddles, and mouldy lifejackets made when they were called "Mae Wests" hung on the wall. Apparently Brown had collected car licenses as far back as 1950, tacking them over knotholes. Alberta, the Wild Rose province, a polar bear from Yukon. A small bird, perhaps a starling, rustled in the eaves, the frantic peeping of chicks audible over the lapping of the water. She climbed a rough wooden ladder to inspect the high shelves, but found only a cracked buoy and a faded old navy ensign, Canada's flag before the maple leaf arrived in 1965. She was about to descend when a messy pile at the end caught her attention. Burlap, often used for winter plant protection. Someone had disturbed the dust pattern. Using her screwdriver, she poked the bundle, sensing a solid mass. Then it moved! Black button eyes and a robber mask stared at her, tiny hands waving, yellow teeth clicking. They both screamed and fled in opposite directions.

In the commotion coming down the ladder, Belle collected a large splinter. Flash clamped in her teeth, she watched her finger blur and clear in the presbyopia of age. God bless the inventor of the needle threader. She would have to wait until she got home, punching pain-override. Closing on five-thirty, the sky was beginning to lighten, she realized with alarm. It wouldn't do to be seen by early-bird boaters or strollers. Chubby Phil Christakos had started to powerwalk at dawn.

Passing the deserted garden made her heart throb more than her finger. Charles had scarcely enjoyed the fruits of his labours. His zucchinis were bombs like hers, the lettuce rotten, the spinach bolting, and the luscious cherry tomatoes portable lunches for chipmunks. Only the root vegetables might be edible. She pulled on a carrot, tapped off the dirt, and stuck it in her pocket.

With her key, she entered the house quickly. Inside all was black as earth with heavy curtains drawn. Even so, she used the flashlight instead of risking a lamp. A quick paw through books and records brought nothing, nor did a perfunctory toss of the couch, chairs and pillows. Next came the tiny kitchen. Charles hadn't lived there long enough to have accumulated much. Except for a new set of dishes, the original cottage fixings remained. She rummaged though the foodstuffs, flour, coffee, feeling silly. Some helpful sprite had cleaned out the fridge and left it open. Next came the bathroom. "Medicine," Brown had said. Like a narcotics agent, she peered inside the toilet tank, pushed on the panelling, and opened the medicine chest, a cheap tin variety securely bolted to the wall. He had been serious about the high blood pressure. A half-full bottle of Norvasc sat next to the aspirin along with cold remedies, bug dope, corn plasters, and Metamucil. Middle-aged Land. Nothing more. Maybe poor old Brown had missed his meds the night before? What else could he have meant?

She turned to the bedroom. Under the bed, not even a dust bunny. In the closet, the beam revealed neat little shoe soldiers. Her fingers probed the floorboards, but the seams were solid. A masculine oak desk seemed inviting, and from a bottom drawer she retrieved a thick envelope. Money! Except with a merry Scot instead of a dour prime minister. Canadian Tire bonus bucks. Some enterprising Canucks had passed them as legal tender in Europe. Charles would have accumulated plenty by paying cash for home improvement supplies. Maybe fifty dollars with nickel and dime bills to fatten the pile. Quite a treasure. She laughed, resisting an urge to stuff it in her jacket. Then she noticed the envelope. Cream vellum. An exact double of Anni's.

For a moment she sat at the desk eyeball to eyeball with "The Anatomy Lesson," stunned against a terrible idea beginning to take root. Another drawer of stationery confirmed the suspicion. The paper belonged to Charles. Still, she defended him. Though he claimed not to have known Anni well, could an innocent exchange have passed between them? A recipe? A shy invitation to dinner unrequited? Mail misdirected, opened by mistake and returned?

Thoughts racing, Belle forced herself to resume the search. In the basement, the smelly oil heater and empty packing boxes made for fast work. Cement floor, cement block walls. What about the crawl space upstairs? The nefarious Paul Bernardo had concealed his documentary tapes of torture and murder in a light fixture, overlooked by the police who had gutted the house. Placing a chair on the kitchen table, she pushed aside a ceiling tile and hoisted herself up, brandishing the flashlight. Dust coated her as she scrambled over the joists, sneezing and dislodging long-abandoned mouse nests, finally dropping back with a grunt. Besides, how could Brown or Charles have played acrobat?

Only the toolshed remained, a sizable, windowless building containing the lawn tractor as well as the lathe and power saws which Charles had been so jubilant to discover. She found the key a perfect fit in the large padlock and, wincing at the metallic squeal, rolled aside the massive doors, closing them before hitting the lights. In the distance, a dog barked a question, and she swallowed nervously. Upstairs was a loft, apparently the repository for Brown's wine-making equipment. Five- and ten-gallon green glass jugs sat mute along with dozens of empty bottles in dusty crates. She opened boxes of corks, filters and other paraphernalia her friend had probably kept in hopes of reviving his own craft, but now the raspberries were fast ripening and he would never sip their jewelled sweetness.

Downstairs was a nightmare, but one last hope. Minuscule drawers of nuts, bolts, and oddments, racks of wrenches and screwdrivers, flotsam and jetsam with a tang of oil and sawdust. She peered underneath the table saw, moved tarps and rolled the lawn tractor away from the wall. Though the front and sides of the shed had exposed two-by-four framing, the back was finished in drywall, lighter spaces indicating where pictures or other tack-ups had gone. A new IDA calendar was turned to July. Flipping along, she noticed that Charles had planned a massive bulb planting for the fall.

Next to the calendar was a large, built-in first aid cabinet. First aid? An old man's fuzzy name for medicine? Inside on a shallow shelf were ancient bandage packages in graduated sizes, mercurochrome gone black, gauze, tape in sticky masses. Strike three. What had she missed? Belle stepped outside for a pee. Squatting in meditation, she noticed that the building backed against a steep hillside with an odd, dark shape on top. When she scrambled up to roof level, she found a ventilation pipe. Root cellars had the same construction. Was some space hidden behind that wall?

Returning on the run, she opened the first aid cabinet and placed everything on the floor, frantic at one last possibility. She gripped the sides, and with a sharp pull, lifted the structure out in one piece, leaving an opening about one-and-a-half-feet by two. Behind it was a clean, well-insulated cubicle containing a new plastic tote box.

Belle reached for the box, touched the cover with shaking hands, jumping at the thrum of a small motor by the shore. Little time left. She unclipped the snaps and opened the top, puzzled at the contents. A large piece of black cloth with flashes of white lay within tissue paper, carefully folded, covering some documents. Setting it aside for a moment, she examined the first item. An old passport. It was Charles. Handsome, young, many pounds lighter. The stamps indicated that for a few years in his youth, he'd travelled widely, Italy, England, Germany. What a wonderful companion he would have been. Then she glanced at the name. James Morris? The same words appeared on a Royal Bank passbook. Her frugal mind was appalled. Over five hundred thousand dollars with only the yearly accumulation of interest, paltry interest lately. Savings accounts were paying three-quarter percent. Only one withdrawal. June 15th. Thirty-five thousand dollars. How many times had she thought about that sum? The envelope, now this. A wave of nausea swept over her. Pictures didn't lie. Charles had another identity, money he never used for himself, even to purchase the property. What else was a lie? Not knowing Anni? Why had he given the money to her, unless…

The sturdy twill unfolded, she held the large garment at arm's length. It appeared to be a priest's cassock. Then a white cloth, a surplice? Other small pieces of regalia she couldn't identify without a lexicon, along with a tiny silver cross on a chain. No diary to serve as confessional. No exculpatory letters. Only a manila envelope containing a black and white picture which morphed Deborah Kerr with Agnes Moorehead, Saint and Manipulator icons. A young bride, seventeen perhaps, taking the veil, the selfsame white wimple that had caught her attention. What was Euphemia to him? Lover? Sister? Both?

With a rue late born, she remembered the precious wooden triptych, those Gregorian chants, the comments about punishment. What did it matter if Charles hadn't been in the Osprey Inlet picture? Never in the picture, yet always there, like Sister Veronica's sinister description. Somehow Anni had detected something wrong at the school, but had moved away before she could confirm her suspicions. Had she recognized Charles' voice more than the bearded, fuller face? Zack had said that Anni was good at voices. What had she done then? A prudent woman in some ways, she wouldn't have acted on mere intuition until checking with Edith.

Belle wanted to run from this place and never return, yet the signals weren't reaching her legs. Too many unknowns. If Charles had killed Anni, had someone killed him? How fractured was the human jigsaw? Had she arrived at the Hill of Science, or was she floundering still in the Fields of Fiction? Truth was straining credibility, even with this palpable evidence. Carefully she repacked the box, safe in its hole. Steve couldn't ignore this, and what he'd say about her collection of facts and fantasies would scorch her ears.

As she locked up and headed for the gate, the scrape of gravel echoed down the lane. A series of painful creaks followed, as if metal were being stretched to capacity. She shrank into the shelter of a thick fir tree, making herself small and inconspicuous. The heaviness of a body falling to the ground made her catch her breath. Then a dark form lumbered towards her on all fours.

TWENTY-THREE

Ed, for God's sake. Do you want to have to carry two canes?" she said as she helped him back over the gate, its wires bent into v's where his feet had pushed.

"The dog put up a fuss, and I came to investigate. And what were you doing?"

"A final reconnaissance. I have to talk to Steve before I can give you any details." The look of consternation on his face paid her in full for the near heart attack he'd caused with his snooping.

Belle trotted back with renewed purpose, calling Steve at home despite the early hour. No answer. Flinging her filthy body into the shower, she scrubbed diligently and dressed for work. The splinter was stubborn, requiring a combination of tweezers, wicked needles and educated guesses. Freya gave her another accusing look, and she forced herself to the mundane requirements of a working life, packing a hasty lunch. "Where do you think your dog food comes from? Three hots, two trots and a cot. OK. Just to the end of the road. Maybe this weekend we can go to Hidden Valley for blueberries."

On the turn, she met Ed with his quad, cane strapped on the back, Hélène and Rusty in tandem, about to forge up the trail to Surprise Lake. "Do me a favour, guys. Take the dog with you. I'm in a big hurry, but I'll explain later."

"No problem. Come over later and have supper with us,"

Hélène said with a motherly grin. "Big pan of cabbage rolls we got at the Garlic Festival. They beat the world record for braided garlic, over two hundred and—"

Belle called over her shoulder, "I may be late, but thanks."

The office was empty at a few minutes to nine. It was Miriam's day off. A slow Friday. But five new listings and two open houses next week. Prime the coffee maker and sprinkle vanilla on the oven racks. Homey fakery. Maybe the life of a private investigator would offer more scope. But in Sudbury? Probably end up staking out gum machine robberies or peeking into motel windows with a camera to catch adulterers, not that it mattered anymore with no-fault divorce. Surely Steve would be at work now. So many details kept to herself. Sister Veronica. Osprey Inlet. And that headlamp. If only he'd taken her seriously, been willing to admit that there might have been another person involved. "He and the family went up north of the Sault to camp out on Superior," a clerk said. "Be back on Monday."

A couple of days, she thought. Maybe there's something else I can do about these loose ends. Who was Charles Sullivan? At lunch time she cruised the Internet for items on the Seaway. A web page for Ontario parks led her to information about the nine "*villages perdus*," lost villages flooded in 1958. Mille Roche, named for its thousand rocky rapids, next door to the major city of Cornwall, now existed only as a series of park islands reached by a causeway. Everything had been relocated at great expense to the government. Houses, schools, public buildings and businesses had been picked up and deposited inland at an equally tiny place called Long Sault. If a Charles Sullivan had been born in Mille Roche, why were there no later records? She closed the file with a click, rummaging through a hundred movie plots.

Perhaps he had never left.

At the Cornwall Chamber of Commerce number, she was greeted by a pleasant woman with the broad Ottawa Valley accent of Scots-English remnants of the United Empire Loyalists, those who had fled America during the Revolution. "I'm trying to locate relatives from Mille Roche for a genealogical chart. We've been out of touch for decades. The cemeteries seemed a good place to start," Belle said, sensing the irony.

"Everyone at Mille Roche was moved to other grounds, some out of the community, but most to Maple Grove. That's your best bet. Try..."

"We're pretty well-indexed here," a man identifying himself as the Human Resource Manager said on her next call. "The government insisted on strict records when the graves were opened. Serious stuff, relocating bodies. What is the name?"

"Sullivan." Her request was met by an odd silence. "Sullivan," she prompted, wondering if they had been cut off.

His voice sounded subdued. "Yes. My grandmother used to tell me their story when she caught me playing with matches."

"Story?"

A sigh issued over the lines. "Some sixty years ago. The entire family was killed in a tragic house fire during one of our worst winters. So many heated with wood. The place went up like tinder."

"No survivors?"

"I'll get the file." There was a long pause, people talking in the background. Her theory had been right. One more piece. Not definitive, blue sky maybe, but who knew what corporeal substance might join it?

"Sorry to keep you waiting. The parents were Percy and Vivian. And two young children. Charles, the baby and his

231

sister Rachel, five. Enough to make you weep. Gran still takes flowers to the grave. Proud to say that the whole town chipped in for a nice marble monument. Top quality. Couple of little angels on top. It's under our most beautiful red maple with a spectacular view of the Seaway."

Belle rang off with bitter satisfaction. Charles had lived in Ottawa with easy access to the small towns of the valley. A cinch to comb newspaper morgues for someone born the same year as he but who had died as a child. Died along with the whole family in a town now underwater. No wonder Steve's records jumped from birth to university. Little Charles Sullivan lay in a grave by the St. Lawrence, stone angels guarding his rest.

TWENTY-FOUR

Back at the office, Belle's emotions ricocheted from disappointment to fury to pity and back again, calmed only by the production and consumption of coffee. She bit into a tomato sandwich lathered with mayo, and munched pensively on the carrot from Charles' forlorn garden. The entire middle of the puzzle was missing, as if macular degeneration had struck. Charles as a priest, serving in unholy alliance with Euphemia in Osprey Inlet, maybe even someplace else before that, pray God not after. Yet unlike his accomplice, he had not been secreted away in a monastery the equivalent of Le Coeur de Repos. Had he left the church of his own will or been forced out? What did it matter? With a creative new identity, he had retrained in an innocuous profession and spent the next decades in Ottawa, Canada's immaculate, if boring home of civil servants. Punishment enough, a cynic would say.

While the cigarette butt had been flimsy evidence to arouse much suspicion, the blinking light and the box of indictments made her suspect that a visitor had been there. Someone connected with his past and with Anni, the woman who had perhaps died at his hands. "Perhaps," a word she couldn't omit. That brutal concept, so far from the civilized man with whom she had shared table, troubled her so profoundly that she continued rationalizing.

The old woman, scarcely infirm of purpose, had been feisty enough to have wielded the stick as a weapon. Perhaps Charles had been defending himself in a protective blow regretted the moment struck. And the probable blackmail that bought the van? Why had she changed her mind? Had she asked for more or regretted the gesture, tried to recapture an ethical edge with the sententiousness that had enraged Patsy? The cryptic comments from the salesman and then Murph added force to that theory. Whatever had happened, threatened the quiet life Charles had nurtured. Even the mildest animal backed to a corner could go wild with fear, like a chained dog guaranteed to bite.

Evening found her returning late from town, irked at the petty details of demanding clients. Belle groaned as the hourly news came on the radio. Eight already. She parked at Fred's restaurant with hopes of a quick meal and was enjoying a Caesar salad when she saw his car enter the strip mall, nosing up to the window. Without modern running lights, he drove with lamps permanently on, European style. Her fork dropped as the old Camaro shuddered to a stop in a cloud of oily smoke, the left beam winking like the monocled Mr. Planters Peanut Man.

Fred shambled in bearing two overflowing baskets of blueberries. He grabbed a coffee and parked jovially at her table. She looked out the window at the car, then at the man, barely able to navigate without a lurch. Surely he couldn't have been involved. "Where's Craig?"

He pointed to the baskets. "Second shift again. We'll get him at nine. There's enough sun for another hour. You just can't keep that fellow down. He's picked twice as much as us. I just hope…" His mouth twitched, and he brushed it with his fingers.

"What's wrong?"

"You know about his past. Guy's fought hard, but a couple weeks ago he tied one on. Disappeared for two days. Just a backslide." He shrugged and forced a smile. "It happens."

Belle pushed aside her salad to concentrate. A calendar tacked on the wall caught her attention, little fishes, waxing and waning moons. "About the end of the month? Full moon?"

Jokes weren't Fred's forte, but he tried a howl like the radio advertising hockey games for the Sudbury Wolves. "Don't tell me you believe in that stuff? Anyway, I think he'll be moving on soon."

"What gives you that idea?" She tried to keep her voice calm, avoid a scare which might stop small bits of information from building to a frightening conclusion.

"Some hints he's been dropping about staying on in Toronto when we drive down to see Garth. Bunk at a hostel for a few nights until he can find a room. Plenty of restaurant jobs in the Big Smoke. 'Course I'd give him a good recommendation. Hate to see him go, though. He's like family."

When she pressed his hand, he nearly jumped. Apparently women had not been part of his life. "I'm going to ask you a question. Please answer truthfully, even if he is your friend. Did you lend your car to him that night he got drunk?"

He hesitated, the cup shaking. "He'd done a double shift. Wanted to see a show at Silver City. Didn't suck on the booze until after he got back. Knew my temper better than to pull a stunt like that."

"Thanks for your honesty. I've got to go and sort out some problems. Where did you leave him?"

"Over the hill from where we saw you that time. What problems? You got me worried. Is he in trouble?" Belle shot him an OK sign, leaving five dollars on the table as she slammed out the door.

"Left his school," Steve had said. "He's lost." Anni at the dentist's side, alert to the subtlest signs of distress. Charles the Enforcer for the depraved Euphemia. And Craig, poor Craig with his broom. All too fast now. As she drove to the fields, foot on the gas pedal jiggling absurdly from nerves, Belle assembled the cast for a tragedy written by an author long dead in a grave on a small island. Whatever the ghastly prologue, nature, nurture, evil incarnate, Act One opened in Osprey Inlet. Act Two, decades later, a chance encounter between Charles and Anni. Act Three, Anni's murder. Act Four, Charles' death. And that was where Craig entered from the wings. Had he met Anni, conspired with her? Or had he seen his tormentor on the street and followed him home, hatred for that face etching itself into his mind like a festering sore?

The parking area was empty. To save time, she pulled as close as possible to the path, squeezing behind a Science North billboard, sticking the van keys under the mat. The berries were nearly finished, only a few wizenings decorating the dry bushes. Besides, the Jays' spoiler series with the Yanks was keeping the fans cheering at home or gathering in the sports bars. Belle climbed carefully in the growing shadows, wary of stumbling on uneven ground. Here the Grenville Front, a highly deformed and metamorphosed zone, met the smoother faces of the Southern province. Rockhounds studied its tectonics, chipped for garnets, quartz and feldspar in its wrinkles. Farther on, in the barest spots decimated by the acid rain, lay traps for even the most careful foot.

There was no one visible across the open stretches. Maybe Craig had given up and hitched a ride to his rooming house, passing her on the way. No problem to thumb a lift in the friendly North. She walked another few hundred yards, scanning the barren hills for movement or sound, dodging miniature oaks and maples sprouting from opportune crevices, natural bonsais older than her father. Several times she tripped, stubbing soft leather loafers on the jutting rocks and scraping skin from her palms. This was getting risky. She was about to turn back, hands aching, when a quiet whistle like a lone piper's tune broke the silence. "Standing Outside the Fire," one of Garth's hits. She squinted at a hunched form far ahead, tinking a metal pot. "Craig!" she called.

He straightened, his lean body silhouetted against the last orange flickers from the vanishing sun, a chimney sweep on the rooftops of London, and he waved eagerly. Her heart doublebeat like a trapped animal seeking exit. Act Five looked like torture, yet did she really fear the man? Violence did not seem his style, passionate though he had been about the kids he protected. "Fred send you out as a search party?" he asked. "Good timing. I've got the last. Nothing else worth bothering about. If you can drive me back, I'll spring for coffee."

That was the longest speech she had ever heard him give. Her better, or perhaps worse half, felt like accepting the offer, then returning to Charles' to collect his wretched secrets and burn them to ashes scattered by amoral winds. "Not tonight, Craig. I have something to ask you."

Leaning against a blackened outcrop, he met her eyes with polite interest, the broad face honest and open, the bearing newly confident. Suppose she never learned the truth? Why not leave this last survivor to heaven? Justice had been served in a clumsy, unofficial way. Craig had taken positive steps to rejoin society, made friends and plans. If he had lashed out at his aggressor, it was small payment for a calculated cruelty that had shackled the prime years of his life. "What is it, Belle?" he asked.

She swallowed the lump in her throat, measuring syllables like bitter medicine, wondering whether the relentless pursuit of facts wasn't worse than the happy peace of ignorance. "I saw you on my road the night Charles Sullivan died."

At the sound of the name, he looked confused. Then his eyebrows gathered in an oncoming storm, a warning Steve flashed in times of anger, yet the rest of his body language screamed for release. He took a rasping breath and then in the shadows, everything happened so fast, the clink of the falling pot, dark berries merging with the rock. His figure pushed past and rushed off, the contrast hard to follow, flat and one-dimensional. She started after him. "Craig! Tell me what happened. Running away won't help."

Common sense argued that she had as much chance of catching him as overtaking a marathoner, but maybe simple words would reach out, make him reconsider. "You didn't kill him!" she screamed, hearing only the rasp of footsteps on stone, the skitter of scree down stark hills. "All you're guilty of is assault."

After a few minutes, cross-country racing, yelling and breathing at the same time became impossible. Belle stopped to rest her wheezing lungs. Why was he so afraid? Of living up to the standards of a law-enforcement brother? Losing a late-found grip on life, though it spelled only a rooming house and cleaning job? Yet that tenuous first step meant salvation to an alcoholic. Sister Veronica's wisdom whispered in her ear. "The victims may feel...partially to blame." No wonder he had never told anyone. Shame and guilt were the most powerful weapons of an abuser, especially one connected with the mighty Church itself.

The terrain grew brutal, overlapping folds of rolling strata turned on their sides like roasted whales, converging into deep pits. Belle peered into the distance until she imagined a shape making its way. A trick of the eye? One of the ghost trees killed a century ago? Jumping a channel, she misjudged the width and twisted an ankle, sprawling onto the ground. For a moment she sat stupefied and gulped back air. Underneath her jacket, her silk shirt was clinging to her back, her linen pants were ripped, and her hands were sticky from plasma. Damn the man, anyway! Craig could sprint clear to Buffalo for all she cared. There was no help if he wouldn't take the hand of a friend. Steve would get the whole mess dumped into a doughnut bag when he got back, and he could sort it out.

Mind travelling faster than body, for a brief moment her eyes left the ground as she wheeled. One foot slipped on a patch of lichens, and she found herself tumbling, knees and elbows bumping like a spastic marionette, her head cracking against rock, finally landing on something mercifully soft. Little Alice down the rabbit hole, she thought, struggling for breath as a black curtain dropped. But I didn't drink any potions, eat any mushrooms. Definitely not mushrooms. She heard laughter, or was it crying? A kitten was trying to make itself heard. Why was the poor creature out in the middle of nowhere?

Fighting back to consciousness brought a nausea which made her retch, shot vinegary bile up the back of her throat. Pain was speaking a language she couldn't decipher, and she squeezed her eyes against its noise. Though everything ached, one particular knife talked with eloquence. The ankle she had wrenched earlier. Better give it a rub. When she tried to move, something stopped her, a contortion of body disconnected from brain. With effort, she raised herself on one elbow. Though a thick bed of moss had broken her fall, one leg was jammed down a deep cleft, narrowing at the bottom. Try as she could, she couldn't get any purchase. And every time she pulled, agony gripped her like a powerful vise. Had she broken her ankle? Palmers had bones of iron. A sprain could hurt as much.

Whatever, the leg wasn't going anywhere, so neither was she.

Shaking her head to clear the cobwebs, Belle tried a more methodical assessment, flexing arms and hands. Her other leg splayed awkwardly underneath, prickly from a pinched nerve. With a deep breath, she stretched it and applied a tender massage. One small relief. She ran sore fingers over elbows, raw as meat. Abrasions, or was it contusions? Fine distinctions muddled. The back of her head hurt, but she could feel no blood, just an egg-sized lump. Probably banged on the way down. How far, though? She swam up through a murky swimming pool, noticing only then that her glasses were missing.

Reality was sinking in as fast as the sun had set. Craig was long gone. He had no idea she had fallen, if that might have made a difference in his frantic escape. But panic was a dangerous option. Wouldn't people come back tomorrow, combing the bushes? She shifted with a moan and snagged her coat on a dried blueberry bush. As she untangled it, the brief optimism blew away like the frail twigs crushed in her hand. Why would anyone return? As Craig had said, the season was over. Even if some hopeful drudge did try for a last pint, this bleak area was over a mile from the edges of the fields. Moonscape, the bare bones of the Nickel City where even a bagpipe would go unheard.

Surely there was some way out, some problem-solving exercise to brainstorm. What would Errol Flynn do? Robin Hood, Captain Blood, Gentleman Jim. Just not Custer, not *They Died with Their Boots On.* The pit itself, full of handholds, posed no difficulty except for her uncooperative leg. Stoic Canadian farmers cut off an arm trapped in the combine, knotted a tourniquet with their teeth and crawled miles across the prairie for help. Somehow she felt glad that she hadn't brought her Swiss army knife. She swallowed with effort, her throat dry. The salty salad was bringing on a fierce thirst. Oh, for a drink of water, a huge bowl.

Then she remembered Freya. Thank God she was safe with the DesRosiers on that timely walk. Expecting her hours ago, Ed and Hélène would be in a frenzy. In the morning, missing-person rules be damned, the old reliables would call up a search, starting God knows where. Parking behind that huge billboard to save a few yards of walking had been a stupid idea. Maybe a fatal one. Gritting her teeth, she retraced her movements. Once word of her disappearance filtered to the restaurant, Fred would put it together, especially if Craig had left town. Discovering the van, they would comb the fields until they found her. Another day? Three? Five? No water and no food. Desperate for a sensation other than pain, her fingers picked at the papery yellow-green rock tripe, the explorer's friend. On one of his many ill-conceived searches for the Northwest Passage, Sir John Franklin and his starving crew had boiled it for soup. She nibbled a tasteless shred, remembering too late that uncooked lichens brought on diarrhea. With a groan, she pounded the rock until her fist hurt. What spectral shape would greet them when they finally found her?

As if in response, a snuffling sounded somewhere above. So close to town, no large predators roamed these hills, but she wouldn't rule out coyotes, or brush wolves as they were called. They had begun moving toward inhabited areas in quest of garbage or small livestock. Ed had chased away one rifling Rusty's empty dog food cans. Still, a loud bluff would handle Wily E. Wasn't the same as a black bear or the cougar in B.C. that had killed a woman defending her children.

When no slavering snout poked over the edge of the pit, Belle sat back, depressed by fresh worries. What would happen to her father? She was his life, a fragile connection to happier memories. If he could save her now, he would, like when her kite had stuck in rotten high tension wires. Childish tugging had brought them crackling and sparking across the quiet, dead-end Toronto street. At her wails, out he'd come on the run, giving her hands a quick glance, then directing traffic and steering onlookers away until the Hydro truck arrived. Barely five-ten, he'd seemed a giant. Huddled on the curb, the tiny cause of furious adult activity, she'd felt her stomach tighten, imagined a painful punishment. But he'd popped her onto his shoulders, trotting up the stairs, both of them laughing. Too bad he hadn't been able to have another ten kids for insurance to see him through old age, especially when the first one had proved a certifiable idiot.

The prospect of splitting the mutual funds with siblings usually dispelled that wish. She wouldn't be tuned to the CBC news tomorrow to see if the TSE hit a new high. That precious bond fund was about to go off like a rocket with the interest rate drop. With eyes closed, she imagined the recovering Canadian dollar high-kicking across the screen. Then she coughed, rubbing her arms. How cold would it get? Maybe seven to ten degrees centigrade, forties Fahrenheit? Nothing to die from tonight, especially surrounded by black rock which held the warmth. Yet it was the third week of August, when a sudden frost could snap the air like an Arctic bullwhip. Belle pressed her cheek to the moss. Soft, velvety, slightly metallic. Nature in sympathy with man. Then she was seven again, swinging up and up. "Higher, Father, higher," she begged, dangling long red braids, dizzy at the flash of blue sky. Somehow her grip weakened and she let go at the arc's high point, falling into vertigo, then plucked out of the air by strong arms. No fancy weight rooms, but what natural muscles, just like hers when they clowned together comparing biceps. He hugged her to his rough tweed jacket, redolent of the cherry blend pipe tobacco Mother forbade in the house, despite her own cigarettes. "OK, honey?" Yes, I'm OK, she whispered, tears bathing her face. But I wonder if I'll ever see you again.

At last, moonrise brightened the scene to reveal the dimensions of the prison. Ten feet by ten, eight feet down, good drainage, no septic, no neighbours, and a damn poor view. Her leg didn't hurt anymore, a dumb and separate thing. In fact she couldn't feel it at all. Suppose it were paralyzed? How many houses or apartments were wheelchair accessible? She might be lucky to find out. Scuttlings of nocturnal animals wakened the night, industrious shrews, skunks, raccoons, squirrels and chippies on the move. Overhead a slender ballerina with legs outstretched crossed the moon, a great blue heron from the nearby wetland, perhaps Surprise Lake. "Why, then, oh why can't I?" she moaned. Suddenly a roar startled her. Too late for Air Ontario, the local carrier. A military flight? The con trail puffed a luminous exclamation point against the sky between incoming clouds, dotted by the faithful evening star of Venus.

Belle napped fitfully, nursing the happy delusion that she was in her wawa bed. Would she ever snore softly in its warm and undulating folds again? Perhaps she should keep awake in case she heard someone, or worse yet, some thing. Her bladder was aching, another humiliation, and why not a moment's surrender for one less pain?

So sleepy. I could have saved a fortune on liquor and cigarettes, she thought in unexpected wisdom. Exhaustion had always been the key for a hyperactive Gemini. She looked at her watch, blessing the decision to splurge on a glow model.

One o'clock. Now that the rock was cooling, the shivers began. Hypothermia wasn't a bad exit, second cousin to freezing to death. Drowning, bleeding, choking, now that was scary. Forget the dramatics. She wore a jacket and pants, and she was dry.

Family, and friends, and dogs aside, it was maddening to leave the solution to someone else. Without Craig, the truth would never be unravelled. Steve might wonder what in hell she had been doing near blueberry fields without even a pan or plastic bag, but with the autopsy report blaming exposure, he'd never connect her death with Charles', never search that toolshed. Tearing down the place in 2050, a new owner would probably toss the box into the trash. It was all so fragmented, so kaleidoscopic without her configurations. Could she scratch a clue, maybe a triangle with key initials, just, just, just in case she was found too late? Her fingers probed the rough granite. And her last lipstick was desiccating into a historical artifact in the bottom of a drawer. She tried her foot again, screaming at the pain, biting her lips to inure herself to the throbbing which would begin anew. Her mind was fading in and out of consciousness, begging her to relax into a torpor, husband all resources, hibernate like a snake deprived of warmth. Live naturally. Wait for the sun. Tomorrow is another day, Scarlett. Then as she passed out, a light rain began to fall.

TWENTY-FIVE

The damn kitten was mewling again, but Belle ignored the cries because she had figured out who the creature was. Still, the little fool persisted, fur wet and matted, calling her name, which made even less sense. It was still dark. Or maybe she had gone blind. Wouldn't that be ironic? Freya would make a perfect guide dog. She clamped gritty eyelids until stars and comets danced wild ballets. Get back to sleep. Think pleasant thoughts.

"Belle!"

"Shut up. I know you. You're me. Go away."

"Belle!" Crazy white beams criss-crossed her face, like a Hollywood opening at Grauman's Chinese Theatre. A tumble of small stones dropped onto her shoulder. At the edge of the hole, a bright yellow plastic poncho flashed. "Up here."

"Craig?" Her voice came from another planet, the tones ragged and plaintive as her lips licked the rain greedily, soothing her throat.

"I'm sorry. I didn't know you'd fallen."

She spoke quietly, marshalling pride against the urge to sob. "I thought you had gone. Left for Toronto."

"Not a chance. I'll get you out." Bracing the flashlight to illuminate the hole, he scrambled down and reached for her arms.

"No, wait. My leg is trapped. And my glasses are gone."

Why did she say that? It sounded so pathetic. Little old crippled myopic woman. Miss Piggy in Lord of the Blackflies.

"Don't worry. I'll be careful. Tell me if it hurts too much."

Craig was as gentle as he was strong. It took agonizing minutes, and more than one undisciplined shriek, but slowly he eased her out of the cleft, shifting a massive chunk of rock with masculine effortlessness. Meanwhile she chewed her cheek and blinked back tears, as much from self-pity as pain. The glasses hung unscathed on a nearby branch. She stretched for them with a wince, then smeared the lenses pointlessly with a wet sleeve. Craig raised one pant leg to inspect her ankle, bulging with fluid, dark where the thin sock had frayed.

"That looks bad," he said. "If we prop you up here…" he perched her rump on a thick cedar root clinging to the rock wall, "I'll be able to pull you from above." Hunched like a helpless ornament, she watched him scale the wall in two quick movements. Then he plucked her from the pit of death, back to the world, clasping her to his chest. Belle felt his heartbeat, strong and fast, a breath quick in her ear.

As he released her, the wind blew against the chill of her sodden clothes as a reminder that she was no animal in harmony with surroundings, not in this unforgiving climate. "First things first. I have to go to the bathroom." He moved away discreetly, and she clambered like a wounded turtle, fumbling with her pants. Wouldn't be the first time I peed on my shoes in the dark on a camp-out, she thought.

"Why I waited, I don't know. I'm already half-drowned. For God's sake, give me one of those," she asked a minute later, as he took out a pack of cigarettes. Sometimes there was power in a jolt of nicotine.

By the flare of the lighter, she watched him light two at

once, Paul Henreid come to life. Sucking back warm smoke, she searched his face in the muted pearl of dawn. "What made you come back?"

"When I found out you knew about Father Jim…"

"Father…?" Of course. James Morris. The name on the passport. "I knew him as Charles Sullivan."

What she said didn't seem to register. Craig wanted to talk, and nothing was stopping him. "I was pretty confused. All I could think of was running." He sighed and brushed rain from his eyes. "My life had been back on track for such a short time. Then it was falling apart."

"Where did you go?"

"Fred picked me up like always. Just went home." He choked back a bitter laugh. "Home, that's a new word. How I wanted to dive into that forty-ouncer of rye. Stared at me like a lying lover. But I saw the faces of the guys at the restaurant and kids like Jedi. Your words kept pounding in my head. I knew you wanted to help."

"So you did hear me. And then?"

"Must have been around midnight. When I figured I had to stick it out, I called your number. Some machine. I can't hack those things. So I woke Fred and got the car to drive to your house." He shook his head. "He wasn't any too pleased until I explained. But he always comes through."

She touched her ankle gingerly. "And I wasn't there."

"I knew something was wrong big time. This was the last place you'd been, so…"

"You found the van."

"That's when I panicked. For the last two hours, I've been looking for you. Guess I got turned around. Everything is the same in the dark."

Belle finished the cigarette, field-stripping the paper like a good citizen despite the rain and pocketing the debris. "DuMaurier. You left one of these at …" A spasm of shaking stopped her words.

With a small nod, he pulled off his plastic poncho and wrapped her in it. "Let's go. You need a doctor."

"Not the Emergency Room again!" Belle threw up her arms in submission, then groaned at the pain. "Still, heavenly after this. Hey, I'm starving. Stop for doughnuts first."

Opting for a three-legged race instead of a fireman's carry, they stumbled back to the car as the landscape lightened. She started laughing so hard at one rest stop that Craig gave her a worried look, as if she were delirious.

The old Camaro had a powerful heater. Those gas-guzzling eight cylinders pumped it out. By the time they got to Tim Hortons, their clothes were drying. Belle called the DesRosiers and found Hélène half-furious, half-crying from worry, so she briefed her and promised to stop for a late breakfast unless the tottering Canadian medical system had landed on life-support.

The admitting nurse took Belle's temperature and blood pressure, then logged her condition on the Alpha Centauri end of triage, number forty-five. Translation: six hours. Balancing on borrowed crutches in front of the bathroom mirror, she washed up in contortionist fashion and surveyed the damage. Scratches and scrapes, nothing fatal. Her hair was matted with dirt and the errant scrap of moss. A piece of rock tripe decorated one tooth. Joining Craig beside a mammoth doughnut box, she sat in an isolated corner across from a collection of glum folks pulled from their beds for medical oddities. The selection included a wailing baby, a trembling grandmother in babushka accompanied by a knitting daughter and miscellaneous beings with white wrappings in conventional places. No apparent gunshot wounds, though.

248

God bless Canada. Belle passed Craig a coffee and grabbed a maple cream doughnut. "We've got all night, or what's left of it. Start at the beginning. You're going to have to tell Steve soon enough."

"Steve? How do you…" He looked bewildered.

"He's a good friend of mine. When you came to Sudbury, he told me that he'd tried to help. Somehow he suspected that something terrible had led to your isolation from the family. He was hurt that you wouldn't confide in him. I never told him about our meeting, but I hoped somehow you'd find each other." She ferreted out a chocolate sour cream pastry. "But time and chance took over."

His deep voice trembled as he took her hand in a familiarity which gladdened. "I've wanted to talk to someone for so many years, back to when I was a kid at one of those residential schools. In Osprey Inlet. Bet you've never heard of it."

"Yes, I have," she said, wishing for forty words for sorrow. "And that's too long to carry such a secret."

"It's weighed me down, you can't know how much. That bitch." He coloured and dropped his voice even though a small television clamped to the ceiling was blaring sitcom reruns. "Sorry. Sister Euphemia, I mean. Why can't I forget the sound of that ugly name?"

"Her picture in an old magazine got me started, but I can't imagine so much evil in such a small frame. Nuns should mean guitar strummers, flying do-gooders, Mother Teresa. This one was a devil in drag," Belle said with contempt.

Craig turned to her with a look of betrayal. "It wasn't fair, Belle. My family lived in a little cabin. At the edges of the reserve. Life was our school. Learning our people's ways. Some might say that we didn't know much of the world, television, video games, but are those things better than knowing how to

249

run a trapline or fish for your supper?"

She shook her head, at one with the view, and he continued. "Then the government decided we should get a real education, whatever that means. I was only twelve when they made us go to that place. First time away from home, so far, too. It wasn't too bad at St. Michael's at first. We got the crap…the stuff we were sent there for, a bed and meals, lessons, something called vocational training. I made a letter holder out of pine." His sigh touched her heart. "But I never wrote anyone, not even my mother. They read the letters, anyways, corrected the grammar and made sure we didn't complain."

"Then she came. Made me an altar boy, gave me treats, clothes, privileges, told me I was her special friend. Soon I learned what she wanted. That silver whistle. Her signal. I threw up every time I heard it. Still," he said, his crinkled, smoky eyes seeing a boy again with the comprehension of a man. "I think I could have been all right if she hadn't pulled him in. He was her brother."

One more piece. As Belle watched him shrink at the pain, the quick sugar fix turned to ashes on her tongue. She asked a question she didn't want answered. "Did he beat you?"

"Didn't have to. She used the idea of him to get what she wanted. Once Father Jim took me aside in the hall, just held my arms and stared at me hard. 'I hear you've been disobedient. Sister likes you. Be a good lad,' he said. He taught us music." Craig blinked and looked at his fingers, one nail torn by the rocks, the thumb bloody. "I used to like music, you know, wanted to play the guitar. He was a pretty good teacher, even though I hated him."

"You were so alone." Had Euphemia attacked any other children? Could she ask him that? "Where was Steve?"

"Steve was four years older than me. Sixteen. He'd gotten

into the navy before I left. They were beginning to recruit on the reserves, weren't too fussy about birth dates for a big guy. I was so proud, and I wanted him to be proud of me. How could I tell him? How could I tell anyone?"

Sister Veronica again. Isolate and devour, a familiar tactic. "And then?"

"Nearly a year. I counted the days, hoping for some dumb reason that Steve would get a leave or something. Fly down out of the sky like Superman to take me home. Or that those two would just go away. She was smart and careful, but one afternoon I made sure someone saw us. A decent lady who delivered the groceries. It didn't take long. A plane landed with government officials. Everyone started running around, giving orders. Like a bomb had hit. We were sent away to a big brick school down on the U.S. border in Fort Frances." He finished the coffee, pulled out his cigarettes and then put them away with an apologetic look to the duty nurse. "The day we got to the city I packed a few clothes and hitched a ride west from a trucker on the TransCanada. Enough school for me."

"You were what, thirteen? How in God's name did you live?"

"You've never been on the road. There are good people and bad. You grow up fast. I could always get a sandwich and piece of pie from any woman home of a morning. Besides, I was a pretty strong kid, like Steve." He swallowed and rebraced himself against the plastic chair. "Wood cutting, gardening, road work, even fire fighting. No questions asked."

"And Sudbury? What brought you here?"

"One town's as good as another for a drifter. But in B.C., an uncle put me up. He said that Steve lived here. It was a way to be close to him, even though I pushed him away with the booze."

While words were flowing like a wound cleansing itself,

Belle tried to steer him back to her purposes. "I'm still not clear how you met Anni and...Father Jim."

His brow furrowed, a blue vein pulsing on his temple. "Anni. That was the name of the woman he kept talking about that night. I didn't get it."

TWENTY-SIX

Belle softened her voice to ease the tension. The worst part was coming. She would have to walk Craig through a painful process. "Anni was the dentist's assistant in Osprey Inlet. Do you remember her?"

He nodded, brightening for the first time in his sad odyssey. "Couple times I went, she was so nice. Like she could sense something wrong. Not the fillings, what was happening to me at the school. But there was always someone along. Usually Father Jim."

"So you didn't meet her here. Did you read about her murder?"

"I don't read too good, Belle. It was him I saw." He opened another coffee and his mouth tightened. "That beard didn't fool me for a second. Not with those eyes."

How different were perceptions. Charles' eyes hadn't been his signal feature, but she remembered them as sensitive and kind. And he'd been a sucker for dogs. Wrong again. "Where was that?"

"At the Catholic church downtown. In the basement, they give out sandwiches and blankets to street people. He was leaving Mass, passed right by me. I froze like a scared animal. The next Sunday he was back. From an alley, I watched where he parked his car. One rear door wasn't locked. On the seat was a phone bill with his address. He'd

253

changed his name. Didn't surprise me."

"So you learned where he lived. And you went out there one night."

He spread out one powerful hand in a poignant gesture of uselessness. "I don't know what I expected. It brought everything back, but I guess I needed that. I walked in from the turnaround, had a smoke by the fence to get up nerve. When he went to the sauna alone, I followed. Took a chance there was no one in the house."

If only there had been, she thought. A vision flashed through her mind, one she'd tried to push into oblivion. Charles' alabaster body luminescent in the moted beams filtering through the small window. "Then what happened?"

His voice quavered in an effort to continue. "It was a dressing room. He looked like God himself in that fancy white robe. Guess he'd found a good job, though he wasn't a priest anymore. All I saw was a bully. 'I'm Craig,' I said. 'Remember me?'" He stared at Belle in clear wonderment. "And he did. He was shaking all over, couldn't catch his breath. Touching at his chest. Then he asked if this here Anni had sent me, something about an avenger. 'Who's she?' I asked."

Belle interrupted him. "I know it's hard, but go slowly. What exactly did he say about Anni? You have the missing pieces to the jigsaw, Craig." For a moment she felt ashamed. Why probe so deeply? For selfish satisfaction?

"Jigsaw?"

"Anni was my friend. I think that Father Jim killed her, but I don't know why. Was it blackmail?"

"He was babbling. Sounded crazy. Something like 'I tried to ato...ato...'" Craig bunched up his fists in confusion, his empty coffee cup dropping to the floor.

"Atone?"

"That was the word. 'I gave her what she asked.' he said. 'Then she changed her mind.'"

Vintage Anni. Playing judge and jury as she did with Patsy and the bear-baiters, meting out punishment without a care for her own neck. But she underestimated the desperation protecting years of quiet security. "What was she going to do? Turn him in?"

"I'm not sure. They argued and then something happened." He spit out the words in contempt. "Always was a coward. That's when I lost it. Gave him one good shot for me and her both. But I'm no murderer, Belle. I left him sitting there in that damn robe. He was crying like I did every night in my bed in the dormitory."

She had to believe him, imagine Charles' relief as his victim stormed out. He'd gone into the sauna, retreated from his aggressor. Then terror pushed an overburdened heart toward its last stand, the robe flung off in the sudden, sharp pain, followed by dark peace, the only real atonement. Had he admitted his sins, sought forgiveness in the final seconds? A higher court would decide. "And then you learned that he had died."

"I got pretty drunk. Took me a day or two to sober up and get back to work." His voice took on an ironic tone. "Fran had started reading the obits aloud, hoping that her husband's name would be there. He left her with HIV, and now he's dying of AIDS."

Belle was somewhere else, rewinding the film. Charles and Anni in that great reckoning in a little room with burnished floors, the old woman wielding her stick like a shillelagh. No script for that scene, no stage directions. The wall clock ticked as she shook off the inertia. Nearly eight a.m. Bad psychology to keep reminding people how long they'd been waiting.

"Steve's got to be the first to hear about this," she said. "Monday he'll be back from a camping trip. Just don't—"

"Belle?" Freed from the paralyzing defenses that had shackled him, he looked as if he might weep.

"Yes?"

"How do you think he'll take it? You know my brother better than I do. Will he hate me?"

"Oh, Craig, no. Never," she said, circling aching arms around him as number forty-five finally came up on Canada's health care bingo.

X-rayed and wrapped in an elastic bandage, Belle's ankle needed no more than a week's rest. Fortunately it had been her left foot, so she could still drive. The aspirins scrounged from the nurse were wearing off as she arrived at the DesRosiers' about noon, her mind nuzzling blunt edges of exhaustion. Freya nearly bowled her over, but she pressed into the soft and familiar fur, accepting a few slurps for good measure. "What lips these lips have kissed."

"Back off, mutt," Hélène said. "Mom's had a heckuva night, and all you did was snore." She helped Belle up the stairs, placed her at the kitchen table in front of a steaming cup of coffee. More brew was the last thing Belle wanted, but her sore hands cradled the warmth.

"Cooking takes my mind off things," Hélène confessed, standing beside a buffet to amaze Martha Stewart. Sausages, back bacon, cornmeal pancakes, blueberry muffins, fluffy eggs dotted with fresh basil, oceans of maple syrup, jams, jellies and juice.

"Popovers!" Belle stuffed a golden globe full of red pepper jelly into her mouth. Between knives and forks and bites and sips, she told them how the past had conjoined to align three disparate people into a fatal triangle.

"If there's one thing I can't stand, it's a hypocrite," Hélène said with a moue of disgust. "Those poor kids. You read about the brutal details at those schools, but it all seems so far away from us."

"Wouldn't have figured Chuck for that stuff," Ed said, heaping his place a third time, stifling a belch. "Manners of a bishop. Couldn't beat a swear word out of the guy with a crowbar. Say, though, no offense about Anni."

Belle made a concerted effort to slow down. Dyspepsia was not in her plans, though she could raid their well-stocked medicine cabinet if necessary. "You know, in another world and time, he might have become one."

After a quick call to Rainbow Country to assure herself that her father was eating like a longshoreman, the rest of the afternoon she spent on the couch, gloating over the bond fund, moping over the drooping science and technology quotes, and wondering if the Nikkei had finally hit bottom. With Circadian rhythm out of sync, she might be up half the night if she grabbed an hour now.

At scarcely an eyelash past supper time, she struggled to the kitchen in a fog, puzzled at a licking sound. Freya worrying a flea again? Where was that noxious aerosol bomb? Apparently the shepherd was making love to her empty food bowl, scouring the sides for residual flavours, petulant that dinner was late.

"A blackmailer in my own house. And I know Hélène gave you plenty of handouts. An extra cup, and that's it."

Along with a bowl of tomato soup, that old creature comfort, she nibbled a few crackers, still full as a boa from brunch. Playing for time, she hauled a bag of garbage to the road. As the top of the wooden box banged, a movement up the hill startled her. A bear, likely a lone male come on rounds, perhaps the prowler which had scrunched by the basement windows one night. He didn't seem disturbed by her presence, resting his rump on a log and questioning her with silence like an old philosopher in a thick and lustrous ebony coat. "Not my garbage!" she yelled, waving her arms wildly. Entire bags of trash often disappeared into the woods, Visa bills, liquor bottles, invitations for a Revenue Canada check. "Get back where you belong." His response was a yawn, or was it a laugh? Some primitive sound mixing both. With a crooked muzzle upturned, he seemed amused at her antics, but she kept her distance. Black bears defending cubs or rummaging for food stored in a tent were no Winnie the Poohs. Then the chug of a pickup echoed, and Shovelnose ambled back into the forest, stumpy tail wiggling farewell.

A brown Ford stopped, and a smiling face greeted her from the open window.

"Heading out for the winter, Nick?" she asked.

"Oh, not for a month or two. Let the snow chase me away," he replied with a grin, patting the truck in a proprietorial gesture. "Say, I owe you."

"What do you mean?"

"Your suggestion. That shop downtown. They took my sketches on consignment. Twenty-five percent commission, but I made enough to trade up the old bomber."

TWENTY-SEVEN

S teve sat on the deck, tapping his boot, clearly miffed at her once again. "I can't believe that you kept important evidence from me. When will you learn?"

"Important evidence, my ear. Ancient history from halfway across the country. How could I have known it was significant? And what was the connection? Anni, Charles and Craig weren't singing 'Sweet Adeline' one short of a barbershop quartet. It was a brilliant deduction on my part, and when I called, you were off playing Boy Scout." She raced off the last words, folding her arms in defiance.

He straightened his back with a glower, ready to score a few final points despite the defensive tone in his voice. "Well, my original idea was on the money. It wasn't the hunters. A savvy old woman wouldn't have opened her door to a stranger. Should have twigged that it was someone around here." He rapped himself "upside the head" as a reminder.

The honest self-criticism struck a rare chord. Steve was a man of great pride. "Don't blame yourself. How could you check the backgrounds of every person on the road? And Charles had just moved in. I wouldn't have suspected him in a million years. Did he fit your profile of a murderer?"

"Who does, Belle? Don't you read Max Haines' crime columns?"

"When I can steal a peek at my neighbour's newspaper.

Think how humiliated I feel!" Her eyes narrowed and she mimed a leisurely cast, reeling in an imaginary line. "Charles played me like a lazy, stupid bass. We strolled through Anni's house looking at jigsaw puzzles. He wined and dined me, went joy-riding in my canoe. What gall."

One corner of Steve's mouth rose. "A cool one, but maybe he liked you. It isn't a crime."

"It should be, the way I attract bodies." She shrugged. "Say, did you ever turn up anything on the Morrises? I wondered where he had gotten that money. And why he kept it under his real name."

"Didn't want it traced to his new identity, I guess, just let it sit there after he disappeared from the Mission. He and his sister belonged to a wealthy Winnipeg family. Meat packing. Last of the line, though. Strange that they both chose the Church."

Their eyes met in unspoken agreement about the destructive pair. Then they both looked up at a familiar chorus of squawks. A black vee-shaped necklace was threading its way south, the few stragglers flapping behind while the timekeeper kept the pace. Beginning of September. The geese were off early. Did that mean a bad winter or an easy one? Then she smiled. "The only good part concerns Craig."

He nodded slowly, his face relaxed and almost cheerful. "The Crown Prosecutor agreed to a plea of no contest to aggravated assault. In view of the facts, it was obvious that Craig hit Morris from a provocation even a saint couldn't resist, pardon the comparison. We got him a suspended sentence with community service at the shelter."

"Is he seeing a counsellor?"

"Every week. And you know, just talking it over is helping the healing process." He paused, let silence grow as he shifted thoughts. "Those lost years. Never saw his home or family. What a price."

Belle watched a squirrel head for the boathouse with a nut in its mouth, already looking ahead to winter storage. "Any plans? Can he retrain? Work with kids maybe? He's a natural at that."

"Sure is. Came for dinner last week. Big celebration. Janet roasted a thirty-pound turkey to make up for all the holidays he'd missed. Now he's Uncle Craig. Heather's his best pal. And he's upgrading math and English at the college. Soon as he nails his level fours, he can enter a post-secondary course. Social Services worker. It's a two-year program."

She took his large hand in hers. How like Craig's it was. "He saved my life, Steve. Something deep inside made him come back. It couldn't have been easy. That decision was a turning point. I'm sure he's going to be fine."

Later that day the phone rang. "It's Sister Veronica. I have something of interest. It came in the mail from Margaret. If you might drop by…"

From the island? Belle felt like squeaking like a delirious chipmunk, but she didn't want to sacrifice dignity to the self-possessed nun. And a change of scene was due. Remove the woman from her element in an effort to crack that damnable superiority. "Let's have dinner if you're free tonight. The Landings at Science North. My treat." She sketched in her discoveries for the nun, who listened with few interruptions, only something which sounded like Latin.

Could this be the keystone, the final piece of information to explain Charles' motivations, reveal his ultimate guilt or innocence? There she was again, trying to exonerate him in the final credits. Yet perhaps Euphemia, the Spider Woman herself, might speak at last from the grave.

261

A chill rain was falling, the wind rising as she parked near the front canopy of St. Joe's. With a welcoming hoot, Zack jumped out of a bright yellow taxi and strolled over, tipping back his Jays cap and grinning self-consciously. "Don't laugh at an honest man. I'm getting used to this. Working evenings and nights gives me time to enjoy the lake. Say, fat guy down the road says you tried to camp without a tent."

That blabbermouth Ed. "A little privation's good for anyone," she answered with a bent smile.

"Now that we know Aunt Anni's killer, do you think that address book will show up at his place, sort of a nail in the coffin?" He didn't seem aware of the unfortunate choice of words.

"If he was smart enough to take it, Zack, to cover the trail back to Osprey Inlet, he was smart enough to destroy it."

At the wave of an elderly man pushing a wheelchair, he hurried over to help. Meanwhile, a tiny white Doulton figurine under a huge black umbrella knocked at the passenger door. The nun seemed embarrassed to be ferried around, casting a wary eye on the bells and whistles of the van's cockpit as she settled into the seat. "This high living is not my usual style. We could have had a nourishing meal in the hospital cafeteria."

Tourist season was winding down at the futuristic complex of Science North. Cars from as far as Texas were returning to check on tumbleweeds, leaving Sudbury to the hardy locals. The waiter gave them a window table where they watched in comfort while a pounding gale lashed Lake Ramsey into froth and foam, sweeping small sailboats toward the marina. With plush carpets and few early diners, the room was quiet and subdued. Belle smiled over a crisp pinot blanc, filling glasses and consulting the menu. "No plain oatmeal or unsalted groats," she said with a teasing smile.

Not a flicker of reaction. "Grains are much underrated. Have you read Bert Greene? He'd approve of this brown rice cassoulet. Made with wild mushrooms, it says."

Belle swallowed hard against a sudden queasiness. "Wild, eh? I'll pass on that. The salmon sounds tempting."

As they finished the meal, Belle waiting on tenterhooks, Sister Veronica delved into a black shoulder bag to retrieve a letter. "I shouldn't be doing this. Margaret had no right to send it on. So impulsive. However, now that she did…" The gaze was steady, her mouth firm, or was it a deadpan smile? Hard to decipher from a poker player par excellence.

"Don't stand on ceremony. The case is closed. What is it?"

The nun sighed elaborately, fingered a silver cross where an emerald winked, and stretched out the moment like Torquemada fine-tuning the rack. "When news of her brother's death reached the island, Euphemia's trunk was opened. It contained only clothes and a Bible, to be portioned out to the needy. We Cecilianists pride ourselves on wasting nothing. But Margaret made sure she attended the examination. And she was able to discover this envelope and retrieve it unseen. For her studies, of course."

With great precision she placed it on the table with a reverence awarded to the Dead Sea Scrolls or the predictions of Nostradamus. Belle's hand trembled to touch the cream rag paper for a third time. What fine taste Charles had. Part of her missed him. A bad part, she guessed, the one which placed wit over wisdom, conversation over charity. Though the waiter was collecting the dishes, all she heard was a pulse pounding in her ears while she studied the familiar copperplate style:

Euphemia:
I write only because I hear you are dying. Since that

nightmare so many years ago, I have had no sister. As my elder and my mentor, you inspired me to follow you into the Church. Only too late did I learn of your devices and desires. I should have read the face of that innocent boy and listened to my heart instead of your false homilies. Though I have tried to start a new and decent life, my soul is a dead thing, and I remain to my continuing shame a craven man with neither the power nor the right to ask forgiveness for either of us.

James

Sister Veronica took a final sip of wine, cocking her head to notice with apparent disappointment that the bottle was empty. "Do you need to show it to the authorities?"

"What would be the point now?" Belle looked across the table, met those doleful eyes in a final challenge. "Did you read it?"

There was no immediate answer, only a pursing of lips as Sister folded her serviette with the patience and exactness afforded an altar cloth. "We are none of us without sin."

Belle smiled crookedly despite the seriousness of the moment. "What does it reveal, though, that only one child was involved? That Charles was essentially innocent? I'd like to believe that."

The compassion was gone, the voice low and uncompromising. "There is a higher power overriding earthly duties. Be that as it may, he felt guilty, and so the letter implies."

"Exactly. And it explains his panic when Anni changed her mind." She lowered her eyes. "But it could have been manslaughter, technically." Would she ever concede that the blow had meant murder?

"God did not write the Criminal Code. You ignore the moral tenor this sad man took to his grave. 'Neither the power nor the right,' his letter said. A shameful hubris. The greatest sin."

"The greatest sin?" What was the hierarchy? Belle shuffled quickly through the Ten Commandments and the Seven Deadlies. Gluttony and envy were going to send most of North America to hell. The waiter arrived with two snifters of Remy Martin.

Sister warmed the cognac briefly over the candle at the table, then swirled it and inhaled. Raising one grizzled eyebrow, she sipped three times before answering. "The greatest sin is believing that your sin is unforgivable. He had not learned. He had not learned at all."

EPILOGUE

A crisp frost had zapped summer into submission with the efficiency of a stun gun. Preparing the property for winter, Belle inspected the branches of her showpiece maple with guarded optimism. Decimated by the 'pillars, it had fought back by sprouting tiny auxiliary leaves to gather strength against the brutal winter. Nearby, the lush kiwi vine drooped. She brandished the pruning shears with vigour. "You're supposed to be self-pollinating. Not one fruit in two years. All show and no go." Then she grabbed a bag of tulip bulbs and headed for the triangular flower bed along the road, pleased that the late dahlias and monkshood were flanked by a pathologically glorious blood-red sumach.

Now that the vegetable garden had been put to sleep, forked up and dredged with manure and lime, it was time for the great zucchini burial, ten-pound jumbos too big to stuff into the composter and too full of organic gold to discard. She had assembled their plump bodies like pods from *The Invasion of the Body Snatchers.* "You're next!" Kevin McCarthy had screamed, running wildly through traffic in an ending so alarming to audiences that a reassuring postscript had been tacked on. Perhaps she should secrete them into basements of problem clients and watch their faces assume that subtle neutral expression as aliens freed them from the burden of emotions. "The house between the railroad tracks and the swamp? With the smelly basement and leaky roof? Perfect, Miss Palmer. I'll take it." She dug trenches, tossed in the squash, then chopped them with a shovel to encourage decomposition. What were the proper words? *Ave atque* vegetables? Memento melons?

With Freya at her side, she started down the road. At the turnaround, she glanced at Charles' property. He would always be Charles to her. Last week it had sold quickly to a family with two kids whose bicycle tracks ringed the dust. She liked to see young faces with their enthusiasm and boundless energy. Already a new plaque sported colourful representations of Mickey and Minnie Mouse: The Blairs, Ken, Judy, Timmy and Jean. In a pile for the trash collection, scratched and gouged, was the Paradise Regained sign. What a corruption of Milton's theology. Paradise Lost was more apt. Better to reign in hell or Ottawa than to serve in heaven. A cardboard box sat nearby, full of ashes, as if they had cleaned out the sauna stove. City folk again. Ashes belonged in the garden. Then a glint caught her eye, and she fingered the debris. A tarnished metal heart-shaped clasp, its tiny keyhole distorted by the heat, unlocked the final chapter. With a tight throat, she closed her hand upon it and turned back down the road.

Like a director in waiting, the brilliant fall had crowned goldenrod and asters lords of the fields. Bliss Carmen might have dwindled to a footnote in Canadian literature, that vagabond poet of the 1890's, but his lyrical soul had seen "the frosty asters like a smoke upon the hills." Distracted by inspiration, she nearly plunged into a heap of bear scat in the middle of the road. Bears don't shit only in the woods. Like many whimsical animals, they enjoy decorating the middle of the path. Shovelnose would be heading for a cozy den. How far back would he go? Would she discover the lair on a snowshoe trek some bright January afternoon? Bears often emerged from their sleep for a mid-winter walkabout.

She followed the dog back to the DesRosiers' place. Hélène was picking the last parsley, and in the garage, Ed had their snowmobile hoods up amid sounds of tinkering and mild cursing. Belle clapped her hands. "Roll out that party barge before the lake freezes. There's one last lake trout with our names on it."

CHOCOLATE ZUCCHINI CAKE

Mix the following dry ingredients:

    2 cups flour
    ¾ cup cocoa
    2½ teaspoons baking powder
    2 teaspoons baking soda
    ½ teaspoon salt
    1 teaspoon cinnamon

Beat together:

    1½ cups vegetable oil
    2 cups sugar
    4 eggs

Add:

    1 teaspoon vanilla
    2 teaspoons grated lemon rind
    3 cups grated zucchini
    1 cup chopped pecans (optional)

Combine dry mixture with wet mixture and beat well.

Bake in greased pans at 350°F for one hour. Makes three small loaves or two large ones.

LOU ALLIN was born in Toronto but raised in Ohio. Her father followed the film business to Cleveland in 1948, and his profession explains her passion for celluloid classics, which shows up frequently in her writing.

After obtaining a Ph.D. in English Renaissance literature, Lou headed north to Cambrian College in Sudbury, Ontario, where she has taught literature, writing and public speaking for the past twenty-five years. Like Belle, her sleuth, she lives beside the breathtaking vistas of a sixty-four-square-mile meteor crater lake where she canoes and snowmobiles, hikes and snowshoes. Her first novel, *Northern Winters Are Murder,* was published by RendezVous Press in 2000.

Blackflies Are Murder is her second Belle Palmer mystery.

Also available

"Lou Allin excels at making the frigid Ontario cold seep into your bones with vivid pictures of life in the Northern wilderness. The book starts at the cold pace of winter and picks up as the thaw draws closer...*Northern Winters Are Murder* is a cozy read."

-Bookreporter.com

NORTHERN WINTERS ARE MURDER

Murder on a frozen lake...

Another freezing winter descends in seeming peace upon the Northern Ontario lake where realtor Belle Palmer lives genteelly with her dog, tropical fishes and classic film collection. But the snow-laden tranquillity is tragically disturbed when a good friend is lost in a freak snowmobile accident on an isolated lake. Or so it seems. Belle and others suspect foul play, but a motive and a criminal prove hard to find. Resort owners, anti-environmentalists and the new local drug dealers may all have had reason to want Jim Burian quietly removed, and information isn't forthcoming. Belle is determined to find out what happened to this decent man, but she is shocked when she discovers what twisted roots underlie this savage crime on idyllic northern ice.

ISBN 0-929141-74-1 / 280 PAGES/ 5 1/8" X 7.5" / TRADE PAPERBACK/$12.95 IN CANADA, $10.95 U.S.